Time wa...
Quinn's s...

The near-silent needles of high-density depleted uranium whooshed through the air in a lethal shower as Quinn tucked and rolled out of the line of whipsawing automatic fire. From half a crouch, he launched an answering salvo of 5.70 mm steel. He scored a clean takedown...but there were others still up and shooting.

"Warning," another VRG readout flashed in a data block above the real-time video display. "Final countdown to detonation commencing..."

In an attempt to distract the shooter detail, Quinn tossed more advanced-design flash-bangs their way, temporarily blinding the NVG-equipped opposition forces. Using the precious seconds he'd gained, Quinn hosed down the opposition with automatically targeted pulses of P-90 fire, killing all of them.

He wasted no time in climbing the access stairs toward the rooftop. His VRG display showed him that only a few minutes remained until the installation shot into the stratosphere in a broiling pillar of flame.

NOMAD
DESERT FIRE

DAVID ALEXANDER

A GOLD EAGLE BOOK FROM
WORLDWIDE.

TORONTO • NEW YORK • LONDON
AMSTERDAM • PARIS • SYDNEY • HAMBURG
STOCKHOLM • ATHENS • TOKYO • MILAN
MADRID • WARSAW • BUDAPEST • AUCKLAND

AUTHOR'S NOTE:

The descriptions of time travel devices and technologies cited in this novel are based on actual theoretical models. While an attempt has been made to keep the segments dealing with the Gulf War accurate in the main, the names of certain principal figures or their specific roles have been changed for the purposes of the narrative.

First edition September 1993

ISBN 0-373-62118-3

DESERT FIRE

Printed in U.S.A.

Things may be the same again; and we must fight
Not in the hope of winning but rather of keeping
Something alive: so that when we meet our end,
It may be said that we tackled wherever we could,
That battle-fit we lived, and though defeated,
Not without glory fought.
    —Henry Reed
    "Lessons of the War"

MISSION LOG ONE:

Strike Vector

1

The warden of Ironstone Federal Prison dragged on a ginseng cigarette as she stared out of her office window. A thick, brown haze of air pollution hovered over the shattered rubble of downtown Detroit like a dirty wall between heaven and earth.

It looked especially grim this morning, and the warden figured that the severe acid-rain storm alert she'd heard on the morning weather report would probably turn out to be as bad as the forecasters had predicted.

Alice Guthrie was glad that she had decided to take the weather forecasters at their word and wear her Kevlar-plastic-weave raincoat to work.

Other than the threatening cloud cover, the outdoor temperature of the spring day was pleasantly warm. There seemed even to be the remote possibility of the sun peeking out once or twice. Despite the early hour and the unpredictable weather, there were already a few of *them* outside the prison gates.

A wave of sickness crashed over the warden as she realized that soon there would be even more of them milling around.

Within a matter of hours, the prison grounds would be thronged. She thought of their blank, soulless eyes and mindlessly beaming faces and shuddered involuntarily.

Her own daughter was... But that was a thought she couldn't continue with. Not now. It was far too painful.

Finishing her noncarcinogenic cigarette, Alice Guthrie consulted her desktop computer's appointment scheduler. She was going through the motions because she knew full well what today's chief business concerned and whom she was scheduled to meet with in her office in just a little while.

Warden Guthrie at once wanted to get the troublesome task over with but at the same time wished she didn't have to play any part in the ghastly charade.

But there was nothing she could do to stop the lawful release of prisoner number 022950.

He had served his time, making parole after only two years of incarceration at Ironstone Prison. The record showed that he was a model prisoner in every respect, and psychological tests demonstrated that he had completely reformed.

Still, Warden Guthrie felt that she would better serve the interests of society by shooting number 022950 down in cold blood rather than permit him to go free.

She would never stop believing that the prisoner was a menace to society, even if society itself had chosen to shut its eyes to the danger he posed.

Warden Guthrie busied herself with some paperwork strewn across her desk, pretending that she didn't hear the chanting that had just started up outside the prison walls.

As THE WARDEN was thinking her private thoughts, the object of those thoughts sat on an examination table in the prison infirmary.

He was there to go through a battery of prerelease medical tests. As well as these, there was the critically important implantation of his BioTrak unit.

The device, no larger than a cherry pit and powered by an atomic battery, was to be implanted in his head as part of the requirements of his parole.

The BioTrak unit would send out a continuous signal that would enable the parole authorities to keep accurate tabs on the prisoner's every movement. With the implant in place, the inmate would in effect be spending his parole in a prison without walls.

It was virtually impossible to remove, neutralize or phreak, and the fact that the BioTrak unit contained a tiny yet extremely powerful explosive charge, easily sufficient to shatter the wearer's head to hundreds of bloody fragments, added an extra incentive to good behavior.

"There you go," the doctor, a bearded young man, said cheerfully, consulting his watch, "the topical anesthetic I gave you should be working by now. Feel numb yet?"

"Yes, I do," returned the prisoner, nodding his head.

He was a man of medium height and build. His features were regular and, except for his eyes, he might have had one of those faces that were quickly forgotten.

But the eyes, the left one gray and the right speckled with what looked like flecked gold, made that impossible. Those hypnotic eyes could not be ignored, and had been the secret of the prisoner's meteoric rise to power and fame.

"Good," replied the doctor, raising a white plastic cylinder about six inches long from a nearby implements table and bringing it quickly to the side of the prisoner's neck. "Just hold still, then. It should all be over in a flash."

The doctor lightly touched the snout of the implanter to the side of the prisoner's neck at the base of the skull. The prisoner experienced nothing more than a momentary tickling sensation as the compressed-air injector inserted the small electronic transmitter.

"All over," said the doctor, putting away the implanter and swabbing the side of his patient's neck with an antiseptic wipe as he inspected the implantation site through a digital magnifier.

A sweep of a hand-held scanner across the implantation site produced a series of beeps and the message, "Biotrak unit 07205-22. Implant successful."

"How does it feel?"

"I don't even know it's there."

"You're not supposed to," the doctor told him with a smile. "And whenever your parole maxes out, we can remove it just as painlessly, quickly and safely." The doctor held out his hand. "Good luck."

"Thank you," the prisoner replied, knowing that the doctor's sentiments were genuine. "I appreciate that. I really do."

From the look in the doctor's eyes, the prisoner knew that he had just won a potential convert to his cause. He felt a sudden elation, aware that his gift for winning hearts and minds was still as strong as ever. As soon as he got out, he would put that gift to use again.

WARDEN GUTHRIE LOOKED UP from the papers that cluttered her desk as the prisoner arrived. In the background she could hear the constant chanting. It was loud now, and she could no longer shut it out of her mind no matter how hard she tried.

With the monotonous chanting came memories of how her daughter had—there was no other word for it—*self-destructed* a few years ago.

She had been a beautiful girl of twenty-five with everything to live for. And then she had become something else . . . first a compliant zombie in a cult, and ultimately a corpse without a heart or liver.

That the man responsible for her daughter's fate now sat in front of her, and that she was about to send that same man back into society, scot-free, filled her with an unspeakable revulsion.

Who would blame her if she killed him right now? Who could deny her the satisfaction of seeing this ghoul die as he had caused her daughter to die just as surely as if he had shot her with a pistol or stabbed her with a knife?

But she couldn't do a thing.

Alice Guthrie was a professional, and she knew that she had to soldier on. The parole board stated that the prisoner was completely reformed. He was to be released. It would serve nobody's purpose if she made a travesty of the system to suit her own selfish needs.

"Mr. Lux Vadim," the warden began. "The federal government says that you've served your time. I disagree with that assessment very strongly. I think you're a danger to society and that letting you go, even wearing a biotransponder implant, might well turn out to be a tragic mistake."

"I'm sorry you feel that way, Warden," the prisoner responded in a velvet-soft voice, his strange, mismatched eyes boring into hers with laser-beam intensity.

Those eyes held the key to the prisoner's power, she knew, feeling the force that seemed to radiate from them, sucking her unwillingly into a bottomless vortex.

"I have completely reformed," he said, his voice tranquilizingly calm, hypnotically soothing. "But may I remind you that my official title is still Reverend. The fact that I have spent time in prison does not change the fact that I am the titular head of a recognized church."

"Very well," Guthrie replied. "*Reverend* Vadim, then. You have done nothing but make fools of the parole board and officials of this prison," the warden countered, shaking off the mesmerizing effects of the prisoner's gaze.

"But you can't fool me. I know who you are and what you are capable of doing. And I warn you, others know you for what you are, too. Step out of line, and you'll wind up right back here, and next time your incarceration will be for the rest of your life.''

"Thank you for sharing your thoughts with me, Warden," the prisoner said, holding her gaze without blinking. "Am I free to go now?"

"Yes," she replied, now eager to be rid of him and knowing that there was nothing more she could say or do.

"Then I won't take up any of your time," he told her as he rose from his chair and turned toward the door. "Thank you again, Warden. May heaven shine on your buffers."

2

"A present, Jimmi."

"Wow, quantum, man! Where'd you get that?"

"That shouldn't concern you," Vadim replied, holding the small plug drug in the hollow of his hand. "You really shouldn't look a gift horse in the mouth."

"I didn't mean to hassle you, man," Jimmi said, snatching away the bright red integrated-circuit chip before the Reverend Vadim changed his mind.

A tall, rangy guy with an accent that spoke of the cornfields of his native Nebraska, Jimmi was serving a life sentence for a brutal rampage of robbery and murder that had left fourteen victims in its wake.

Vadim had found Jimmi useful in the performance of odd jobs. He had found out quickly that Jimmi had a talent for pack-ratting things. He also had performed the more unsavory tasks that a model prisoner of the reverend's ilk could not allow himself to be given credit for.

A number of prisoners whom the reverend had found troublesome during his stay at the Ironstone correctional facility had been sent to a better place by his cell mate and trusted friend.

"It's just that, I mean ... " Jimmi went on, fingering the chip's smooth red surface, "this here's some expensive shit, man."

"Indeed it is, Jimmi," the reverend replied with a short laugh. "But as a parting gift it's the least I can do for my most trusted associate while I languished here in durance vile, a man with whom I have shared my most intimate secrets."

"We *were* pretty tight, man," Jimmi said back, nodding his head. "That's a natural fact."

"As inseparable as a great white shark and its sucker fish," the Reverend answered his cell mate.

"Hey, what do you mean by that crack?"

"Just my little jest, Jimmi," the reverend assured his cell mate with a pat on the shoulder. "At any rate, I want you to think of me while you enjoy this vintage hardware narcotic. It's your favorite memory chip, Jimmi."

"Wow, superquantum, man!" he exclaimed as he looked from the "plug" to the reverend, forgetting all about the slight he'd just received. "You mean..."

"That's right, Jimmi. Woodstock," he replied. "Every glorious minute of that legendary rock festival held almost sixty-six years ago in August of 1969 as seen through the eyes of a nineteen-year-old hippie zonked on Owsley acid. It's seven straight, mind-bending days of sex, drugs and rock and roll, Jimmi. You'll love it.''

"I'm all choked up man," Jimmi replied abashedly, his dull brown eyes growing moist. "What can I say?"

"Simply let me see you place my humble gift in your socket, Jimmi," the reverend replied softly. "That's all I need to warm the cockles of my cardiac region."

Vadim watched Jimmi lift the memory chip and insert its pins into the thirty-two-pin socket connector that had been bioengineered into the side of his skull.

The hardware narcotic immediately took effect, patching the virtual-reality memories that it contained directly into Jimmi's hard-wired brain, which plug-drug users called a "McBrain."

"Wow, this is too much," Jimmi replied as he began to relive the Woodstock music festival, tapping his feet and snapping his fingers. "Hey, we'll get together after I get out of stir?" he asked.

"Don't worry," the Reverend Vadim replied. "We'll certainly stay in touch. Be well, Jimmi. Time flies and so must I."

Vadim left the cell, with Jimmi staring at the steel-plate ceiling as he lay on the lower bunk, hearing, seeing and feeling the vintage rock of a bygone era.

THE THRONG of chanting, shaven-headed acolytes began to cheer in wild unison. A mad frenzy of discordant voices filled the air as the milling crowd saw the Reverend Vadim walk to freedom through Ironstone Prison's main gate.

Uniformed members of Vadim's private mercenary army were already waiting to meet him as he left the prison gates. Instantly they formed a protective cordon, forcing back the reverend's own impetuous followers in order to usher him safely into a waiting electric limo.

The media was on the scene, too, and newspeople were already shouting questions at him as the reverend rushed toward the waiting stretch.

"What are your plans now?" asked one of the newspeople.

"To integrate all subfunctions with the universal dharma," the reverend replied. "Such has always been my root path."

"Will you be returning to your space station headquarters, Reverend?" another newsperson asked him, shouting to be heard over the deafening roar of the surging crowd.

"All data emerges, disemerges and becomes non-data," he responded. "The lotus has opened, and from within its mysterious depths the arrow of Arjuna flies to heaven."

Vadim was already nearing the limo. While a crew of his blacksuited mercs held back the surging, chanting crowd that was desperate to touch his person, other flunkies were holding the door of the limo open for him.

"Reverend!" another newsperson shouted above the din. "A report has just come in that your cell mate, a man named Jimmi Jones, has just killed himself in an apparent drug-induced suicide. Have you any comment on this breaking story?"

"This is indeed tragic news. I just left my good friend Jimmi only a little while ago," the reverend replied, pausing before entering the limo. "If this news is true, then I grieve deeply for my young friend. He had so much to live for."

With that, the Reverend Vadim slid completely into the limo's dark interior. He was bracketed by two bodyguards, one of whom immediately slammed shut the rear door. A third hardman sitting behind the wheel of the electric vehicle sent the limo screeching toward the highway outside the prison.

Behind the opaque windows of the large bulletproof vehicle, no camera lens could pick up the broad smile of deep satisfaction on the reverend's face as he thought about his late friend Jimmi. Dead men, after all, told no tales.

3

The aerospace plane, or ASP, skimmed the near edge of space, cruising at hypersonic speeds in excess of Mach 5.

The ASP was at an altitude of one hundred thousand feet. The sky was an inverted bowl of polished ebony, and the curvature of the luminous blue earth below could be seen from the cockpit. In the crew compartment of the sleek, delta-winged passenger aircraft, the commuter flight was progressing smoothly.

The captain thought about enjoying a cold stein of draft beer laced with just enough hallucinogenic drugs to put him in the mood for some fun and games with triple-breasted women when the scramjet landed at Sydney, Australia, less than two hours after departing the greater Boston area out of Logan International Airport.

Aft of the crew compartment, passengers in the wide-bodied aircraft enjoyed complimentary drinks, noncarcinogenic cigarettes, and five hundred virtual-reality cable channels available on their 3-D eyephones.

Traveling in the first-class compartment just aft of the cockpit, on his way from a meeting with a client and en route to a symposium on international techno-terrorism before returning to home base for some much-needed rest, one of the passengers was watching an all-news channel on his complimentary eyephones.

The scene depicted the besieged entrance to Ironstone Prison, where the religious fanatics who dubbed themselves "Motherboarders" had turned out in droves to witness and cheer their leader's release from two years spent behind bars.

"This is indeed tragic news. I just left my good friend Jimmi only a little while ago," Reverend Lux Vadim replied to a reporter's shouted question regarding the unexpected suicide of his cell mate, then quickly disappeared into the back of the limo, which promptly drove away.

The drug overdose had caused Jimmi's brain to malfunction. As neural circuits popped, a massive cerebral hemorrhage caused blood to pour from his ears, nose and mouth. He was dead in a matter of seconds.

In his first-class seat, the passenger on the transonic flight switched off the eyephones. Removing them from his head, he tucked them away in the pouch on the back of the seat in front of him.

His jaw was set, and his gray eyes narrowed to tight slits as he stroked the point of his angular chin. A female flight attendant passed and asked if she could get him anything, perhaps sensing the tension the passenger felt. The passenger shook his head and politely turned down the offer.

At the moment, the man named Quinn, also known to a select few by his code-name, Nomad, desired a great many things, but nothing on his wish list was within the flight attendant's power to provide. Chief among his wants at the moment was for the Reverend Lux Vadim to be sent back to prison immediately.

Quinn's thoughts turned back to events that had taken place some two years before.

They had been events leading to the arrest, trial, conviction and incarceration of the Reverend Lux Vadim for atrocities he had committed against all humanity.

Quinn had played a pivotal role in these affairs. As the scramjet sped through the ultrathin atmosphere of near-space, Quinn's mind sped backward to another time and another place....

THE PLACE WAS Los Angeles, and death was in season. A series of grisly mutilations had plagued the nation's second-largest city, spreading panic throughout the urban population.

Bodies were turning up, their organs apparently removed with surgical precision. It was apparent that an individual or group was going around and taking out the organs, though for reasons then unknown.

The best theory that the Los Angeles Police Department Corporation had to go on was that they had been removed from healthy bodies and then sold on the black market for transplant purposes.

Quinn had been hired as a consultant by the Los Angeles Police Department Corporation to conduct a probe into the serial killings. The multiple fatalities had stymied the cops and had sent politicians of every political stripe clamoring for the violence to end.

Quinn's private security organization, Intervention Systems, or IS, had placed agents on the street in undercover roles. From one of these undercover assets, who had been recruited by the Reverend Vadim's followers, came a critical lead that was to be the first break unraveling the twisted meaning behind a baffling spate of senseless violence.

Converts new to the fold were disappearing from the reverend's Church of the Divine Motherboard, the IS agent had reported. On the surface, at least, there appeared to be no pattern to the disappearances. Followers joined the Motherboarders and left just as quickly in a constant ebb and flow.

It was discovered that the disappearances had been carefully orchestrated to exploit the normal changing of the guard as cover. The candidates selected for killing and subsequent organ removal were those whose absence would not attract undue attention. Those who would not be missed easily or quickly were fated to die.

Quinn's ongoing probe of the Motherboard Church had led to the piecing together of the grisly process by which acolytes were culled from the group, euthanized and then surgically cannibalized so that their body parts could be harvested and sold at black-market auctions to meet a worldwide shortage fueling a desparate demand.

Organ transplants had been perfected, and when faced with the choice between life and death, many terminally ill and affluent patients did not question closely where and how the donor organs had been obtained.

Those selected were taken to several "retreats" established outside the city. The retreats were actually psychological-conditioning centers where the Motherboarders were brainwashed using shock neuroprogramming techniques and potent psychotropic drugs.

Once they had been changed into catatonic zombies, little more than living robots, they were induced into signing away all their wordly possessions to the Motherboard Church. Since many of the new converts were wealthy, this strategy reaped an added king's ransom in plunder for the Motherboarders. Once this was accomplished, the organ donors were taken to their place of euthanasia, the reverend's headquarters.

This was a station in space. It was named Sunyata, after the Hindu word for ''suchness,'' or the ultimate reality. After the fact, the media made much of this name, for it had a gruesome double meaning. To the Reverend Vadim, the ultimate reality was death.

There, in the station, the organ donors were slaughtered like barnyard animals. Their organs were removed from the freshly euthanized bodies and stored cryogenically.

After piecing together the mechanics of liquidation practiced by the Motherboard Church, Quinn's next task was to prove that the Reverend Vadim was responsible for masterminding the organ theft and sales operations on the black market. Quinn got his chance when word came down to him about a secret organ auction where some of Vadim's black-market body parts would be sold to the highest bidders.

Spearheading a bust of the auction, a Los Angeles Police Department Corporation task force led by Quinn seized dozens of surgically removed hearts, livers, spleens, bladders, colons and other human viscera taken by Vadim from his victims.

Using genetic imprinting and other forensic technologies to prove that the organs had originally come from murdered Motherboarders, Quinn succeeded in putting across his theory to the World Police Agency. The reverend was arrested on the basis of the evidence that Quinn and his IS operatives had compiled.

Vadim was tried and convicted, though not until a great deal of deliberation and courtroom pyrotechnics had taken place. Vadim's personal fortune of billions of dollars had enabled him to hire the best lawyers in the business to defend him.

In the end most claimed that Vadim might have walked if it had not been for Quinn, whose testimony had led to the conviction that had put the reverend in a federal correction facility.

Learning that the reverend had recently qualified for parole, Quinn had been among those who had pleaded with the courts to keep him locked up for the rest of his life, if need be. But the courts had overruled Quinn.

The Reverend Vadim had reformed, they claimed. He was a changed man, one who had paid his debt to society and could now live a productive existence. Brain scans and expert testimony had backed up these assertions. Vadim was fit to be released.

The purpose of prison, society's watchdogs had told Quinn, was not to warehouse criminals, but to turn them into useful members of society. These were not the primitive days of the twentieth century, after all, they added. These were enlightened times.

Quinn had answered at the parole hearings that the Reverend Vadim could as soon be a useful member of society as an infectious virus could be a friend to mankind. The reverend was a disease, he had argued, one as deadly as a cancer.

But he had been overruled....

THE FLIGHT ATTENDANT came by again. "Are you sure you wouldn't like me to get you something, sir?" the attractive greenette with fashionable purple eyes asked Quinn, her smile suggesting something other than a drink or sandwich.

"No, thank you," Quinn replied, shaking his head. Turning, he caught sight of his reflection against the mirrorlike surface of the double-paned glass, backed by the seamless blackness of space. His jaw was tight and his lips were drawn back in a snarl. But it was the eyes in the reflected image that held Quinn's attention.

He now knew why the flight attendant had been so solicitous. The eyes staring back at Quinn were the eyes of a man in pain. And the source of that pain was the man who had just been freed from Ironstone Prison.

4

Some months after the Reverend Vadim's release from Ironstone Prison, the world bore witness to an amazing exodus. It was called the Day of Ascension.

At airport terminals across the continental United States, from Los Angeles to New York City, planes chartered by the reverend's organization were taking off in a mass migration never before seen on earth.

Their destination was Sunyata.

In its high orbit more than twenty thousand miles above the planet, the space station looked down upon the spinning blue globe from which the aerospace planes took off on their skyward journeys.

Among the thousands of acolytes heading for the runway-to-orbit-capable aircraft was Mike Bodhi Tree. Mike was the unhappy product of a broken home. He had run away at an early age, earning a meager and precarious living as a teenage prostitute who worked the mean streets of Los Angeles in order to stay alive.

He had been picked up off the streets by one of the mobile recruitment teams sent out by the reverend's Church of the Divine Motherboard to scour the city streets for new converts to the cause.

Like most other recruitment targets, once the mobile team hooked Mike they easily reeled him in. The teams rarely lost a recruit. Nor was Mike given a chance to think too long about the possibility that he might have made a tragic mistake in going with the Motherboarders. From the moment that the mobile team had picked him up, the cult began the process that would culminate in turning him into one of its own.

While it put hot food into Mike's belly, the cult put their twisted doctrines into his vulnerable mind. Soon his head was as bald as a cue ball and his worn street clothes had been replaced by flowing white robes of a phase-one Motherboarder clone.

After days of psychological conditioning and the ingestion of mind-altering drugs that his food was laced with, Mike had moved on to the next and final phase of his membership in the Motherboard Church. He had "volunteered" to be implanted with a hardware drug module interface. This would permit him, his keepers told him, to be "plugged directly into the great cosmic motherboard" and become a phase-two clone.

The name he had been given at birth had been changed as Mike underwent the initiation ceremony from which he would emerge a full-fledged Motherboarder. From that moment on he adopted the surname "Bodhi Tree."

Mike saw visions of the paradise that awaited him through being plugged directly into the divine motherboard as a phase-two clone. The integrated-circuit chip that was inserted into his skull interface showed Mike images of the destruction of the wicked and the rewarding of the just.

Seas of fire, lakes of burning lava, swarms of pestilential killer bees and other hellish plagues tortured the unbelievers. Most of humanity died horribly under these afflictions, for humanity was wicked and evil and rotten to the core.

Mankind deserved to suffer such a fate, preached the Reverend Vadim. Only those who joined his church as holy clones would be saved. Only the Motherboarders deserved salvation by becoming one with the cosmic circuit of Mu, the divine mother.

Now, on the Day of Ascension, Mike Bodhi Tree as a phase-two clone, trudged with the crowd toward the waiting scramjet. There he was seated and sat quietly, lulled by the alpha waves coming from the chip in his skull.

Songs praising the glory of the lost mother continent, Mu, were struck up as the scramjet began rolling down its taxiway. Mike joined in, joyously singing "my interface is in thy hands, oh Mother."

Quickly getting airborne, the ASP reached transonic velocities and rocketed upward toward the microatmosphere and microgravity of near-space, where the mothership Sunyata waited to receive him into her electric bosom.

"IT IS perfection itself," the Reverend Vadim cried with joy as he looked out into the blackness of space through one of Sunyata's oversize viewing windows.

The station was a dual-keel type, constructed of a network of modular components linked by connecting nodes. Immense solar collector arrays were pointed at the sun at all times, gathering solar energy for conversion to electrical power.

A spinning hub at the center of the station maintained an artificially generated earth gravity of one g. Also at the station's central hub were the main docking platform, housing launch and landing facilities for space shuttles, aerospace planes, orbital tractor vehicles and other craft.

Glistening silver specks were approaching from Earth as the Reverend Vadim looked down on the shining blue orb below, and he knew that these were the planes that contained his followers, drawn to him like filings of metal to a powerful magnetic field.

"They come by the thousands. How many have we, Tabor?"

"I've lost count," Donald Martin Tabor replied gruffly.

He was a stocky man with thickly muscled arms and a barrel chest. His head looked small by comparison with the rest of his body, especially because of the crew cut that he sported, accenting the hollows beneath the high bones of his skeletal cheeks. "Enough, anyway," he concluded with a laugh.

"Fine. That's how I like it," Vadim answered the former circus strongman and longtime associate, for it was Tabor who had managed the Motherboard Church in the reverend's absence. "Is the Earth-based operation on-line yet?"

"Yeah," Tabor replied, nodding. "The plug factory in Elay is ready to begin production."

"Uh-uh. I meant the new megachips, Tabor," Vadim stressed. "What about them? Don't jerk me on this."

"Well," answered Tabor, drawing out the one-syllable word and spreading his hands, "that might take a little longer. But not too long."

"Make sure it doesn't, Tabor," Vadim replied, turning to the large window in which the planet Earth hung against the blackness of outer space. "And above all, make damned sure you don't get caught."

THE REVEREND WALKED OUT onto the rostrum. He was resplendent in his flowing white robes, almost godlike.

"Chips socketed on the great cosmic Motherboard," he began. "I bring you tidings of salvation, hosannas of praise, proclamations of glory," he went on.

A cheer went up from the assemblage of phase-two clones in the great hall. In the crowd was Mike Bodhi Tree. Like the rest of the acolytes filling the great hall of worship, he applauded the appearance of the reverend with all his heart and soul. A deep hungering to merge his being with the spirit of Mu, she who had installed the motherboard at the dawn of history, filled Mike's soul.

"Now I shall channel Abraxas, the high priest of Mu," the reverend said. "It is he who hid the crystals of power before that terrible day when Mu sank beneath the waves forever. Now the spirit of Abraxas will discourse through these lips of flesh. Listen well, for he speaks for the ancient mother."

A hush fell across the assemblage.

The reverend's features changed as he underwent a complete transformation. His eyes became hollow black orbs staring out from infinite depths. His lips trembled. His body seemed to shake and shudder as if seized by terrible convulsions.

"Ahh..." the deep voice that came from his lips proclaimed. "Abraxas comes forth!"

Channeled through Vadim, Abraxas spoke and prophesied from his place in the spirit realm. The Muan priest did not have good news to report. He told his faithful flock about the cataclysm that would soon strike the earth below.

Mountains would quake and split apart like ridges on a crust of rising bread. The planets would swing out of orbit like beads spilling from a broken string as the sun enlarged to fill the entire sky, burning all living things before the coming of redemption for the faithful.

The Reverend Vadim, said the voice of the Muan priest, had been released from Ironstone Prison just before this tragedy would strike.

The cataclysm would befall the nations of mankind in the twenty-first century because of the same wickedness that had doomed his own people millions of years before, on the primal continent of Mu, the land of the mother.

"Debug your flesh program!" cried the spirit of Abraxas from Vadim's lips. "Cleanse the virus of ignorance from your source code! Socket your chips upon the bosom of the cosmic motherboard!"

At the conclusion of the ceremony, Mike Bodhi Tree was among those "clones" who volunteered to donate their flesh to the motherboard. With gladness in his heart, he signed a standard waiver form legal under the National Euthanasia Act of 2010 and was led to a far chamber of the space station.

When the group to be euthanized was assembled there, a technician punched a series of keystrokes into a computer keyboard. A code number flashed on the computer screen, along with a message: terminating number 0987-655.

The plug module in Mike Bodhi Tree's McBrain instantly sent out a lethal signal and induced a massive cerebral hemorrhage.

Mike's eyes rolled up in his head within a second. Even as the blood from his rupturing McBrain began to ooze from his ears, nose and mouth, he was being wheeled on a gurney into an operating room.

There, medical technicians in sterile gowns waited to harvest the precious organs before necrosis set in and they lost all commercial value to the Motherboard Church.

5

The warehouse stood on a burned-out city block that itself occupied a place on a forlorn grid of trashed streets. Riots sparked by food shortages and fanned to flames by the mob's lust for destruction had claimed most of the buildings here years before.

Now there was not a lot of the original architecture left standing and nobody in their right mind would have even thought of building there since the riots.

Constructed of cinder blocks and concrete, the warehouse dominated the bleak, eerily desolate landscape of what Los Angelinos, and indeed the rest of America, called the L.A. Burnout Zone.

Outside its walls, in the barren city streets, all appeared deceptively quiet. Inside the lone warehouse, it was another matter entirely.

The earth below the two-story cinder-block building had been tunneled out extensively into a network of huge concrete-walled bunkers. Hardware-narcotics-manufacturing plants and research-and-development facilities had then been installed into every square foot of this subterranean facility.

Tabor, the reverend's chief enforcer, had come down to Earth from the space station Sunyata to oversee the operation. He toured the facility, determined to get the production of the mega chips started before the reverend lost patience with him.

That, he had learned, could prove hazardous to the health.

QUINN SAT before the console screens in the darkened interior of the surveillance van parked on a street on the perimeter of the Burnout Zone.

The only source of light came from the banks of blinking data terminals that crammed every spare inch of wall space in the vehicle. The only sounds were the click of computer keys and the whirring of disk-drive mechanisms and high-speed printers.

The Black Shadow satellite imaging platform used by Intervention Systems was about to come on-line.

In moments down-linked telemetry flashed across the console viewscreen as the Black Shadow satellite made another of the scheduled high-altitude passes over the city that night.

The computer systems inside the van recorded every byte of data sent down from the orbital imaging platform. Sophisticated sensing filters combed the digitized surveillance telemetry utilizing artificial-intelligence encoding.

The computers had been programmed to search through the stream of telemetry for indications of drug manufacturing, and the intelligent machines went about their task with speed and efficiency.

Quinn was aware that the Reverend Vadim knew his business and had perfected his modus operandi. As shrewd as he was insane, Vadim would have taken care to use thermal-imaging countermeasures to hide any drug-manufacturing activities in the Burnout Zone.

Stealth would ensure the continuance of his illegal industrial activities, and Vadim would have installed the best systems that money could buy, if he acted true to form.

The sensitive cameras orbiting in space had now come on-line, transmitting real-time video of the desolation below.

The screens relaying satellite imaging data showed Quinn a slow pan of the landscape of South Central Los Angeles. The bleak urban grid was covered by rubble, looking just like the urban combat zone that in fact it was.

As Quinn watched the telemetry, the signals-processing computer, which had been filtering the transmission for signs of illegal drug manufacture, flashed him a message indicating that he might have hit pay dirt.

"High probability of match parameters detected" read the text block that had popped up over the images beamed down from space. Quinn keystroked in commands that told the computer that the data was to be saved for another look-see after the satellite had completed its pass.

After a period of time, the Black Shadow surveillance platform had completed its sweep across the skies far above the city. Now all of the millions of bytes of visual data that the "overhead system" had scanned and recorded was logged into the mass memory of the computers on board the van.

There were thirty-odd possibles, announced the computer after it had analyzed all the discrepancies it had detected from the satellite scan.

All the possible sites exhibited thermal signatures that seemed to be incongruous with their apparent function. A chimney, for example, would display a heat pattern that normally would be different from that made by the engine of a car.

In each of the "possibles" flagged by the computer, there was a discrepancy between the known thermal signatures of the objects and those that had been detected by the overhead imaging platform. The very fact that it looked as if someone had taken precautions to disguise the thermal signatures made the flagged sites look suspicious.

Of course, these readings could also be attributable to environmental causes, or even artificial factors that were of nonhuman origin, such as debris blocking a ventilation duct in such a manner that the dispersal pattern of escaping heat was such that the computer flagged it as suspicious.

Item by item he painstakingly scanned the Black Shadow recon satellite's transmitted data until his eyes hurt and his mind throbbed. Quinn was driven by the haunting images of the victims of Vadim's ghoulish crimes, and by his obsession to prevent the same obscenities from happening all over again.

Hours later he had narrowed down the field to three high-grade target sites. The satellite had done its work, and now had come the moment for Nomad to take a closer look from a different observational perspective. Quinn swiveled in his chair and switched to another viewing window on the main computer screen.

He selected the menu option called Launch Drone.

Within moments the remote-piloted vehicle, or RPV, lifted silently from the roof of the van. The drone soared to a height of eighty feet, then began cruising across the darkened city in a westerly direction, heading toward the first site that Nomad had targeted for a closer look.

Clutching a yoke-type piloting device, Quinn steered the rotor-powered miniature aircraft across the dark, cloud-streaked skies.

Television and thermal-imaging sensors arranged on its outer hull in a phased array sent multimode data to the stationary van. Quinn steered the drone aircraft with such dexterity that it seemed the distant machine was an extension of himself.

Within a matter of minutes the pilotless drone had reached the first of the preselected surveillance sites. Quinn slowed the RPV's forward speed and put it into a holding pattern above the initial target site—a building where an unusual thermal pattern had been detected by the computers. Quinn lowered the RPV to investigate the target close in.

On the rooftop he saw the reason for the odd patterns: a group of winos were sleeping there, and their body heat, in addition to the smoldering remains of a cooking fire, had been the cause of the discordant readings.

Taking the drone up again, Quinn piloted the unmanned surveillance aircraft toward its next target site. This, too, turned out to be a dead end. But on his third try, Quinn found what he thought might in fact be pay dirt.

He zoomed in the image on the screen before him. There was the telltale structure—a system of metal vanes that was part of a roof-mounted ventilation duct that had looked suspicious to the computers, as in fact it did to his own eyes. He called up Image Enhancement on the computer's icon menu.

The image of the duct was zoomed up and digitally refurbished. What Quinn saw on the viewscreen convinced him that the structure, which on close inspection appeared to be made out of hundreds of thin metal tubes, was definitely out of place on the rooftop of the warehouse.

Quinn called up Comparison menu on the screen. The computer's artificial-intelligence drivers matched the image to entries in a digital library containing the specifications of millions of technological components of U.S. and international manufacture. In a matter of moments it flashed the message "Match probability ninety-eight percent" to Quinn.

The definition of the object was a thermal interface distorter, part number EV-78901.

It was manufactured by Cybertron Military Supplies of Greenville, Texas, as a niche product for what the on-line parts description said was "for changing the thermal signature of vehicles and structures and to facilitate evasion of detection by both ground-based and overhead imaging platforms with a high order of effectiveness."

Quinn phoned Cybertron Military Supplies and was linked to its computer by high-speed modem.

"Thank you for calling Cybertron Military Supplies," the androgynous voice of a service computer answered when the line engaged. "None of our sales representatives are here at the moment, but if you would like to engage our on-line data base, please do so at your first convenience."

Quinn's own computers were soon linked to Cybertron's, and the military supply company's data base yielded its most protected information to the security clearance that Quinn had electronically "forged" to gain access to the system.

The hack was illegal, but if he could save one life that Lux Vadim was destined to take, then Quinn was not above hacking the Cybertron computer. His system penetration provided him with the data that the part had been sold to a reseller outfit known as Data Integration Products of Los Angeles.

Quinn checked further, closing down the Cybertron hack and clandestinely entering the computer systems of several banks, commodities exchanges and even the federal courts system to secure the data he required to nail Lux Vadim to the wall.

Data Integration Products, it turned out, was actually a shell corporation leased to an offshore corporate entity, the South Breeze Conglomerate, based in the Cayman Islands, B.W.I.

By now Quinn knew enough to convince him that an on-site inspection of the warehouse was warranted. Placing all systems on standby, Quinn prepared to pay the warehouse an unscheduled visit in the dead of the night.

6

Some time after the moon had set over the city of Los Angeles, one of two wandering homeless men drinking cheap wine cut with hallucinogens chanced to glance up into the starlit sky. The one who had looked up suddenly cried out and pointed his finger at the stars.

"Yo! Check that shit out!" he shouted to his companion.

He had seen what appeared to be a huge bird or bat flying directly overhead. The frightening apparition glimpsed by the homeless man was silhouetted against the field of stars, its immense wings propelling it across the heavens at a fantastic rate of speed.

"Don't see nothing, man," the wino's companion answered with a shake of his head.

He had followed his partner's pointing finger and seen nothing out of the ordinary in the sky above. Except for the outlines of the skyscrapers in the distance, and the seamier skyline of the squat buildings in the Burnout Zone, the night sky was as empty as the bottle of cheap hootch he's just chucked into a rubble-strewn lot.

"It was there, I tell you!" the first man cried out. "I seen it! Some kinda giant fucking bird!"

"You been drinking too much rotgut, man," the second wino told the first. "You're losing your mind. Lemme take you to the euth center."

"Fuck you, motherscut!" the first man protested, shoving the second man in the chest. "Maybe it's me who's gonna take *you* to the euth center!"

Instead of shoving back, the second man drew a long combat dagger. Without saying another word he plunged it into the belly of the first derelict. Blood began to gush and he turned the knife in the wound, drawing it up from navel to clavicle and feeling hot blood gush all over the filthy rags he wore as his buddy's entrails ruptured.

"You should'a kept your stinkin' mouth shut," he said to the mutilated corpse as he wiped the bloody blade with the dirty scrap of a discarded cellophane bag. Hearing the sound of growling as a feral dog pack sniffed the blood scent on the wind, the second man got scared and ran away, his thoughts already turning to how he could cadge the money for a fresh bottle of LSD wine.

The second man would not have been as skeptical had he looked at the skies a pulsebeat sooner. Then he would have seen the winged figure pass almost directly over his head.

That figure was now approximately a quarter mile from the vacant lot where the two men had argued over the apparition that the first had seen in the night skies overhcad. But it had been no bird, bat or other flying creature that was glimpsed by the dead man who had spoken up.

What had been mistaken in the darkness for an animal was in fact a highly sophisticated machine.

Its wing were mechanical, linked to an onboard computer processor that controlled their upsweep and downbeat with precisely timed rhythms, while rear elevons and control surfaces made up the tail assembly.

The device was an ornithopter, and it was piloted by the man called Nomad.

The target zone flashed on the virtual screen as invisible lasers painted the ground below and sub-miniature computer hardware enhanced the image, throughputting a constant stream of tactical data.

Quinn circled the warehouse as he subjected the strike site to a series of multiple-mode scans. Thermal imaging continued to yield evidence that the site was a likely candidate for search and interdiction: a great deal of effort had seemingly gone into dissipating the thermal patterns rising from the warehouse.

Using his wrist-top keypad, Quinn punched in a fast command sequence. The ornithopter's navigational computer immediately put the unique, movable-winged aircraft into its automatic-landing sequence.

The rapid beating of mechanical pinions against the cool night air was the only sound that disturbed the stillness of the night as Quinn's combat-booted feet touched down lightly on the rooftop of the building below.

Inputting another sequence on his wrist-top keypad, Quinn unfastened the wings and fuselage of the ornithopter from the quick-release fittings that fused the various components to his body. In previous eras, fliers talked of "strapping aircraft to their backs." Now that expression had finally become a reality.

Each of the ornithopter's wing, tail assembly and airframe elements neatly collapsed and folded up into modular units that Quinn stashed quickly in the darkness of the warehouse rooftop.

He might need these components later for escape. But if anyone but himself tampered with them, computer-linked antipersonnel submunitions would go into autodestruct mode, blowing away all traces of the advanced-design flying machine.

Invisible to night-vision instruments, Quinn trod stealthily across the rooftop on specially cushioned boots. All forms of thermal imaging and passive infrared scanning were defeated by the stealth suit that encased his body in a cocoon of virtual invisibility.

The unique combat garb functioned by breaking up the thermal patterning produced by the human body. It accomplished this feat by means of a criss-crossing network of microthin plastic tubes sandwiched between the fabric of the stealth suit.

This mixed pattern of heat and cold could be "sculpted" to match the thermal signature of the surrounding environment. This was to prevent the production of "black holes"—areas of negative thermal activity—which would be telltale giveaways of attempts to conceal a heat source.

Also unique was the battle mask worn by the striker. The virtual-reality goggles or VRGs, Quinn wore covered most of his head area, the two large sensor arrays fronting the goggles resembling the eyes of a predatory mantis.

The VRGs constantly scanned the combat environment with invisible Q-switched lasers, sonars and radars, mixing the scans or selecting one mode above the other according to the situational dynamics of the ops zone. Constantly updated tactical data could be flashed on the virtual screen for use by strike personnel in real time.

The VRGs could also be cybernetically linked to one or several personal defense weapons, such as the P-90 CAW, or close assault weapon, that Quinn now ported, enabling him to put a pipper, or "death dot," on the target display. This in turn would automatically trigger the weapon and release computer-guided burst fire.

Moving swiftly, Quinn found an entrance on the rooftop and crossed toward it. Although this access point was secured by an electronic keypad lock, it wasn't a problem to the cybernetic warrior on the roof. Quinn unshipped a lock decrypter mechanism from one of the gear pouches on his stealth suit and proceeded to phreak the lock.

He placed the lock decrypter over the keypad of the lock. At once the decrypter went to work, intercepting and decoding the locking sequence. In a few moments, the message "lock decrypted" flashed across the LCD display window.

A few seconds later the lock had been popped right open. Swinging the door open, Quinn stole down a set of fire stairs. Probing ahead of him, the invisible laser beams of his VRGs scanned the strike perimeter. No sign of threat was detected in the darkness below.

At the foot of the stairs, the striker's on-board audio amplifier picked up the sounds of voices. The upper stories of the building were pitch-dark, and Quinn moved with the confidence that he could not be seen in the absence of light.

This was not the case for the two mercenary troopers who were making the rounds of their patrol perimeter below. The fact that the patrol walkers wore passive infrared night-seeing goggles explained the reason for the total darkness.

The strategy behind their security patrol activity was to capture penetrators in the darkness who could not see them coming until it was too late. This strategy was about to backfire.

Nomad passed directly in front of the two-man perimeter patrol, the heat signature of his stealth suit making him blend into the enveloping darkness. Through his VRGs he could clearly see his targets as easily as though it were high noon. They were staring directly at him, unaware of his presence despite the image-intensifying goggles that jutted from their masked faces.

Using the buttstock of the P-90, Quinn lashed out at the jaw of the first sentry. The man let out a grunt and crumpled to the deck, knocked unconscious. The second man heard the dull thud of the body toppling to the floor nearby and whipped his weapon toward the source of the sounds.

He saw nothing, except for his partner lying in a heap on the floor.

"Scudder?" he called out, sweeping the muzzle of his AUG bullpup left and right, unsure whether to go toward his partner or not. "Scudder, what the—"

A savage side kick to the merc's head, using the side of the foot as a striking point, made what seemed like a bright flash of lightning explode inside his brain. Knees buckling, the second merc collapsed with a loud grunt onto the deck a few feet from his partner.

Quinn checked their conditions with the VRGs set on bioscan tracking mode. A graph showing vital signs traces of Quinn's victims confirmed that they had not been seriously injured, but would remain unconscious for some time.

To make certain that the unconscious security crewmen would present no further threat or raise any alarms, Quinn unshipped a roll of duct tape and used strips he cut from it to bind their hands and feet and to gag their mouths.

Some things couldn't be improved upon, and as far as securing captives quickly and efficiently went, the sticky silver tape was an old, reliable solution. As he left his immobilized captives, Quinn was certain that they would remain on ice for the duration of the assault.

7

In the glassed-in booth that looked down onto the main mezzanine of the assembly line, Tabor was on the secure satcom uplink to the space station Sunyata.

"Make sure that production quotas are raised by three percent," the voice coming from the face on the phone's viewscreen commanded Tabor. "Quality-control standards have been piss-poor, too."

"I'm working on it," Tabor told the Reverend Lux Vadim. "But it's rough. These new people, they're green. Don't forget that all the old pros are gone."

"I'm well aware of that, Tabor," Vadim said. "Nevertheless, I want to see results. That's what you're paid a great deal of money for, in case you've forgotten."

"Production levels *will* rise," Tabor promised. "I personally guarantee it."

There was sudden static over the connection as the face on the screen began to waver, then break up as noise bands crisscrossed the screen. The space station Sunyata was passing out of telemetry range overhead. Soon all transmission would be cut off.

"Keep me posted," Vadim said, and quickly severed the connection link.

As the screen blanked, Tabor spun around on his heel and walked over to the observation window.

In the drug factory below, he could see the shaven-headed Motherboarders busy at their work stations. They were engaged in various activities ranging from testing the chip matrices to assembling the finished product, ready to be shoved into the skull sockets of plug-drug junkies across America.

Tabor took out a noncarc cigarette and popped the self-lighting cap on its end. He inhaled ginseng-flavored smoke and cursed under his breath as he continued to scan the activity down below the observation window of the sky suite.

These people were no damned good, he thought as he shook his head in disgust. They just plodded along like robots, which, of course, they were.

The secret was in the supervisory people who could speed up the process and squeeze every drop of productivity out of the "clone" labor force.

But all of those upper-echelon people had gone down with the reverend when he had been busted a few years ago. They were either dead, had taken a powder or were waiting to max out behind the bars of cells in the federal penitentiary system.

No way was Tabor going to up production quotas the way things were going. He could see the handwriting on the wall.

He turned and walked out the door of the sky suite. He would have to talk to the new supervisors he'd just hired. Somehow, he'd have to get his point across to them. If promises of more money wouldn't work, then he would just have to put the fear of God in them. Maybe, he thought, he should kill a few right now, just to set an example for the others.

ELAPSED MISSION TIME was nearing the twelve-minute mark. Quinn crossed the warehouse area to inspect some of the shipping cartons stacked against the bare concrete wall. The boxes bore markings indicating that they contained nonprescription drugs and medical supplies of various kinds.

Using his wrist-top keypad, Quinn punched in a command string that placed his VRGs in real-time recording mode. The data block reading "video recorder active—elapsed time 00:00 seconds" flashed on the upper right corner of his virtual screen before popping out of existence again.

Lifting up one of the storage cartons from the warehouse floor, Quinn was not surprised to find that the carton seemed to be feather light. Using a spring-loaded knife to slit open the box, he found that it was completely empty.

Repeating his search throughout the storage area, he discovered that the remainder of the boxes were just as empty as the first carton he'd checked.

This confirmed Quinn's impression that the warehouse was only a shell and that the entire building housed a front operation for the genuine business being conducted elsewhere on the premises: illicit plug-drug manufacture, most likely.

Before turning his attention away from the storage cartons, Quinn panned the VRGs across the empty boxes littering the floor, recording the crime scene as evidence against the Reverend Vadim.

Because he did not have a warrant, his search was not legal and would not hold up in court. Nevertheless, there were those who would be highly interested in the data he brought back, obtained according to Hoyle or not.

With the VRGs still on video-recorder mode, Quinn crossed to one of the exits and used his lock decrypter to silently open the door and defeat its intruder alarm.

The passive IR sensors built into the corridor's smart walls failed to register the passage of the stealth-suited striker as Quinn hustled down a flight of stairs that quickly brought him into the lowest levels of the building.

At the foot of the steps he came upon another door, this one bearing only a crash bar and no lock.

Reaching toward his right wrist, Quinn punched up farfoon mode on his wrist-top pad.

Standing stock-still, he listened for a while. From beyond the door came muted voices, the jingling of metal fastenings, the rustling of fabric and the noises made by the soft treading of footsteps.

"Analysis" read the data block superimposed on the VRG screen after Quinn keystroked another command set on his wrist-top pad and artificial-intelligence hardware initialized. "Security station fifteen yards beyond door...eighty-four percent probability of three guards on station."

Quinn hit a key on his wrist-top pad. The screen immediately flashed him a wire diagram in glowing red that indicated that on the other side of the door the corridor made an L-shaped blind turn before opening out onto a security station. Three-dimensional green-colored wire diagrams showed human figures seated at a console station beyond the bend.

Switching the VRGs to full-automatic scan modes, Quinn reached down and pulled the doughnut-shaped P-90 CAW from the Velcro quick-draw fastenings at his thigh. A targeting pipper automatically appeared on the virtual screen as he silently pushed against the crash bar and swung open the door.

Invisible lasers swept the corridor and redrew the VRG screen to process new data streaming in from the ops zone. Numerals indicating the distance to the security station around the corridor's L-bend augmented the wire diagram in glowing red as Quinn darted around the corner, bringing him into the line of sight of the guards occupying the security station.

The 3-D wire diagrams indicating the figures of the guards began to move as the first guard recovered from his initial shock at scoping the black-clad striker in the high-tech battle mask. In Quinn's cyberspatial viewing envelope, the three guards were immediately assigned targeting priorities.

As the first guard spun around, simultaneously drawing the weapon holstered at his hip, Quinn put the death dot at the center of the reticle that had appeared over the diagram of the target's head.

A trigger squeeze on the P-90, and a silenced autoburst of precision-targeted 5.70 mm fléchette fire rotored from the black plastic doughnut in Quinn's gloved fist, hurled with lethal accuracy at the target simulation on his VRG screen.

Quinn scored two more takedowns in quick succession after the first guard was terminated clean and fast. The two other security personnel had both made the wrong moves, reaching for their Glock side arms instead of raising their hands in the air. They had paid the price for acting in haste rather than surrendering.

Moving quickly to the guard station, Quinn subjected the combat zone to a fast perimeter scan. The VRGs reclassified the strike environment's status as threat neutral.

Holstering the CAW, Quinn crossed quickly to the blood-spattered security console and unshipped the phreaker he had brought with him.

Before deploying the phreaker, Quinn wanted a full schematic of the mission site. If one were available, the main security computer was the place from which to get it.

Locating an RS-232 serial port, Quinn attached a cable to the twenty-six-pin interface and punched in a command set on his wrist-top keypad. Within a matter of seconds, the VRGs' on-board computer had found the floor plan of the site and copied the data to its high-capacity bubble memory.

Now it was time to put the phreaker into action. Punching a command set into the keypad on the small black box, Quinn placed the phreaker beneath one of the consoles. Its magnetized surface held fast to the metal housing. Quinn checked the security console screens and noted with satisfaction that the area of penetration continued to remain tactically sterile.

Hunched over one of the keyboards of the security station, Quinn tried to patch a playback of the past six to eight minutes of monitoring the area onto the security screen. Again, to his satisfaction, the screen showed no indication of his presence.

This told Quinn that his phreaker was functioning properly. Its integrated circuitry would continue to override the security channel with its own signals, spoofing the perimeter security sensors.

Rising from the security station after inputting a ten minute warning to personnel timed to coincide with the detonation of the charges he'd brought, Quinn again reached for the lethal black doughnut holstered at his thigh. His VRGs indicated that its clip was seventy-five percent full of 5.70 mm rounds, and Quinn decided to pop a fresh clip into the magazine well that sat vertically atop the P-90's receiver.

The VRGs had also redrawn the virtual screen to display an updated 3-D wire diagram of the area based on the floor plans that Quinn had copied earlier. Following the glowing digital arrow, Quinn continued on his probe through the three-dimensional maze of cybernetic space.

8

Tabor was in the matrix room, looking at Armageddon.

Projected onto the wall was an immense blowup of a Wire hardware drug chip, the core layer known as the "matrix."

A technician was explaining how this new plug drug, to be called "Armageddon," would be twice as potent as any drug of its type that had been manufactured before.

"We've squeezed in a million more transistors," the tech explained proudly to Tabor. "A hit of one of these can be incredibly addictive."

"What's the downside?" Tabor asked the techie. "And why hasn't production on this line been instituted yet?"

"Well," answered the tech a little sheepishly, "there have been some problems in our development cycle. I'll show you if you'll permit me."

He asked Tabor to come with him. They went from the projection room into the research wing. Here a thick pane of double-layered viewing glass gave vantage into a testing area, backed up by a recording camera aimed inside the room.

Beyond the large glass panel were two shaven-headed Motherboarder clones in their flowing white robes. The acolytes were sitting on the floor, staring at the walls with blank expressions on their faces.

"Everything ready?" the tech asked a woman seated at a console filled with multiple viewscreens and flashing digital displays. At her nod of assent, the tech turned to Tabor and said, "They can't see or hear us. The glass is one-way."

"I assume that these two are testing the new chip you're developing," Tabor surmised, inspecting the experimental subjects through the large pane of shatterproof glass.

"That's correct. The prototypes are identical to ordinary plugs except for the fact that they can only be activated from the remote console here."

He gestured toward the tech at the console. "Care to see a demonstration?" he asked Tabor. "I have to warn you, it may get a little hairy."

"I'm ready," Tabor told him, waving his arm impatiently. "Just do it."

"Corinne, please initialize," the tech said.

The woman nodded and input a series of commands. "Showing deep alpha wave readings," she announced, her eyes tracking across the array of data terminals. "They're feeling the effects."

Tabor watched the Wireheads inside the glassed-in room begin to stir from their catatonia. Suddenly their motions became spasmodic.

One began repeatedly striking his skull against the shatterproof window. Soon blood began to streak the double-walled glass. The other walked, fell, picked himself up and repeated the process all over again.

Seconds later the test subjects began lashing out at each other. The one who had been banging his head on the window grabbed hold of the other's shoulders and bit into his face, sinking his front teeth into the fleshy skin of his right cheek just below the eyelid and pulling his head sharply back with a tearing noise.

Flesh ripped away, and an eye popped out of its socket, trailing a bloody cord of nerve fibers behind it. As the eyeless subject was gripped by agony, the attacker bit him again, stripping more flesh from his face.

"Gas them," the head tech said to his assistant, "we've seen quite enough."

The tech at the console quickly input a series of commands at her keyboard. Tabor immediately saw a greenish haze fill the glassed-in testing chamber as nerve gas was ejected from nozzles in the ceiling and floor.

Both subjects inside the observation chamber quickly dropped to the deck and all movement ceased, except for an occasional twitch and the seepage of blood from the bitten-up face of the badly lacerated subject.

"We have to kill them when they go haywire," explained the tech to Tabor. "Once the plugs are initialized, we can't turn them off again." He looked away for a moment. "As you can see, we've got some problems with this new chip matrix," he finished.

"How many of them have you tested it on?" Tabor asked.

"Dozens," the tech replied. "I can get you the exact number if you really need it."

"Not necessary, just keep working on the problem. In the meantime, I want production increased on the regular flavors of our standard line of hardware narcotics. That order comes directly from upstairs."

"The man himself," the head tech grunted as he nodded. "All right, I'll try my best. You'll see results in twenty-four hours."

"I'd better," Tabor threatened. "Or the next poor suckers in that room might just be you and Corinne."

GRASPING IT by the feet, Quinn dragged the body of the taken-down security guard behind some cylindrical storage modules marked with the yellow-and-black sign indicating the presence of hazardous substances.

With the schematic of the underground installation beneath the dummy warehouse building in the Los Angeles Burnout Zone mapped into memory, Quinn had followed the flashing broken line on his VRG screen to the power station of the facility.

Having terminated the guard, Quinn now unshipped a high-energy explosive charge from one of the ordnance pouches on his black action garb. The fist-size black cylinder bore an LED readout panel at one end. Quinn calibrated the munition for delayed detonation.

Before exiting the zone slated for total demolition, he scanned the strike environment with his virtual-reality goggles.

The storage modules yielded components that were critical to the creation of silicon masks used in the manufacture of integrated-circuit chip matrices, the basic components of illegal hardware narcotics.

Tapping a series of keys on his wrist-top keypad, Quinn asked his on-board computer to flash him data on the next prioritized target site.

The VRG screen promptly showed him a glowing box that highlighted the part of the 3-D wire diagram showing the next sublevel of the multistory underground installation one story below his present position.

Guided by his on-board computer, Quinn negotiated the corridor, avoiding a contingent of security troops who came around a sudden dogleg in the passageway after a threat warning popped up on his screen. When they were gone from sight, he stole into a storage area that the VRGs indicated was a storage dump for highly flammable chemicals.

This area he also slotted with demo charges, using another of the small black superexplosive cylinders he'd unshipped from its carrying pouch.

After leaving the storage area, Quinn soon came to yet another doorway. Phreaking the lock, he pushed inside and found himself within one of the observation suites high above the production line area below.

He crossed the carpeted floor to the picture window and looked down into the manufacturing level. The VRGs were still on video-recording mode. While Quinn scanned the activity below, he punched up wrist-top commands telling the computer to cue him if it found a match with any of the Reverend Vadim's known associates among the personnel in the factory.

Within seconds a zoom window appeared at the center of the real-time video picture. The zoom window showed a close-up shot of the face of a target subject. He was speaking with a tech in the production facility many stories below the sky suite.

The data block above the zoom window informed Quinn that he was looking at Donald Martin Tabor, who was a convicted felon and a known associate of the Reverend Lux Vadim.

Saving this data to random access memory, Quinn exited the sky suite. A threat warning popped up on his VRG screen and he was immediately confronted by a group of security guards emerging from an elevator a short distance along the corridor.

Though startled, the guards reacted at the sight of the blacksuited intruder in the bizarre headgear. As they reached for the micro-SMGs holstered at their hips, Nomad put the targeting pipper on the first takedown and squeezed off a burst of precision-vectored P-90 automatic fire.

As he retargeted and fired again, a second and then a third target was terminated by 5.70 mm needlepoint rounds cycling from the lethal doughnut of black plastic in the striker's gloved fist.

But the fourth and final target was luckier than his brackets, and he'd had a split second advantage while Quinn took down his companions one by one. He managed to skid around a blind corner as a round bored into the wall a fraction of an inch from his face.

Quinn shifted position and saw the guard reaching for an alarm button set high on the wall. Even as the pipper touched the edge of the glowing killbox on

Quinn's virtual screen, the striker knew that it was too late to silence the merc before all hell broke loose.

THREE STORIES BELOW in the manufacturing pit, Tabor heard the sudden din of sirens shrieking from everywhere at once. Jerking his head up at one of the large, flat, digital security screens that projected from the wall above, he saw a security camera shot of the black-clad striker hustle around a bend in the corridor and disappear from the frame.

Tabor didn't know who or what he had just been looking at and he didn't care. All Tabor needed to know was that he was looking at trouble. Big trouble. He had seen that at a glance.

"Damn!" he cursed.

Pulling the micro-SMG from its shoulder rig nestled beneath his jacket, Tabor left the manufacturing level on a flat-out run. Somehow he had to get things back under control. Tabor's job security and his life depended on taking down the man in black.

9

Quinn had ducked into an elevator car, his destination the warehouse rooftop. The elevator rose several levels at his voice command, then came to an abrupt halt.

From a command node outside the elevator shaft, one of the mercenaries had tripped an emergency circuit breaker and stopped the rising car as it ascended toward the warehouse above them.

"You don't have a snowball's chance," a voice said from the speaker grille of the car in place of the simulated voice of the elevator. "We're restarting the elevator. When you reach the next level, lay down any weaponry immediately or you will be shot."

An emergency hatch with a quick-release bolt covered a section of the roof of the elevator car. Quinn put the pipper on the flashing box that framed the release lever and fired a 5.70 mm round that struck the lever and popped the hatch.

Jumping up, Quinn closed his gripper-gloved fingers around the sides of the hole in the roof. Pulling himself up, Quinn waited, crouched in darkness at the top of the car. When it once again came to a stop he heard the muted sounds of shouting voices.

The sonic disrupter grenade no larger than a ball-point pen was clutched in his hand, and a moment later, as its doors silently opened and the guards rushed the elevator, he dropped the grenade through the hole. The electronic "flash-bang" went off in a heartbeat.

Strobing laser flashes and earsplitting high-decibel noise was generated by the small black cylinder. The shattering combination of effects produced an instant suppressive effect on the human central nervous system.

His pursuers were incapacitated, Quinn jumped back down into the elevator car and used a flurry of lashing foot blows and bludgeoning swipes of the buttstock of the P-90 to take out those who were still capable of putting up any resistance.

He was out in the corridor in a matter of seconds, and he followed the flashing yellow broken line on the three-dimensional wire diagram of his VRG screen, which led him toward an emergency exit stairwell.

The stairwell brought Quinn back up into the warehouse from which he had entered the subterranean research-and-development levels of the drug production facility. Back in the lightless environment of the warehouse, his VRGs automatically switched over to night-vision capability.

A brace of mercenaries equipped with night-vision goggles confronted him there within a matter of seconds. Whether or not they had an inkling that the stealth suit rendered Quinn virtually invisible to their image-intensification apparatus, they were taking additional precautions.

"Warning," flashed the VRGs, "Active infrared emissions detected."

Quinn realized that the enemy had augmented the passive infrared detection systems of the NVGs they wore with active IR. Emitters attached to their NVGs were pulsing out beams of infrared radiation. Against active IR, the stealth suit operated at only limited effectiveness levels.

Now capable of being seen, Quinn became a target of coordinated bursts of time-on-target fire from the caseless 4.73 mm fléchette bullpups packed by the patrol personnel.

The near-silent needles of high-density depleted uranium whooshed through the air in a lethal shower as Quinn tucked and rolled out of the line of whip-sawing automatic fire.

From a half crouch, he launched an answering salvo of 5.70 mm steel at the opposition. He scored a clean takedown as one of the hired guns grunted and fell spread-eagled onto the floor, but there were others still up and shooting.

Time was not on Quinn's side.

"Warning," another VRG readout flashed in a data block above the real-time video display. "Final Countdown to detonation commencing. Fifteen minutes and counting at mark..."

The mark was signaled by a one-second beeptone indicating to Quinn that he would need to deal with the mercs quickly and decisively or be caught at ground zero himself when the small yet lethal munitions he had slotted throughout the installation detonated.

When the charges went up, the entire complex would become a blazing mushroom cloud, disintegrating everything above and below ground in a devouring firestorm.

Quinn broke right and left as more lethal heat was directed his way. At the end of his zigzagging run he took cover behind some modularized cargo crates that were stacked against one of the warehouse walls.

In an attempt to distract the shooter detail, Quinn tossed more advanced-design flash-bangs their way. As the neural disrupters detonated, strobing light combined with deafening sound effects overloaded the IR sensors, temporarily blinding the NVG-equipped opposition forces.

Using the precious seconds he'd gained by this maneuver, Quinn hosed down the opposition with automatically targeted pulses of P-90 fire, killing all of them as they groped sightlessly in the dark.

He wasted no time in climbing the access stairs toward the rooftop, while his VRG display showed him that only a few minutes remained until the installation shot into the stratosphere in a broiling pillar of flame.

WHILE QUINN was quick-assembling the ornithopter on the warehouse rooftop, attaching the ten-foot carbon-fiber laminate wings to his arms and the lightweight magnesium-aluminum alloy airframe to his back, Tabor, accompanied by two mercenaries, was roaring out of an underground garage in an armored vehicle.

The viewscreens on the dashboard of the truck showed a variety of scenes relayed via down-link from different vantage points inside the installation.

On the screen labeled Warehouse—Low Light, Tabor's security forces were firing their bullpups as they chased the black-clad figure, who seemed to be more than a match for his entire crew.

Who was that guy? Tabor wondered. He'd never seen anything like him before.

A high-low tone sounded from the dashboard grille as a face appeared on one of the viewscreens linked to a console back at the production level.

"Sir, I've got some bad news," the man reported as the sound of gunfire was heard in the background. "We lost the guy. He was fast and tricky. I'm afraid he turned in a high body count."

"Just keep—" Tabor began, when suddenly a tremendous explosion shattered the night to pieces.

Tabor saw the sudden blinding flash of almost supernatural brilliance before he heard the thunderous sonic pulse that followed a heartbeat behind the hell-white detonation flash.

The ten-ton armored vehicle was suddenly rocked on its oversize, run-flat tires by a tremendous shock wave as the warehouse blew itself to kingdom come.

"Damn that bastard!" Tabor cursed as he fought the steering wheel to speedball the vehicle through the streets of the Burnout Zone, thinking about all the things he would do to the intruder if he had the luck to meet him face-to-face.

10

A hot night wind blew across South Central Los Angeles as Quinn launched himself into an empty black void.

In the window on his VRG screen, he could see the glowing numbers running down to the zero mark as the computer clock ticked off the time remaining until the countdown terminated in mass destruction.

Only a matter of seconds remained until the demo charges blew and the hardware narcotic plant blew straight to hell in a searing pillar of flame.

Linked cybernetically to the on-board navigational and flight computer on the ornithopter, Quinn pushed the flight envelope to gain maximum speed and lift.

Using the thermals rising from the shattered streets of the Burnout Zone, Quinn succeeded in climbing to three hundred feet before the primary explosion took place.

There was an earsplitting boom from below as the countdown reached zero and the charges ignited, right on schedule.

A heartbeat later, the entire top story of the warehouse building below and to Quinn's rear disintegrated in a seething cloud of incinerating fire.

In the space that asphalt and concrete had occupied only a matter of moments before, a roiling mushroom of yellow-and-black flame erupted skyward. The fireball expanded like a balloon as it zoomed high into the night. Within a matter of seconds the envelope of incandescent gasses and micropulverized rubble had attained a dizzying altitude of several hundred feet.

Quinn had gained more altitude and distance from the blast site as the demolition charges he had placed had exploded. Helped in his upward climb by the shock wave and sudden updraft from the superheated gases produced by the explosion, he soared higher and higher with each passing second.

Yet Quinn knew that the superheated bubble of gases could roast him alive. He felt the sudden rise in temperature as he rose into the turbulent night air, and he was bathed in the flickering white light of the blast as the thermal pulse of the explosion washed over him with pounding waves of broiling heat. Without warning, the gases in the capillary tubes lining his stealth suit burst as they expanded beyond the tolerance limits of the tubing.

The fabric of the stealth suit began to smolder, and his on-board computer started to fail as operating temperatures began to exceed the VRGs' performance specifications. Severely buffeted by yet another powerful shock wave from a final pair of explosions, Quinn began to plummet earthward.

Then, only a matter of feet before striking the jagged rubble on the ground directly below, the danger had suddenly passed. The intense blast heat began to ebb as the leading edge of the superheated gas bubble began to withdraw toward the nucleus of the firestorm that was beginning to burn itself out.

As he began to rise, shakily in the turbulent air, Quinn realized that he had narrowly escaped serious injury or death.

His mechanical pinions beat against the disturbed air currents as he gained altitude and leveled off at a stable cruising altitude.

There was a vehicle below, negotiating the shattered streets at high speeds. Judging by the route it was taking, Quinn had a gut feeling that the armored van contained escapees from the burning installation.

He punched in a combination on his wrist-top keypad and directed his VRGs to zoom in on the vehicle below. From the blurred outline of half a face reflected in the side-view mirror of the truck, the VRGs' on-line computer was able to construct a match.

"Match probability sixty-five percent that face belongs to Donald Martin Tabor," the text block on Quinn's virtual screen stated, then winked out of existence again.

The match probability given by the computer was high enough for Quinn to proceed with an interdiction strike on the vehicle below.

Increasing power to the ornithopter's carbon-fiber wings, Nomad swooped down in the direction of the truck on a low-trajectory attack vector. He had already unshipped the P-90 close assault weapon.

As he held the black plastic weapon in one hand, the target below was already framed in the glowing cross hairs of his virtual screen.

"WHAT THE HELL is *that?*" asked one of the men riding shotgun in the back of the armored van.

"It's got wings!" shouted the other one, a look of awe on his beefy face. "It's some kinda mutant bird, man. Christ! I can't believe this is happening!"

Tabor swiveled his eyes up through the windshield and peered above the truck. Against the starlit night sky, he saw the gliding winged shape and caught a gleam of the multiscan sensors of Quinn's VRGs.

"That's no bird, you idiots," he shouted back at his gunsels. "It's the same bastard that wasted our people. Blow him out of the sky!"

At once the two mercenaries in the back took up the hardware they ported. One of them got behind the 7.62 mm MAG machine gun whose black snout jutted from the rooftop of the van. As he pointed it up at the sky, the smart weapon's targeting computer automatically acquired the flying form, computing range and azimuth as it continued to track the airborne target. Fire bratted from the big gun, and glowing tracers lit up the night as the triggerman behind the heavy gun opened up.

Quinn's VRGs had spotted the armament below, and he took evasive action as he put the pipper on the target and loosed a salvo of 5.70 mm fléchette fire from the P-90 that razored downward with computer-guided accuracy.

Tabor lost control and crashed against the wall of a building to the right as the burst of 5.70 mm penetrator rounds pierced the hull of the armored van. Its front end collapsed under the impact of the high-speed crash. Cursing as he gunned the van's engine, Tabor tried unsuccessfully to get the stricken war wagon in motion again.

The surviving hardman in the back pushed open one of the van's rear doors and jumped to the street, the black wedge shape of an advanced combat rifle jutting upward in his clenched fists. As the red pencil line of the bullpup's targeting laser arrowed upward, he opened up with a 4.73 mm burst at the strange winged target. But a precisely placed bullet to the head sent the gunman sprawling in a tangle of arms and legs to land in the rubble.

As his final bodyguard went down, Tabor took matters into his own hands. He brought out a man-portable HEMP, or high explosive multipurpose, rocket launcher.

Tabor had had enough of playing around. It was time to get serious with the birdman. He would make him trade his mechanical wings for the wings of an angel. The 80 mm, thermal-seeking beauty perched on his shoulders would blow him sky-high.

Tabor tracked his target via the image-intensifying targeting scope, and as the HEMP unit's laser tracker sighted in on the heat signature of the flying figure, he hit the fire button.

With a loud *ka-thunk!* and a furious rush of back blast, the HEMP round streaked from the launch tube and vectored up into the black skies.

ALTHOUGH TABOR DID NOT realize it, Quinn was now highly vulnerable to acquisition by an infrared seeker round. The effects of the superheated thermal cloud had bubbled away the gases that rendered his stealth suit invisible to heat-emission imaging sensors. The HEMP rocket's seeker head could now lock on to him—and it did, homing in on the areas at the roots of his wings where the motors that powered each upstroke and downstroke were generating heat.

The rocket-powered warhead was a lot faster than Quinn was. He could not run from it and he could not evade it. Only a single strategy was feasible: make it de-acquire by forcing a break lock.

To do this, Quinn flew directly toward the round, bombarding it with laser energy from his VRGs' front-mounted sensors. Overloading the rocket's sensors, the energy bombardment secured a break lock on the warhead. The missile veered to one side just before its proximity-fuzed warhead detonated.

But the explosion took place close enough to send Quinn reeling from the skies. With one ten-foot wing almost useless due to shrapnel strikes, he went spiraling down to the rubble-strewn streets of the Burnout Zone.

TABOR HAD his Glock 25 SMG clutched in a two-handed grip, having tossed aside the now-useless HEMP firing tube. A graveyard grin twisted his features as he headed toward the prone figure, eager to deliver a put-away stroke to his downed and apparently injured adversary.

So intent was Tabor on killing his blacksuited antagonist that he took no notice of the stream of fuel that had been leaking steadily from the rear of the truck ever since it crashed.

Struggling to stand after plummeting to earth, Quinn saw Tabor hustling toward him, the deadly silhouette of the weapon he clutched waving menacingly against the sky. A dagger of pain stabbed through his side, and he fell back with a groan, almost blacking out.

Then something cold touched his face, its sharp odor stinging his nose to bring him around. Quinn's pulse raced, he had smelled the stench of gasoline. There in the moonlight, he could see the rainbow stream of fluid stretching from where he lay to the rear of the damaged truck.

Grimacing in pain, Quinn reached for his bullpup assault weapon, knowing there were only a few heartbeats left until Tabor put a salvo of bullets into him.

But the P-90 had shaken loose from its breakaway rig on impact. Having skidded several feet, it now lay too far away for him to take hold of. Instead, Nomad reached for the less accurate backup piece holstered on his chest. Drawing the double-action SIG he aimed the small plastic handgun at the gas spill.

The 10 mm bullet ignited the trail of gasoline that flowed along the ground. Quinn grunted as burning fuel splashed on his clothing. But flame was also racing up the spill line toward the leaking gas tank of the stalled armored van as Tabor raised the Glock 25 SMG in both hands and walked the red pencil line of laser light toward the writhing figure on the ground.

All at once Tabor saw the flame and understood its meaning. The knowledge of what lay in store filled his mind with horror. Spinning, he dropped the Glock and tried to run from certain death. But he had reacted too late to save himself. In a second the burning fuel had ignited the truck's gas tank, causing a tremendous explosion.

Razor-edged shrapnel from the ruptured tank sheared through Tabor's body as the truck blew sky-high with a deafening bang. Jagged shards of plate steel went pinwheeling through the night, and scorching yellow tongues licked obscenely from blazing fuel spills. The tires of the wrecked truck melted to become foul-smelling puddles as fire swaddled the vehicle in a cocoon of flame.

Quinn picked himself up from the killing ground as Tabor's funeral pyre lit up the shattered streets of the L.A. Burnout Zone. He discarded the useless wings of the irreparably damaged ornithopter.

Like Icarus, he had fallen to earth as fire scorched his artificial wings. But unlike his predecessor, Quinn had survived the crash to carry on the fight. Tabor was down, and the drug operation was out of commission. Next it would be Vadim's turn to fall.

11

"You demons have corrupted my interface! But you have not reformatted my soul!"

At most, the kid calling himself Govinda Software was no more than twenty-one. His skin bore the waxy paleness that was characteristic of most of the Reverend Vadim's followers Quinn had seen. The eyes were the worst part.

They were empty black holes, the mirrors, not of the soul as the poets had it, but of a brain already damaged by lengthy exposure to hardware drugs and months of psychological conditioning.

"Maybe you're right," Quinn told the kid. "Maybe we are demons. But what are you? You're not even human anymore, pal."

"I am a node on my savior's network, a pixel on his screen," he replied. "If I walk in the light of his raster I will fear no evil."

The room was soundproof and electronically cloaked against hostile surveillance measures. It was impenetrable to even the most sophisticated eavesdropping techniques.

Behind the one-way mirror, the members of the special task force that Quinn had set up to deal with the threat posed by the Reverend Vadim watched the progress of the cult-deprogramming encounter.

Since Quinn's bust of the hardware drug facility in the L.A. Burnout Zone had gone down, and the subsequent viewing of the data he had collected during the strike, the World Police Agency, WorldPol, had opened a new case file on the reverend.

While there were as yet no smoking guns to firmly link Lux Vadim to the illegal hardware drug facility, enough questions had been raised by the search data to warrant further efforts to penetrate Vadim's quasi-religious organization.

From other reports that had come trickling in over the course of the months that the Reverend Lux Vadim had reestablished himself on board the Sunyata, his space station headquarters, evidence had surfaced that he had renewed his trafficking activities on the organ black market.

"You think the reverend is your savior? Then maybe you don't know who and what you're really dealing with," Quinn said, trying to get through to the kid despite the walls that had been erected between his mind and the truth. After hammering away at him for the past ten hours, he had yet to see a crack in the Motherboarder's mental conditioning.

"The guy is dirt, plain and simple," pressed Quinn. "He uses jerks like you. He sucks you dry, then throws you away. Lux Vadim is a master manipulator."

"My write-protection interface locks out your lies," the kid said in a faraway voice. "My program integrity remains uncorrupted. Praise be my data, for it is saved."

"What do you know about the Reverend Vadim?" Quinn asked in a softer voice, now trying a different tack.

"That he integrates all systems into the feedback loop of suchness," the kid replied. "That we are all microprocessor chips plugged into the infinite cosmic motherboard. Get thee behind me, demon! You do not write to my screen! You have an ugly interface!"

"Look at *this* screen," Quinn insisted, going to a console and starting up the taped data on the reverend's case file. The large, flat digital screen showed a younger version of Vadim being led through a crowd of newspeople. He was wearing handcuffs poorly concealed by the jacket that one of his flunkies had draped across his hands, and his head was bowed with guilt.

"This video was shot after Lux Vadim was arrested for ripping off his own company to the tune of at least a billion dollars. You know what his company did?

"It manufactured electronic components for aerospace and defense. You know what those components were made out of? Shit, kid. Pure, unadulterated shit."

Quinn punched up another command sequence on the console keyboard. The giant digital screen immediately flashed to a scene all too familiar to the world's viewing audiences, one that had become iconic. It was telemetry of the Mars Mission astronauts trapped in a space vehicle that was burning up in the atmosphere.

The face of Sismondi Napoleon, the Mars Mission commander, begging for help as his crew went through the hell of slow oxygen starvation, bore the signs of a mind driven half-insane by the torture of his predicament.

More sickening images of the doomed astronauts flashed on the screen, until the last member of the crew died in fits of horrible convulsions.

"Those components were made by Vadim's company, Centurion Development," Quinn said as he froze the final image of death. "They were what malfunctioned during the Mars Mission. Backup systems failed, too. Your Reverend Vadim is responsible for killing those twenty-four astronauts, just as surely as if he'd shot them all with a gun."

The kid stared blankly at the terrifying images on the giant digital screen. But this time he said nothing in his own or the reverend's defense.

"It was after serving his first prison term that your 'savior' began his 'religious conversion,'" Quinn went on. "But that was all a put-on. Vadim was washed up as far as the technology industry went. Who wanted to deal with a convicted racketeer who had lined his pockets at the expense of the Mars astronauts?

"So Vadim became a 'reverend' and started channeling what he claims is some high priest of this fictitious lost continent he calls 'Mu,' the mother.

"But he was, and is, still the same piece of garbage he'd been before. Only this time instead of selling faulty components to NASA, he sold a philosophy that was every bit as faulty and every bit as dangerous to those who believe in it."

"He channels the great Abraxas, high priest of vanished Mu, mother continent of all mankind," the kid retorted hesitantly. "Abraxas speaks through his voice, and in union with his spirit we are patched into the great motherboard of Mu."

"Vadim is as phoney as a three-dollar bill," Quinn persisted, shaking his head. "He channels nothing. He sees nothing. He is nothing. It's all an act, a twisted charade designed to take in suckers like you, kids and adults who are so alienated by an admittedly lousy world that they're ready to grasp any straw to keep their sanity.''

Quinn unfroze the image on the screen and punched up another video sequence to replace it. This one was even more startlingly graphic in the horror that it displayed. The scene on the screen depicted a grim tableau reminiscent of the liberation of the Nazi death camps at the end of World War Two. As the video panned across the bleak room, the corpses on the tables were exposed in ghastly detail.

All of the cadavers showed the evidence of extensive removal of organ tissue. Some of these gruesome surgical specimens had their abdomens propped open with clamps and their entrails excised, lying on the table next to the mutilated human corpses.

With other mortal remains, it was the skull that had been sliced open and a ragged hole remaining where the brain had been surgically excised. Still other cadavers were missing limbs, eyes and other assorted body parts.

''This is what got your savior, your high priest of Mu, your holy master, thrown into prison the second time, my misguided young friend,'' Quinn went on, unconcealed disgust now clear in his voice. ''This is just one of the illegal organ-extraction facilities that were linked to the Reverend Vadim.''

"He was not convicted for that," the kid blurted out, no longer repeating catchphrases by rote, and something other than blankness had come into his eyes.

"Maybe that's what he told you," Quinn said. "And he had the savvy to kill any witnesses that might have turned on him. Just like Adolf Hitler and Saddam Hussein, two men he admires and calls reincarnations of the holy spirit. He wasn't convicted on all charges, but he was convicted just the same.

"But he was behind it all. Just the same as Hitler was behind the concentration camps of the Third Reich. Just the same as Hussein massacred tens of thousands of his own people. I know it and you know it, kid. You're not that dumb."

"I...I...am...a node on...my savior's network..." he stammered, beginning to rock back and forth. "If I...walk in...the light..."

Suddenly the kid's composure had cracked, and he began sobbing disconsolately. He leaned forward, his elbows resting on the tops of his knees as his body was racked with sobs brought on by suffering and emotion.

Quinn had broken through, he realized finally. But now would come the hardest part of all, as well as possibly the most dangerous. He would have to turn the kid, convince him to become the eyes and ears of WorldPol in Vadim's own backyard.

Quinn watched the Motherboarder weep uncontrollably. He went over to the water cooler in the corner and drew a cup of deacidified water.

"Here, kid," he said. "Drink this. I'll be back in a little while. Then we'll talk some more."

SUNYATA CIRCLED the earth twice every twenty-four hours. On board, some five hundred of the reverend's followers lived and worked and prayed in their orbital commune.

On the earth below, thousands more Motherboarders lived in giant communes that the reverend had established across the globe, each of them in turn responsible for bringing new blood into the fold.

But in the space station Sunyata, the elite of the reverend's acolytes lived in their own version of heaven. Believing that they were close to the infinite suchness of the cosmos, they cast their thoughts toward the distant stars.

Now the faithful assembled. In the steel belly of Sunyata, the great meeting hall quickly became filled to capacity.

An array of enormous flat digital screens encircled the vast womblike spherical space. The screens were blank at present, but as soon as the hundreds of acolytes were seated and ready, the screens flashed instantly to life, filled with the image of the Reverend Vadim.

"I channel the great Abraxas of Mu," he intoned. "With his help we will rewire the human consciousness and receive alien signals from distant galactic realms."

"Receive alien signals from distant galactic realms," the assemblage chanted in unison as they opened their minds to the reverend. The reverend was seen to shudder and gasp as the spirit of Abraxas, the high priest of Mu entered his consciousness.

"The Reverend Lux Vadim is now in sleep mode. I, Abraxas, have made my program active. I bring thee greetings from the mother continent. I wish thee peace, prosperity and cooperative multitasking."

"Peace unto you, Priest Abraxas," the assemblage chanted. "We patch our souls into the great motherboard."

Now the eyes of Vadim became filled with tears, and he flung his head back as he raised his hands to his watering eyes.

"I weep, my children, oh how I weep!" wailed the Muan priest Abraxas from the lips of the Reverend Vadim.

"Why do you weep, Great Teacher?" they cried in unison. "Pray, tell us why you weep."

"I weep for the planet, oh my children," the voice cried out between tremendous sobs. "I weep for the cosmic motherboard. For there are those who persecute us, those who would rip our circuits from the motherboard and recycle us into the junk pile of dark oblivion.''

"Who are they?" cried the audience. "Why do they persecute us?"

"Oh, my children, they are demons, they are demons of WorldPol! They wish to destroy all our good works, to screen dump the boot record of bodhidarma and call down the pestilential darkness of total systems failure. Even now they are plotting to take us away, to kill us all in their chambers of torture!"

"What are we to do, great teacher?" the masses cried in chagrin. "Tell us what we must do!"

"Hold fast to the motherboard. And prepare for the great systems crash that may take place if our enemies assault us. When they come to tear our pins from the motherboard, we will never go willingly. Sooner than let them take us, we will all die!"

"Yes," they chanted. "Never will we leave the motherboard. Instead, we will die. Our pins will never be removed! In death our interface will shine forever in the light of heaven's screen!"

MISSION LOG TWO:

Lethal Envelope

12

Govinda Software's heart beat like a jackhammer. He had forgotten what it was like to be terrified after months of Motherboarder conditioning had numbed his mind.

But that had changed since the intensive week-long deprogramming effort conducted by Quinn. Now he remembered the sensation of fear with painful clarity. Now Govinda Software was stricken with panic.

But once the psychological conditioning had been reversed, he also experienced a great anger welling up inside him. It was an anger that at first Govinda directed at himself for being dumb enough to allow himself to be used by the reverend's organization, to fall for his clever lies.

But in the course of the deprogramming experience, that initial self-contempt had been redirected. It had finally come to be leveled against the true cause of Govinda's suffering, the Reverend Vadim and his soul-destroying machinery that masqueraded as spiritual enlightenment.

Govinda Software had consented to go back into the Motherboarder fold as an informer for WorldPol. He had also consented to have his left eye temporarily removed from its socket. In its place, WorldPol biotechnicians had implanted a subminiature audio-video, or AV, recording unit. The unit, despite its tiny size, was highly accurate and had a data-storage capacity that was the equivalent of hundreds of conventional videotape cassettes.

The AV implant recorded everything that he heard and saw for the following thirty days. The implant automatically activated when he awoke and remained dormant when he slept, sensing and responding to the changes in brain patterns.

Now, some thirty days after the implantation, it was nearing the time when Govinda would be through with the reverend and the Church of the Divine Motherboard forever. A specially chartered extraction team headed by Quinn was standing ready to take him out of the operations zone and give him a second chance at life.

Govinda had been informed that he was scheduled to depart from one of the reverend's earthbound retreats for the space station Sunyata the following day. He realized that he had to seize the moment at once or risk it being lost to him forever.

Once he was on the space station, he doubted that he could easily be rescued. He realized that the data stored inside his eye socket AV implant made him a target for elimination by the Motherboarders.

In the course of the past month, during which he had acted as a human camera in the bowels of the reverend's organization, Govinda Software had borne witness to things that had turned his stomach.

Often he had come perilously close to expressing revulsion at the sights to which he was exposed. Such a lapse would have proven fatal. Any deviation from the blank stares of a Motherboarder acolyte would be immediately noticed.

The worst part of the entire grim charade came when Govinda witnessed the vivisection of a live subject for the purpose of removing the organs from the body for resale on the black market.

The scene where this took place was in an operating theater. The room was hidden beneath the facade of a warehouse on the waterfront of the San Francisco Tenderloin district.

"Praise to the lifeblood that nourishes the Motherboard," the shaven-headed surgeon muttered as he made incisions in the pulmonary artery just above the Arch of the Aorta leading away from the beating heart, his actions directed by impulses from the IC chip that was socketed in his skull.

There was no blood flow from the beating organ because the pulmonaries, carotids and other arteries and veins had been shunted off into a pump that drew off the blood and sent it to a storage vat, from which it would be packaged for resale, as well.

After a few more deft strokes of the laser scalpel, the clone surgeon had freed the last scraps of spongy epicardial tissue that had adhered the heart to the rib cage.

Reaching down and muttering more thanks to Mu, the surgeon lifted the heart free, blood trickling down his surgical-gloved hands. The others in the operating room chanted more blessings on the beating organ as it was placed at once in a cryogenic storage module.

At that moment Govinda realized that he could no longer stand to be in the room watching the obscene spectacle play out.

Fortunately he was ushered from the surgical chamber of horrors and told that he was to be honored with the sacred task of being the courier entrusted with bearing the cryogenically preserved heart to the aerospace port. From there it would be taken from him and flown to its final destination, a private hospital facility somewhere in Southeast Asia.

Govinda was in the company of two of the church's "spiritual guides" as he began the journey to the aerospace port. Now was the time to signal the WorldPol agents who would be waiting the signal that he needed to be immediately extracted.

To activate the warning signal, he had been told to concentrate hard on his code word, a unique phrase that would trigger specific brain wave patterns.

The tiny electrical impulses in the brain waves would be picked up by the sensitive processor in his AV implant and turn on a transponder beacon engineered into the implant, enabling his "guardian angels" to home in on his position.

As he arrived at the aerospace port, Govinda Software thought hard. He thought about his code word harder than he'd thought about anything in his life. He chanted it silently to himself like a mantra, and this time Govinda was praying for a different kind of salvation than the reverend had promised him.

"WE'VE GOT A SIGNAL," the tech manning the telemetry console declared with sudden excitement. At the touch of a button, a warning signal was transmitted to commo units ported by all members of the extraction team, regardless of their respective locations.

The tech had been part of a site team monitoring the equipment around the clock during the course of the past thirty days. The console was constantly manned on three daily duty cycles and never left unattended in anticipation of the incoming signal.

"Where?" Quinn asked the technician via portable commo as he reported back to the site base. He was several miles distant from the monitoring station, but he received the message instantly via the small satcom unit linked to a cellular net.

"Punching up the coordinates now," said the tech. As the map grid lit up on the large digital screen in the control room, a smaller but identical map flashed on the wrist-top screen of Quinn's satcom cellular phone link.

Artificial-intelligence filters crunched numbers, already interpolating possible destination points by analyzing the routes that the vehicle carrying Govinda was taking.

"The aerospace port's a strong possible," the tech declared, interpreting the data.

"I'm on my way over there," Quinn informed him. "Get the rest of the extraction team in gear. This might turn out to be a messy one."

"You got it," said the tech, who had already punched the dedicated key on his console keyboard that relayed the telemetry to the extraction team standing by.

Within a matter of seconds, all members of the extraction team had received their instructions and were racing to their designated rally point at the scene of the operation.

AT THE AEROSPACE PORT, Quinn linked up with the extraction team. The four men and two women were counterterrorism experts working for IS under contract with WorldPol, and together they had staged dozens of successful extractions in their time.

Some ops didn't go that well, though. Quinn hoped that this round wouldn't be one of those. He had bonded with the kid during the grueling deprogramming session, and wanted to see him come out of this bad situation intact.

The hand-held tracer's screen that was linked to the transponder in the AV implant in Govinda's eye socket displayed a target icon representing Govinda Software. The flashing icon was progressing through the schematic of the main departures building, twisting left and right as Govinda followed the corridor network.

Quinn punched a button marked Pos, and the tracer's screen showed him map coordinates corresponding to Govinda's position, as well as the distance of the target from the extraction team's rally point.

Issuing instructions for the team to split into groups that could offer mutual support and spread out to work the airport terminal, Quinn hoped that Govinda could keep his act together long enough for the snatch operation to be successfully carried out.

The flashing screen icon on the tracer showed Quinn vital-signs data, including a highly elevated pulse rate. Govinda was freaking out, Quinn knew, as he drew closer and closer to the departure gate.

What Quinn could not see from the tracer data was the sweat that had begun to bead the Motherboarder's face as he tried desperately to keep the blank expression from changing into one that betrayed the panic he felt inside. His keepers, the "spiritual guardians" assigned to watch over him, had noticed the perspiration and had asked him a couple of times if he was feeling all right.

Govinda had repeated the usual platitudes that Motherboarder acolytes used to answer questions, and his companions had lapsed into sullen silence. But he had caught them watching him suspiciously out of the corner of their eyes, and Govinda knew that they were not buying his response.

When extraction team's first visual contact was made by one of the three groups circulating through the airport terminal, Quinn cautioned them all to take it easy. Quinn moved in as close as he dared, getting a visual confirm himself as he rounded a turn in the corridor and caught sight of Govinda up ahead beyond a crush of bodies. He put away the tracer unit and eyeballed the subjects of the op.

The two men with the kid were heavies. Although they sported the cleanly shaven heads and the baggy clothes of the rest of the Motherboarders, they didn't walk like robots and their powerful bodies and hard, alert faces marked them as anything but "clones." Their gait was springy, and they surveilled the area with the wariness of professionals.

Quinn moved into position for a fast snatch, but just then his worst fears were realized. Govinda had begun to crack completely. He had reached the point of snapping, the point where he could no longer hold his mounting terror back any longer.

He had begun to shiver and shake as he blew his cool. Gesturing frantically, he was quickly engaged in a scuffle with his two guardians. The hardmen bracketing him had become alert to danger. They spotted Quinn coming toward them in a second flat and recognized that he was trouble. They tried to hustle Govinda away from the crowded terminal while dipping under their jackets in grabs for weaponry.

The 10 mm MAC 12 SMGs were already in their hands, the double-action subguns automatically cocked and unlocked their lasers seeking targets.

Yelling for the crowd to get down around him, Quinn raised and aimed the P-90 bullpup at the hardguy closest to him. As the red laser line of the MAC 12 swept his way, Quinn triggered a 3-round burst of 5.70 mm fléchette fire.

A put-away burst of needlepoint steel rotored from the muzzle of the black plastic P-90. There was little ballistic spreading, and the burst pattern hit the target with all the shots placed squarely within the heart zone. A hole edged with flayed flesh opened up on his upper left chest as the MAC went flying and landed with a tinny crash on the hard floor, followed in a pulse beat by the gunman himself.

"Get down!" Quinn shouted at the kid as pandemonium spread through the terminal lobby. Govinda tripped over his own two feet, dropping the cryogenic container with the frozen human heart inside it.

The container skidded and broke apart as it hit the floor. The cryogenically preserved heart fell out of it and lay in a gathering pool of melting blood and ice.

Seeing the teams converge on him and realizing that he was finished, the second gunman dropped his weapon and stuck up his hands. He faced his captors with a smile on his face and bit down on something in his mouth. Almost instantly he began going into convulsions. His eyes rolled up in his head as his legs went limp, and he sagged to the floor. It took several minutes before his arms and legs stopped jerking.

Going down on one knee, Quinn bent over the now still corpse of the gunman. He held his nose to the dead man's lips and sniffed. There was the strong odor of bitter almonds coming from it. ''Cyanide,'' he said to the rest of the extraction team.

It was an oldie, but still a deadly.

Getting up, Quinn crossed to where some of the team members already had Govinda in custody. To his relief, he got a nod of reassurance from one of them as he approached the kid.

13

Early-morning darkness shrouded the clandestine launch facility located in a remote section of the Nevada desert. The ready room for Operation Redball was housed in a geodesic dome which looked out across a heavily guarded private spaceport.

On the covert runway, a cluster of sleek black aircraft with wings that were angled steeply forward toward the nose assembly stood poised for immediate takeoff. The ASPs were capable of runway-to-orbit flight.

Their scramjet engines could not only generate transonic flight speeds in excess of Mach 5, but could also breathe the microthin atmosphere of near-space, using it as a basis for internal combustion.

Once reaching their orbital trajectories in the airless void of near-space, the ASPs would shunt over into their solid-fuel propulsion systems, enabling the transonic aerospace craft to cruise beyond the gaseous envelope of the earth's atmosphere.

Waiting inside the ready room, Quinn was among those personnel who had been assembled inside the geodesic dome to face a digital screen to receive preflight instructions via a global teleconferencing link.

The force was largely comprised of World Police Agency elements, though it was under the leadership of the North American Air Defense Command, and under the direct command of Brigadier General Maxwell Swope of the USAF, the United States Aerospace Force.

Quinn himself was a deputized member of the WorldPol-NORAD strike team, his presence deemed vital due to his technical knowledge both of the target and of the single man who was the object of the strike force's coming action, Reverend Lux Vadim.

The team's destination was the space station Sunyata, and the NORAD-WorldPol strike force was tasked with apprehending the reverend, who was charged with violating antiracketeering laws, and taking into custody the members of his organization.

At all costs, Sunyata itself was not to be damaged.

To assault the space station with direct firepower would mean immediately condemning hundreds of innocent civilians to certain death. Such an outcome conflicted with the objective of the NORAD-WorldPol strike, which was aimed at saving lives, not taking them.

"As of now, Operation Redball has commenced," the general said via the teleconferencing link to the assembled aerospace strike force element.

The general went on to explain that the spacebound assault would commence as soon as all of the separate components of the mission had reached suborbital trajectory.

While these elements included aerospace planes at the razor-edged strike point of the operational pyramid, the broad base had also pressed several obsolete space shuttlecraft into service. Though outdated, these legendary aerospace craft, which had ushered in the age of routine ground-to-orbit missions, were still dependable. They would be used for ferrying prisoners taken into custody back to earth, and HAAWACS—high-altitude AWACS—aircraft would serve the command, control, communications and Intelligence role in the mission.

"Two days ago the two Phalanx Domino–class surveillance satellites shown here on the screen were secretly fitted with jamming upgrade packages," General Swope went on to say. "When the jammers go on-line, the Sunyata will be effectively blind to all video, audio, radio and telemetry reception.

"If we're lucky, we should be able to dock with the station, which will recognize us as a scheduled supplies flight. If our luck isn't as good as we hope, then we issue the target spacecraft a warning. Above all, a paramount rule—we fire only if fired upon."

The general asked for questions and received none in return. The team members were professionals and all of them had individually rehearsed the roles they were expected to play.

He dismissed the strike crew with a curt nod and watched, via the large digital screen in front of him, as the elements of the crews filed toward the hyper-jets that were waiting on the runway. Then he himself left to man the mission's command, control, communication and Intelligence center on board the lead HAAWACS aircraft.

As THE ASP REACHED orbital trajectory, the Phalanx Domino satellites turned on their jamming modules and began spoofing the target with an array of powerful electronic countermeasures.

"What was that?" asked the chief technical officer of the Sunyata's space operations center. The chief technician, like the members of his crew, was among the few personnel on board the station who were not themselves Motherboarders.

"Don't really know," the puzzled ops manager answered. He was looking at the sudden wave of static that had just passed across the viewscreen.

"Did you run a systems integrity check?"

"Doing that right now, boss," the ops manager reported. "All parameters read green, lean and mean," he went on, raising his hands in exasperation.

"Then it's sunspots," the chief tech told him. "Call me if you catch another glitch like that again. And don't wake me up unless it's important with a capital *I*."

"You got it, chief," said the ops manager, and watched the phone screen wink off. He grabbed for the turkey sandwich he had been eating just as the glitch once again passed across the monitors, this time totally unseen.

BENEATH the electronic masking laid down by the Phalanx Domino satellite, the strike ASP came arcing over the Sunyata's visual horizon.

This was when things could get hairy, Quinn knew as he scanned one of the bulkhead viewscreens that showed the video input from the ASP's nose-mounted sensors. The orbital station loomed ahead of the assault force, highlighted against the starfield of space.

The Sunyata was a composite of several generations of space stations. Planned originally as a space-based facility for manufacturing pharmaceuticals, the first station had been assembled in orbit in the closing years of the twentieth century using a node-

and-module building scheme developed by NASA in the 1960s.

The venture went bust, however. For the next few decades, the station had changed hands several times, each turnover resulting in a new layer of modules being added to the original structure.

Like the other members of the Redball strike-and-rescue team, Quinn's flak vest was emblazoned with the word WorldPol in bright, high-visibility characters.

His weapon was standard issue, a Heckler & Koch LSW caseless bullpup rifle with a three-hundred-round magazine that contained 4.73 mm fléchette ammo. In addition to the bullpup, Quinn also carried stun grenades, plastic handcuffs, a wrist-top comm unit and emergency medical field kit, all of which had been standardly issued to mission personnel.

Within a few minutes, the captain of the ASP transmitted a ten-minute alert to the strike team members via intership commo. "Right now we're flying in under the electronic curtain," Quinn heard the captain's voice rasp in the earphones of the protective helmet he wore. "Weapons are to remain safed until we are successfully docked."

In the cockpit of the ASP, the captain punched up the automatic telemetry that exactly duplicated the call sign of an aerospace craft expected by Sunyata for a scheduled resupply run.

The bogus telemetry was transparent to the computers on board the Sunyata's command center. They would not be able to tell it apart from the real "eighteen-wheeler" scheduled to make the delivery.

In fact, the space command center had been tracking the aerospacecraft ever since it had reached orbital trajectory without either the chief technician or the ops manager suspecting that anything might be amiss.

"Flight 903, you are cleared for docking at bay number four," said the operations manager as his face appeared on the viewscreen in the ASP's cockpit. "Hope you guys brought some Scotch with you. The commissary's dry as a bone."

"Thought you religious people only ate brown rice and stuff like that," the captain of the aerospace plane replied cheerfully as another console screen displayed the progress of the ASP as its automatic-docking sequencers brought it into a slow-motion collision with the station's number-four docking bay.

"That's for the 'Motherfuckers,'" the tech answered derisively, corrupting the word by which the occupants of the station were commonly known. "In this section, you got the burgers-and-beer contingent."

"Well, don't worry, partner," said the captain as the ASP's nose locked with the grapplers arrayed in a ring around the landing bay, "we got plenty of everything. Plus a few surprises."

"I'll get an off-loading party right down," the tech said. "Love surprises, especially good ones."

"Roger that," the captain answered back. "This one's as good as it gets. Out."

As soon as he signed off, the captain relayed the order to the strike force personnel in the crew compartment that the ASP was securely docked.

All weapons were now to be moved from safe to unsafed position, and all combat gear and body armor was to be strapped into place.

The strike was a definite go.

14

The off-loading detail was comprised of elements of the Sunyata's operations staff. Off-loading was a jealously guarded privilege because it enabled these personnel to skim some off the top for the sole use of the crew dogs on the ops staff.

"Man, I can't wait to wrap my mitts around a cold brewskie," one member of the detail said to his partner as they watched the LED readout showing that the airlock was cycling down. "Here they come now. Yeah, yeah, come to papa, baby!"

Pressure had equalized, and the airlock was already in the process of sliding open.

Their jaws dropped as the off-loading party were confronted not with the delivery men they had expected, but a group of heavily armed commandos rushing toward them from out of the airlock.

Bullpup autoweapons were pointed menacingly at them by grim-visaged assault personnel, and the unloading detail was quickly subdued. Once the prisoners were taken into custody by the Redball strikers, they were ordered to lie down on the deck while they were handcuffed and read their rights by their captors.

At almost the same time, General Swope in the mission control center in the HAAWACS relayed orders that would set the next phase of the strike into motion. The three other strike aerospacecraft that were orbiting just out of the visual and radio horizons of the Sunyata were now to converge toward the station at flank speed.

One element of the strike detail was moving through the corridors of the space station to occupy the Sunyata's main operations area. Here it was to prepare the docking modules for the arrival of the other ASPs.

While this element began its critical tasks, the main body of the strike force rushed toward the inner rings of the space station and secured these priority areas, as well.

The station was arranged in the form of concentric circles, with life-support areas located on the outside rings and the living quarters clustered toward the central hub.

With the peripheral layers of the station secure, the central nervous system of the station was next in line to fall under the control of the Redball strike force.

WITH QUINN ON POINT, the detachment of strike force personnel negotiated the corridors of the space station. The primary target of this elite assault element was the Reverend Vadim himself.

The tracer device clutched in Quinn's hand—identical to the unit that had led the extraction team to the confidential informant earlier—was now tuned to the BioTrak transponder beacon that had been implanted inside the reverend's skull.

"I have a fix on our target," Quinn said in only a short while, noting the map coordinates flashing above the glowing wire diagram representing the station's interconnecting corridors.

The tracer's screen icons indicated that their quarry was located just beyond the next bulkhead. Only a few twists and turns of the corridor network now separated the strike team from the Reverend Vadim.

Quinn's strike detachment reached the final bulkhead between them and the target icon within a matter of minutes. "Get into position," Quinn ordered the three other members of the point team as he placed a lock decrypter over the locking mechanism of the door. "We're going in," he said.

Punching in the initialization codes that activated the delocking mechanism, Quinn stepped aside and let the computer-controlled burglar tool do its work.

He crouched by the door, the black wedge of his H&K gripped in both his hands as he tensely waited to lead the team inside the moment that the door slid aside.

The decrypter did its work, and the pneumatically controlled bulkhead slid into its niche in the double-baffled wall a few moments later.

Quinn moved into the chamber beyond on a half crouch, the rest of his crew jumping in after him and breaking to left and right. Quinn's bullpup weapon was already probing for target acquisition, sweeping the room as his eyes took in the scene before him.

In the foreground was a large free-form sculpture of burnished metal. Beyond, a shaven-headed Motherboarder in a flowing robe squatted in the lotus position at the center of the room, sitting like a thing made out of stone. Apparently deep in meditation, the seated acolyte did not stir at all.

A heartbeat passed, and Quinn's combat-stressed senses told him that something was wrong with the apparently tranquil scene.

Something was very wrong.

In a pulse beat he knew what that dangerous something was.

The robed figure had jumped to its feet in the center of the room.

Beyond a doubt it was not the Reverend Vadim.

Quinn realized with a flash of insight that the reverend had either removed his BioTrak skull implant or was able to suppress its beacon and create a phreaker unit of some kind that would duplicate its signal.

"Don't move, and don't think," Quinn commanded the shaven-headed Motherboarder clone who faced him with a blank expression on his or her face, as it was impossible to tell the clone's gender. "Lock your hands behind your head."

At first seeming to heed the shouted instructions, the figure raised its arms high overhead. But then the clone began to shiver uncontrollably. Its entire body had suddenly begun jerking and shuddering as the clone seemed to struggle to draw breath.

The clone's face was turning blue, and now the blank expression of a Motherboarder clone was replaced with a sudden grimace of extreme pain, mounting to intolerable limits.

Soon a faint wisp of smoke rose from the center of the clone's chest, from beneath the flowing white robes.

"Get down! *Fast!*" Quinn shouted his warning at the rest of the team as he took a dive behind the protection of the steel free-form sculpture that he had noticed as he'd first entered the room.

A deafening bang filled the room as Quinn hit the floor. A ball of blinding white light expanded to the edge of consciousness. It was not the light of nirvana.

It was the radiation of sudden death.

THE REVEREND VADIM slung the heavy pack across his right shoulder. The pack contained a small fortune: millions of dollars in international credits.

He had already crammed a score of fifty-and sixty-round ammunition modules into his pockets. These went into the small black plastic autopistol he had charged and which now hung from a breakaway shoulder rig for quick deployment.

A weapon with more stopping power than the autopistol hung from a strap around his back. The M-20 caseless autorifle was loaded with explosive-tipped fléchettes and was equipped with a laser range finder that would automatically trigger the weapon when the beam touched a vital targeting area.

The Sunyata was under attack. Soon the space station would be in the hands of the government.

But Vadim had been expecting something like this to go down all along. Forewarned was forearmed, and if Vadim was anything, it wasn't stupid. He'd had his backup plan all worked out and was now about to put that very plan into effect.

Not far away, an escape craft was waiting. The aerospace plane was kept in a continual state of readiness, in anticipation of the reverend's potential need to make a hasty exit from the Sunyata if the station came under attack.

Now that this contingency had materialized, he would waste no time getting on board the ASP and using the aerospace plane to escape the long arm of WorldPol.

Before he took his final leave of the Sunyata, there was just one more thing that he needed to do. He took a remote unit from his pocket and input a special access code on its small keypad. A series of beeptones and a message that flashed across its LCD screen informed him that the device was now ready to receive the special coded instruction that he had prepared for it.

The special instruction was simple: set the auto-destruct timer to blow the Sunyata and all personnel on board on a trip through outer space to the fringes of the universe.

15

Covered with chunks of blast debris, Quinn slowly picked himself off the floor, brushing pieces of the ceiling off his body armor. A dense, foul-smelling cloud of munitions smoke now filled the chamber. In a single destructive instant, everything in sight had been trashed.

As for the androgynous Motherboarder who had been used as a human bomb, he or she was nowhere to be seen, having been blown to bits and splattered all over the place by the high-energy explosion.

Quinn's first action on recovering was to check on the status of his team. Though far from the blast center when the bomb exploded, one of his people had been killed by a chunk of flying glass that had sheared off the side of his head.

Another team member had sustained serious injuries when razor-sharp fragments of a metal bulkhead had ripped into his groin, from which blood was now seeping.

Quinn turned to his emergency medical kit to help attend to the badly wounded team member, then used his portable commo to order up the assault force's emergency medical support unit on the double.

Quinn also had another concern to deal with in the aftermath of leading the arrest detail into the booby-trapped room.

The escape gambit orchestrated by Vadim had been a brilliant if lethal piece of planning and execution. He had deliberately countered the tracking implant, either by removing it entirely, which was doubtful to Quinn, or by generating a spoof signal, which was more than likely.

Quinn had no doubts whatsoever that Vadim was at that moment carrying out an escape bid that he had planned down to the most minuscule details. It was sure to succeed unless Quinn managed to find him and take him down before he fled the Sunyata.

No other suitable explanation existed for why Quinn's team had not found their quarry. Vadim had been conclusively placed on board the Sunyata prior to the commencement of the NORAD-WorldPol raid. Unless he had somehow managed to evade some of the most sophisticated surveillance tactics and technology available, Vadim was still somewhere close by.

In the excitement of the explosion's deadly aftermath, Quinn had forgotten to check his tracer unit. Pulling the unit from the Velcro quick-release mounts that secured it to his belt, he punched up a data screen. Vadim's icon was still there, blinking steadily on and off, although its position had shifted. This confirmed to Quinn that he *had* created a spoof signal to distract his pursuers.

"Can you hold down the fort till the medical support unit arrives?" Quinn asked the uninjured team member who was administering first aid to her wounded comrade.

She answered in the affirmative, applying a pressure bandage to the still-bleeding wound. "Get that son of a bitch," she said, then looked down at the semiconscious figure on the floor. "Murchison's had it."

Receiving acknowledgment, Quinn rushed from the blast site, following the transponder icon on the screen.

MINUTES AFTER THE RAID on the Sunyata had commenced, the WorldPol-NORAD strike force had issued a communiqué to the world news organizations. The announcement declared that the joint task force had secured the space station. Seven fatalities had occurred during the operation, three sustained by task force members, the others by personnel on board the station.

As the breaking story traveled across the global media network, the Redball mission manager on board the HAAWACS plane initiated a secure transmission to the ground base station almost one hundred thousand miles below his high-altitude orbit.

"Activate Corona," General Swope said.

"Roger that," said the base station. "ETA for Corona is ten minutes."

Corona was the code name used to denote the convoy of space shuttles that had been orbiting well out of the Sunyata's radar and visual horizons. The shuttles of the Corona phase of the mission would pick up those on board who were being placed under mass arrest. Then they would ferry the prisoners back down to Earth to complete the most ambitious bust operation in history.

The strikers had directed their strongest efforts into corralling the elite guardian element of the Motherboarders.

At the hard nucleus of Vadim's operation were the paramilitaries with the guns and security training. Vadim's mercenary forces were not mere drones. They were full partners in Vadim's scams. Since many of them were former commandos, they were thought to pose the highest risk to the raiding forces.

With the elite elements now in full custody and presently being advised of their rights under both respective national laws and World Police Organization statutes, the strikers easily cowed the more docile acolytes into submission.

These rank-and-file clones were instructed to move toward the large central meeting hall, which was located at the inmost ring of the Sunyata station. There they would be identified, informed of their legal rights and processed for earth-bound transference.

The first of these rank-and-file prisoners was now being directed toward the waiting space shuttles to begin the trip back.

When the last personnel had been vacated, the station would be confiscated under the RICO anti-racketeering statutes as constituting the material assets of a continuing criminal enterprise, and a WorldPol force would be left to man the station until the case was processed by the judicial system.

THE TRACKER'S steady pings began to rise higher in pitch. The constantly changing audio output indicated that the target was within twenty-five yards of the hunter's position.

Quinn ported his LSW autoweapon as he neared his quarry. The bullpup weapon was fully charged with a 4.73 mm caseless round in its chamber and several hundred more fléchette bullets in its butt-stock magazine well.

The LCD readout panel on the side of the H&K's black plastic receiver indicated that all its systems, including laser autotarget designator, were fully operational.

Suddenly Quinn glanced up at one of the flat digital screens slanted from the ceiling. All over the station the screens transmitted Vadim's channeling of Abraxas throughout the Sunyata, as well as constant messages aimed at maintaining the spiritual purity of the Motherboarder clones.

The last screen Quinn had passed had borne three messages in succession: "Blessed be function 02H"; "My dharma is my search path"; and "Buddha was a time traveler."

But there was another message on the next screen, one that made his blood run cold: "Warning: mothership Sunyata will auto-destruct in twenty-two minutes. All personnel please clear the area."

The striker immediately pulled his commo unit from his belt. "This is Quinn," he said. "The base is set to self-destruct. This is a Juke Box emergency. Evacuate immediately."

"Impossible, the station is secure." It was General Swope's gravel voice on the comlink. "Nobody's reported hearing any alarms."

"Vadim silenced the alarms," Quinn replied, "but he apparently forgot about the monitors. See for yourself."

Quinn held up his commo unit, pointing its TV camera toward the screen and holding down the video zoom button.

"Hot damn!" General Swope shouted as he saw the message, relaying the alert immediately.

"I copy that as Juke Box emergency condition," said the strike team leader on board the ASP that had shuttled the strike force up from Earth to the Sunyata's orbital ring. "Do you affirm?"

"That's affirm," Quinn replied, and signed off.

Quinn's comset immediately crackled with the repeated, hastily issued instructions for all personnel to head for the shuttles and hyperjets that would clear the doomed space station as soon as possible.

But the squawking from Quinn's reholstered comset had alerted another figure who had stopped in midstride and flattened his body against a wall.

Cold sweat poured down his face, and the fists grasping the wedge-shaped bullpup tight to his chest were white at the knuckles. His mismatched eyes were wild and desperate as he heard the footfalls approaching the blind turn in the corridor that he knew lay only a few feet away.

Pivoting suddenly, Vadim darted from cover as his quarry negotiated the turn. The beam of his laser autotargeter shot out in a line thin as a razor's edge and as red as fresh blood. Quinn sidestepped as a rotoring burst of 4.73 mm caseless autofire lashed his way, pockmarking the bulkhead behind him.

Tucking sideward as the crimson death beam again sought him out, Quinn hit the floor on a fast shoulder roll inches ahead of a new burst of caseless needles.

Rolling full around and popping back up to a half crouch, Quinn jerked the H&K bullpup to chest height but could no longer acquire a target. Vadim had taken the hit-and-git option. The ratcheting of gunfire was still echoing in Quinn's ears, but Vadim was nowhere in sight.

Vadim was at that moment under the dogged-down cockpit canopy of the ASP that he always kept ready and waiting for immediate departure, his fingers playing across the preflight section of the plane's control panel. The hypersonic aerospace vehicle was set to initialize all flight systems as soon as he entered his personal access code.

Taking the Sunyata's corridors on a run, Quinn reached the docking module bay. Four tubular modules ringed the bay at compass points. The red warning light flashing above one of them indicated that Vadim's getaway scramjet had achieved final separation from its docking module.

The hard charger saw right off that Vadim had beaten him to the punch. Even if he could have reached the docking module, Quinn could not have opened the module's air-lock hatch. He could not survive the airless vacuum of space long enough to draw a bead on the departing plane.

In order to intercept, Quinn needed to get his hands on the controls of another ASP. Since the three other modules in the bay were empty the only other such aerospace craft in the vicinity were those of the strike force. But the assault squadron was docked along the rim of the station, while Quinn was now at the station's inner hub, thousands of feet away from that point.

It was then that Quinn saw to his surprise that in fact one of the three remaining docking modules had a second ASP berthed in the tubular enclosure. A tarp was partially hiding its nose assembly, making it nearly invisible in the darkness of the tube as Quinn squinted through the small viewing window.

But as he waited for the inner air-lock hatch to slide open, Quinn still doubted that the plane would prove functional: the fact that it was covered with a tarp indicated it was probably either down for repairs or used as a source of spare parts.

Pulling off the tarp, Quinn climbed into the teardrop-shaped cockpit of the orbit-to-ground-capable craft. He was familiar with the controls of the advanced tactical fighter. To his surprise, the hyperplane was fueled and ready to go.

Though prudence dictated that he run a full systems check, Quinn initialized the ASP's systems right away. He couldn't afford to wait and would just have to take his chances.

Departure sequencers automatically began un-docking the plane from the module, closing the inner air-lock door and pumping out the atmosphere to equalize pressure before opening the outer door. Even as the plane backed out of its tube at the bottom of the space station's hub, Quinn had turned on the craft's track-while-scan radars.

A target icon immediately flashed on the cockpit's main tactical screen, representing the ASP piloted by the Reverend Vadim.

According to the accompanying data block, the icon's position was already nearly a thousand miles from his own position and would quickly progress beyond the range of his long-range search capabilities. Quinn had to make tracks or risk losing his quarry altogether. Opening up the throttle, he sent the ASP streaking through orbital space at high Mach numbers.

16

The first of the aerospace planes and space shuttles was pulling away from the doomed station. Shortly before their arrival, the ASP piloted by Nomad streaked away from the Sunyata on an earth-bound flight trajectory in pursuit of his dangerous quarry.

Quinn closely monitored his scopes, mindful both of the now considerable distance that lay between himself and the screen icon representing his quarry's ASP and the distance between himself and the Sunyata.

The space station hung in orbit like a stick of TNT with a slow-burning fuse, ready to burst asunder. It was only a matter of time before it blew to nuclear smithereens.

Suddenly the autodestruct sequence terminated by cycling down to zero. The booby-trapped reactor core that had been rigged to double as a subkiloton nuclear bomb exploded immediately into an atomic fireball of just under a hundred tons of dynamite in blast yield.

The nuclear-detonation flash lit up the heavens as the Sunyata went critical. By this time most of the other escape craft had already succeeded in putting enough distance between themselves and the station that they survived.

But those few aerospacecraft that were closest to the epicenter of the blast were not as fortunate. Quinn's cockpit real-time video display was whited out as the fast-growing perimeter of the fireball stretched out its searing tentacles and consumed a space shuttle and an ASP at the same instant. The aerospacecraft exploded, it and the shuttle becoming two more brilliant fireballs that merged their seething fire with the plasma cloud and shock waves of the detonating Sunyata.

Anger at the latest mass murders filled Quinn's heart and soul. But he had to accept the strong possibility that he might never succeed at bringing Vadim to justice because of the speed of his escape.

Quinn was now the only force that stood between Vadim's complete escape and the retribution before the world that he deserved. Quinn had to be good; he had to be very good in order to apprehend Vadim.

IN THE COCKPIT of the escape ASP, Vadim kept flicking his eyes to the threat icon that flashed on his multimode screen.

Although he had spotted the long-range contact on his scope as soon as the aerospace plane had left the Sunyata, Vadim had assumed that it was merely the first of the assault force's shuttle craft to leave the station behind. He had calculated that his own escape had gone unnoticed in the confusion.

But in the aftermath of the explosion that had consumed the Sunyata in a ball of nuclear hellfire, the Reverend Vadim realized that the ASP registering on his computer-augmented radar scope was not only far closer to his scramjet than the other vehicles now on earth-bound trajectory, but that it was in fact following him.

To test out his suspicions, he executed a series of evasive pitches and yaws that swung the transonic craft to port and starboard. Just as he figured, the pursuing aerospace plane hugged his tail cones.

It was following him down, all right. That was now a certainty.

Well, thought Vadim, that was okay, too. The ASP was not only fast and stealthy, but he had ensured that his escape vehicle came complete with an assortment of deadly attack options, just in case he was faced with the current contingency.

Punching up a command set on his console keyboard, he selected one of the icons representing a Killshot air-to-air cruise missile.

This was a modified ASAT, or antisatellite cruise missile, designed for orbit-to-airpace use. The advanced tactical warhead was capable of reaching multi-Mach speeds on its path to its target.

It was also as "brilliant" as they came, an Einstein among missiles, designed by the weapons genius Newcomb Straker before his untimely death.

With the computer-enhanced radar scopes set on track-while-scan modes, Vadim used a trackball pointing device to first select the Killshot icon. Hitting Auto as the trackball cursor touched the screen selection "button," he instructed the ASP's battle-management computer to take care of the rest.

It was so easy to kill, he reflected, when you could just fire and forget.

THE SUDDEN GROWLING in the cockpit informed Quinn of a threat confirmation. This electronic warning tone was echoed by the console screens, which lit up as a launch signature was recorded by IR sensors positioned in the nose of the ASP.

Because no radar signature was detected, threat identification systems acknowleged the incoming round as a thermal seeker by default. The thermal "tail chaser" had already acquired his aerospace-craft and was locked on to the ASP's scramjet exhaust nacelles. It was fast, too, closing on him at a speed of Mach 4 and increasing its terminal velocity by the second.

To his dismay, Quinn realized that the ASP was not equipped with any missiles of its own. Why the plane had not been outfitted with defensive arms was immaterial.

Suspending all further thought, Quinn performed a ninety-degree wingover maneuver. The ASP accelerated as it traded altitude for speed, its nose assembly glowing an incandescent white from friction with the outer atmosphere at the transonic velocities that it was traveling.

A quick check of his instrument scopes told Quinn that his quarry's ASP was again widening the gap between them and that the Killshot round had only been momentarily sidetracked by his evasive maneuver. It was now apparent, too, that since Quinn could not outpace the incoming warhead, he would have to go for the break lock option.

As brilliant as the air-to-air cruise missile might be, blind spots were inherent in any targeting system's design. All systems that either radiated energy, passively sensed energy or used a combination of both seeker methods to acquire and track targets had blind spots.

This round, whatever its strong points, would have its own blind spot, too. Quinn had to find and exploit that blind spot in order to create a break lock condition.

Quinn was flying in darkness now, but ahead of him, just across the line between night and day—called the global terminator—he saw that the sky was lightening. If he could move quickly enough, he might yet beat the Killshot round to the punch.

But he had little time in which to push the ASP's performance envelope. The multi-Mach round's speed was increasing steadily, and it was eating up the distance between it and the ASP with each passing second.

Pulling back the side-stick controller that throttled the ASP up to its maximum cruising speed of Mach 6, Quinn shot the transonic scramjet toward the horizon.

His instruments reported that the ASP was dangerously overheating as he approached the terminator. The LCD temperature gauge on the cockpit console was already red-zoned. He had no choice but to disregard the warning and keep up the pressure because the high-velocity cruise missile launched by Vadim was steadily gaining on him.

The incoming tail chaser was now less than a mile away, his instruments reported. In only a second or two, the rocket-powered, stub-winged cruise missile would reach its detonation zone.

At that point its proximity fuze would initiate an explosive airburst. The splinter zone created by the detonating warhead would catch the speeding ASP in its lethal perimeter, destroying the aerospace plane utterly.

A pulse beat passed, and then Quinn saw the blinding ball of light. It was the light of the sun that was exposed just around the hemispherical curvature of the global terminator.

He was flying over the Southern Hemisphere, and the sun was large and bright as it filled the black sky overhead, causing Quinn's helmet visor to automatically opaque in order to screen out the intense light and protect his eyes from solar radiation.

The stub-winged round on his tail was only a second or two away from detonation. Quinn pushed the side-stick controller all the way to its final stop, continuing to ignore the engine-overheat warnings the ASP was giving him.

The scramjet went into a steep nosedive as it plunged almost straight downward, air friction and g forces on its airframe causing the entire aerospace plane's fuselage to shudder violently, threatening to break it completely apart.

Quinn paid no attention to the tremendous forces that were capable of sending him into G-LOC, gravity-induced loss of consciousness, at any second. His eyes were riveted on the track-while-scan window in his multimode display scope that showed the path of the Killshot missile behind him.

For a moment it seemed to hesitate in its deadly course. Then, with the brilliant disk of the sun eclipsing the thermal signature of the ASP it was chasing, the round veered sharply to starboard, then swung to port again. Its targeting microprocessor was confused. Quinn had achieved his break lock.

Then, with almost surprising suddenness, the round exploded. Quinn was too far away from the splinter zone to be destroyed, but the ASP was close enough to be struck by the spreading envelope of razor-sharp fragmentation particles of prefragmented steel.

Some of the fragments struck one of his forward-canted wings. The ASP, its airframe already near the point of disintegration because of the titanic g forces that buffeted the fuselage from every angle, now gave a final shudder as one of its scramjet engines flamed out, and the hypersonic vehicle pitched crazily across the skies.

17

Quinn hit the restart button on the ASP's main console panel. The on-board computer executed a series of precision-timed restarts, but none of them were successful in reversing the partial flameout induced by the shrapnel burst.

Fighting to keep from blacking out from G-LOC, Quinn grappled the frozen side-stick controller in an effort to level the aerospace plane out. With one of its wings all shot up, the ASP bucked and shuddered, refusing to respond to Quinn's efforts to steady the vehicle.

Slowly, as the ASP lost altitude and descended into "thicker" air, the violent convulsions began to quiet down somewhat.

Imminence of breakup flattened out to mere balkiness as Quinn grew assured that the worst of the crisis had passed. In the space of two dozen seconds, he had descended hundreds of miles from the point where he had first put the ASP into its steep downward plunge.

But where was he now? Quinn punched up his GPS and the ASP's global positioning system immediately flashed his current position along lines of latitude and longitude on one of the cockpit's multimode viewscreens.

Quinn could see that the ASP was far off its original northwesterly glide path, having veered eastward to such a degree that its course would soon slingshot it across the southernmost tip of the Florida panhandle.

Using the trackball on the instrumentation console to pop up another window on the multimode display of his main scope, Quinn called up track-while-scan radar.

The long-range scan revealed no sign of the ASP that he had been pursuing through the skies for thousands of miles. What it did show was that the remainder of the strike force aerospace planes and space shuttles were moving out of orbital trajectory and into their atmospheric cruise vectors. They would soon be landing on earth-bound bases, presumably having sustained minimal blast damage.

Going for a long shot, Quinn popped up another display window on his main scope and tried to obtain a probable position fix on the flight vector of Vadim's ASP.

The artificial-intelligence hardware crunched the numbers and gave Quinn the finished data in the space of a pulse beat.

According to the data on the scope, there was a high probability that the ASP was flying toward the southwestern sector of the continental United States, based on its previous heading, speed and other performance factors.

Quinn shunted his ASP into a pursuit trajectory, hampered by the lack of speed as a result of flying on only a single burner and able to go no faster than a relatively slow Mach 3.

He was running dangerously low on fuel when a target icon popped up on the track-while-scan window of his multimode radar screen. Quinn's pulse quickened; he had found the needle in the haystack and he was again on Vadim's tail!

The computer-enhanced display calculated the distance and probable destination of the target scramjet, which flashed on a pop-up window on the multimode cockpit screen. Quinn saw from these displays that the ASP he was bird-dogging through the skies was hundreds of miles downwind of him and moving much faster than he could in his blast-crippled vehicle.

The pilot of the fleeing space plane had by now probably seen him, too, and that added to Quinn's problems. Pushing the wounded bird to the max,

Quinn followed, flying as much on determination as on fuel reserves and burners.

THIS WAS the end of the line.

Vadim felt the entire airframe lurch violently as all three landing gear bit down into the crusty surface of the desert salt pan, the remnant of what had been an arm of a shallow inland sea millions of years ago but was now flat as a board and dry as a bone.

He could feel the baking Nevada desert sun beating down on him through the clear polycarbonate cockpit canopy of the ASP. He knew that outside the dome the mean daytime temperature rose to highs in excess of one hundred twenty-five degrees Fahrenheit. That was hot enough to fry your bacon and eggs without your having to light a fire.

But Vadim also knew that if he allowed himself to be captured by WorldPol, the heat would be turned up a great deal higher. Hot enough to fry *him,* he would not escape the death penalty for blowing away scores of innocents on board the Sunyata—never mind his other crimes.

But Vadim had no plans to go that route. In fact, his plans called for an escape of an entirely different sort. Instead of being sent into the afterlife, he would send himself to a previous lifetime.

He had piloted the ASP to this location for a specific reason. Not far from where he had landed was a way out of his predicament that nobody besides himself had even dared to consider as a serious possibility.

The heat of the afternoon was searing in its intensity as he stepped down from the ASP's cockpit. It stifled him and dazzled his eyes as he hauled his gear out of the cockpit, setting the autodestruct sequence in the scramjet, which would blow the ASP to useless wreckage and destroy it beyond any attempt to reconstruct it.

Desperately he ran from the landing site because he knew that the plane would explode in only a few minutes. At last he hit the blazing-hot desert sand behind a jumble of large boulders.

The scramjet aircraft blew up with a tremendous boom, and a wave of heat even more searing than the scalding Nevada sun washed over him as the fireball expanded from the burning wreckage in all directions.

Climbing back up to his feet again, he watched what was left of the ASP burn for a few long minutes.

A smile of satisfaction played across his gaunt features, plucking at the corners of his thin, bloodless lips. If his luck ran true, then WorldPol might even get the impression that he had crash-landed and burned up in the wreckage.

Then he suddenly remembered the damned tracker implant that was still pinging away inside his skull. Even Vadim had not yet been able to figure out a way of getting rid of the infernal contraption without blowing his brains out at the same time.

The reverend was about to turn from the blast site as the flames began to die down and the charred airframe wreckage blackened, when he caught sight of a distant flicker of light on the far horizon.

The glint was like that made by a fast-moving aircraft, still high up and far away, and a wispy contrail of exhaust trailed the pinpoint of light that seemed to crawl across the seamless azure sky. He held his hands up to shade his eyes and frowned.

A gut check said that, yes, it had to be Quinn up there.

Cursing the man he detested above all others, Vadim shouldered his pack of money and weapons and hustled away from the burning wreckage. The sun filled the sky and the air was hot enough to scald his lungs. But he didn't have far to go before reaching the point of no return.

Then nobody, not even Quinn, would be able to touch him.

WHEN THE SECOND ENGINE flamed out, Quinn knew that he had finally run flat out of luck. There was no mystery about what caused the flameout: his readouts told him he had run out of fuel. There wasn't any way he was liable to cure that problem, short of working a miracle, and he had exhausted his supply of those.

Far below him, rising up from the brilliant white expanse that Quinn knew to be the Nevada desert, a plume of black smoke marked the spot where the aerospace plane he had been following had come down to earth again.

On the face of it, a crash was the most likely explanation for the visual evidence below. But there could be other explanations, too, including a deliberate effort by Vadim to cover his tracks. Quinn would not be satisfied until he had the opportunity to take a close-up look at the landing site with his own eyes.

Quinn's altitude began sharply dropping as the ASP went into a glide slope beginning at approximately thirty thousand feet.

Because the ASP, minus hundreds of pounds of fuel, was now much lighter than it had been when he had first set out on the chase, and because it was also an aerodynamically stable craft, Quinn was able to keep the angle of descent from deteriorating into a full-out tailspin.

Soon he was cruising a few thousand feet above the desert. At this altitude he felt the sudden lurch that would have bounced his head off the cockpit dome were he not strapped securely in his seat as the lightened ASP swept through thermals rising off the superheated desert floor.

Down at this low altitude, the air was turbulent, but the high-energy thermal currents also helped to give the airframe desperately needed lift and keep it airborne much longer than a controlled descent through calmer, cooler air would have done.

Keeping his eyes on the dense pall of black, sooty smoke that rose up from the crash site a few score miles away and over a thousand feet below him, Quinn fought the stick controller to keep airborne and squeeze every last ounce of velocity out of the tortured airframe.

He was helped now by surface effect, the added lift that aircraft pick up when gliding very low over landmasses or across water.

Thanks to the aerodynamics of surface effect, the ASP scudded across the flat landscape like a desert eagle swooping after its prey, and Quinn realized that he would make it to the site of the apparent crash in one piece—*if* he was lucky.

Within minutes his extended front landing gear bit down on the hard, flaky crust of the salt flats. The other two hind gear touched down in similar fashion seconds later.

The ASP began rolling forward, not needing a drag chute or the reversal of its thrusters since its landing was hundreds of times slower than its normal supersonic landing speed of approximately Mach 2.

Pausing to wipe the sweat from his brow, Quinn pneumatically retracted the cockpit canopy bubble. Climbing out of the cockpit, he turned on the ASP's transponder beacon and reclosed the cockpit canopy as the transponder sent out a continuous radio signal that would be used for later retrieval by search teams.

Next he set about inspecting the crash site. There was no sign of organic debris amid the smoldering wreckage of the airframe, no sign that Vadim had perished in the crash.

In fact, Quinn did not believe that it had been a crash so much as a deliberate attempt to scuttle the plane.

The scattering of wreckage, for one thing, was not consonant with how pieces of a crashed aircraft would spread. The wreckage was uniformly scattered and in large chunks, the effect that a blast from a stationary explosion would cause.

Quinn pulled his GPS unit from his belt pouch and got a position fix on his location. He was, as the ASP's instruments had told him earlier, on federal lands.

In fact, he was not far from Groom Lake, a site he knew from prior missions to have been used by the military and other, more esoteric entities, as test areas for a host of clandestine projects.

Replacing the GPS, Quinn unshipped the tracker unit from another pouch. Activating it, he picked up a clear signal from a source whose code number designated the icon as belonging to Lux Vadim.

Quinn began using the tracker beacon as a guide while he unshipped his satcom commo device. It was time he turned in a situation report to the mission command center.

18

It was amazing how quickly the body became dehydrated in this baking heat, thought the reverend to himself as he approached the cool shadow cast by the towering red sandstone mesa. Not that it mattered much, though. In just a little while he would be out of the heat of the day and in a pleasantly air-conditioned environment.

Despite his "conversion" to a cult religion and the preachings of life on a new and higher plane after his imprisonment for racketeering in the wake of the Mars Mission deaths, he had made certain that the umbilical cord to his previous existence had not been completely cut. That previous life had centered around his company, Centurion Development Corporation, and the high-technology industry that the company had served.

His clients had included advanced research-and-development projects for DARPA, the Defense Advanced Research Programs Agency, the CIA and certain highly placed foreign sources, among others.

A crooked smile corkscrewed across the Vadim's dust-caked and already sunburned face as he recalled the fact that the keys he held to a variety of skeletons in people's closets had ensured that his stay in prison was relatively short and his time behind bars had gone easy.

His intimate knowledge of the dirty little secrets of the Pentagon's top brass—and a few CIA projects so black that the world would be turned upside down if even a syllable leaked out—had also ensured that he would breeze through the parole board hearings, despite the highly vocal pleas for his continued stay behind bars.

It was one of those dirty, dangerous and highly damaging secrets that the reverend was now counting on to assist him in pulling his chestnuts out of yet another fire. A solid reason, not mere chance, had brought him to his destination. He had piloted the ASP to this remote corner of the Nevada desert because it was the covert site of one of DARPA's most ambitious military technology projects—Project Toymaker.

At another place and time, the portals of the Toymaker project would have been guarded by a contingent of Special Forces troops. Not so today. Intelligent machines were counted upon to do all the grunt work that humans shunned, and even now Vadim knew that a line of hidden sensors had long since picked up his thermal signature as he approached the mountainside. Computers had relayed the data to a command post deep within the mountain that now cast its long, cool shadow over him.

But the wafer-thin flash ROM identification card he carried in the pocket of his flight suit ensured that the computer did not trigger any alarms. The card emitted a weak field of coded magnetic pulses that identified its holder as a person carrying the highest access priority. The card bestowed ask-no-questions authority on a level so high that it permitted the holder to come and go at will.

Such a high-priority clearance would not cause the base computer, which monitored the perimeter, to issue an interdiction alert. In addition, the card would unlock and slide open the pneumatically controlled blast door hidden around the opening of a small box canyon at the mountain's base.

His feet crunching on pulverized rock as he entered the canyon, he slid the flash card from his pocket. He sighted the dull metallic finish of the blast door amid the gray-brown of wrinkled granite and inserted the flash card into the slot beside it.

The steel door, otherwise impervious to shock forces up to those produced by a subkiloton nuclear blast, slid effortlessly aside with a faint whirring sound.

He slipped his card back into one of the pockets of his "zoom bag" as the door closed behind him once again. He entered the sterile corridor with brushed-steel walls that lay beyond the computer-actuated portal.

The base was largely robotically controlled, staffed by only a handful of technicians at any given time. Even security forces were severely restricted on a tightly controlled need-to-know basis.

This situation was due to both the fact that Project Toymaker was arguably the most ultrasecret project yet developed by the U.S. Government and the fact that robotic security measures considered highly dependable were in force to guard the base perimeter.

The former factor had motivated the overseers of Toymaker to keep even the number of security troops deployed on site to the smallest possible minimum, while the latter had meant that the base could be plausibly denied if the need ever arose to disclaim any knowledge of its existence.

There were enough trained killers on base to drastically change Vadim's plans, though. But if he had to deal with them, so be it. As always, he had come prepared. He checked the LED readout on his black, wedge-shaped 4.73 mm bullpup assault weapon.

All systems were go.

Wielding the bullpup, he moved quickly, with the deftness of a man to whom the layout of the base was well known, toward the mission objective hidden deep within the mountain's labyrinthine depths.

As GOOD AS HE WAS, the trooper never knew what hit him.

With point-and-shoot accuracy, thanks to the weapon's laser autotargeter, Vadim opened up with the M-20 bullpup, spraying the security station with dozens of explosive-tipped fléchettes.

Launched with computerized accuracy, the multiple detonations came so close together that the individual blast pulses merged in what sounded like a continuous peal of thunder.

When it was all over, the shock attack had taken out the entire security detail on the first level of the covert installation.

The strike objective that Vadim was seeking would be found another level down. Swiftly getting into the elevator car, he rode it down to the limit, watching the status lights on the panel overhead move from left to right as they tracked the car's descent from surface level all the way down to level one.

When the elevator doors opened some quarter mile below the desert, Vadim was pumped up on adrenaline to take on the brace of fresh troopers that came at him from down the corridor.

Already holding the electronic flash-bangs in his hands, and wearing goggles and ear protection that would render him unaffected by the paralyzing effects of the detonating submunitions, he tossed the two black cylinders at the advancing troops.

Cocooned in disruptive sound and light waves, troops sank to their knees, convulsing in pain as the corridor filled with ultrasound highly damaging to the nervous system while strobing lights further disoriented the visual senses.

With the troopers incapacitated and unable to put up even token resistance, the reverend had himself a relatively simple task of killing all of the personnel in the corridor. Almost casually he walked through the mass of writhing, moaning figures who lay on the floor.

He fired burst after burst, until he had killed every last member of the base security detail.

At the end of this corridor, he saw the sign warning unauthorized personnel that they were about to enter a restricted area and that only those bearing the highest security clearance were allowed access beyond that point.

The data on the flash ROM card in his pocket gave him that privilege, and he inserted the card into the slot in the wall near the door. Its autolocking mechanism permitted him instant entry.

His pulse hammering in his ears in anticipation of the incredible discovery that lay just beyond the door, the reverend pushed against the crash bar.

He knew that after he walked through that door, nothing in the world might ever be the same again.

19

Quinn's commo unit bleeped.

"We're receiving reports of a crisis situation going down near your position," the gravel voice of General Swope apprised him via comsat down-link. ".I'm sending a detail down right now."

Quinn checked the coordinates relayed by the airborne command center to his GPS unit. They matched the last known point at which the signal that he had been following had faded.

"What am I walking into?" Quinn asked.

"Can't tell you," Swope reported. "Subject has a one-zero priority code. Need-to-know regs are in force."

"To hell with 'need to know,'" Quinn shot back. "I'm looking at getting my ass shot off. That's *my* need to know."

"All right. I'm clearing you under emergency provisions. It's a spook installation. A special technical project is being conducted there."

The Operation Redball commander told Quinn about the concealed entrance to the base, code-named Gamma, and added that his mission ID card would now open the door.

Already walking in the shadow of the high sandstone mesa, Quinn could soon easily pick up the impressions left by recent footsteps in the fine gray sand. The trail led directly toward the box canyon from which the entryway to Gamma could be accessed. Finding the concealed doorway, Quinn input the emergency access code issued him by General Swope at the keypad beside the pneumatic hatch. After a series of beeps and other electronic sounds, the door slid open.

Munitions smoke billowed out of a sterile corridor with brushed-steel walls. With the lancing red line of his weapon's laser projector tracking through the obscuring fog, Quinn entered the secret base, his bullpup ported, his senses alert.

Soon he came upon the first of the corpses that littered the corridor in pools of their own blood.

THE HEART of Project Toymaker was a sphere thirty feet in circumference. The sphere was made out of a transparent polycarbonate material.

The immense, clear-walled globe stood at the center of a large operations area filled with banks of sophisticated mainframe computer equipment. Consoles containing monitors, keyboards and banks of readouts occupied the rest of the floor area.

Vadim was sitting at one of those consoles. His oddly colored eyes were wide with deep concentration as he keyed in command sequences from memory at the keyboard in front of him. Sweat had begun to bead his forehead and upper lip as he focused all his attention on the precise series of keystrokes necessary to initialize the unit.

And that was the dicey part. Vadim knew he had to get the codes exactly right the first time because every passing minute made capture more likely and there would be no second chance.

The huge sphere's interior was already beginning to light up with a soft, pulsating glow. Scintillations of light danced inside this throbbing cloud of power, and a low whine, barely audible at first, had started to fill the room until it pervaded every corner of the command-and-control center.

He had done it!

Certain that he was on his way, he set the digital timer on a small explosive charge as he logged in the final command sequence and rechecked the data on the monitor screen one last time.

Satisfied that the program was up and running, he gathered his gear and placed the demo charge beneath the console, where it attached itself magnetically. The charge would detonate a few minutes after he entered the sphere.

If all went well, he would be free. If things didn't work out, he would be dead.

But those were the breaks, and Vadim had the satisfaction of knowing that he would be dead anyway if he allowed himself to be captured.

He stepped toward the sphere. There was a hatchless opening through which a single person could walk unobstructed.

He stood at the center of the sphere. Swirling motes of colored light circled around him in a quickening vortex that merged to cocoon him in a glowing, flickering plasma cloud filling the transparent shell.

There was a momentary feeling of disorientation, as if every cell in his body were being dispersed. Then, as he began to translate, he saw something through the clear walls of the sphere that made him laugh out loud. Fate, he knew, had been kind to him in the end.

What Vadim had found so amusing was the sight of Quinn bursting into the restricted area, weapon in hand, just as Vadim translated completely.

IT TOOK A SPLIT-INSTANT for Quinn's situational awareness to take in the totality of what was happening in the large research zone he'd just entered.

As he stormed into the restricted operations area, he heard the earsplitting whine of the dynamo effect generated by the powerful electromagnetic pulses that powered the Toymaker sphere.

His attention screened out the banks of flashing digital readouts and console data screens at either side, focusing tightly on the sphere at the center of the spacious area. As though viewed through a screen of milky light, he could dimly see a human figure.

Quinn raised his weapon but as he prepared to fire he saw the milk white radiance suddenly darken.

Within the space of a pulse beat it had gone completely black. The interior of the sphere looked as though it had been suddenly filled with black enamel.

Just as quickly the blackness vanished. Once more the clear polycarbonate shell of the sphere showed nothing within. The human figure that Quinn had seen inside the strange device for a fleeting instant was gone.

Letting his weapon drop to point toward the floor, Quinn approached the enormous globe-shaped machine when a warning tone sounded and the screen of the tracker hung at his waist flashed him threat data.

Across the screen a graphic display was painted of one of the control consoles. A glowing red triangle highlighted a small cylindrical shape that the tracker's microprocessor indicated was magnetically attached to the underside of the console.

"Warning...threat parameters match M45 high-energy fragmentation mine," read the accompanying text block.

For a split instant Quinn wondered if there was enough time to disarm the mine. But the M45 made the decision for him. It exploded with sudden violence, ripping apart the console and sending sparks flying in all directions as dense, choking smoke billowed through the air.

Far enough from the blast to escape injury in his body armor, Quinn was nevertheless hurled several feet across the room. As he picked himself up from the floor, he grabbed a fire extinguisher from a wall and put out the fire.

As the blaze flickered out beneath the quenching halon spray, Quinn stared at the smoldering wreckage of the console, realizing that Vadim had just evaded him completely.

If Quinn's hunch was right, Vadim might just have sent himself on a one-way trip to a place that put him beyond the reach of WorldPol forever.

20

Like wildfire, the repercussions of what had gone down at Gamma Base had rapidly spread to every corner of the globe. Secret, hastily convened and high-level meetings became the urgent focus of political centers of gravity from Washington to Beijing, from Moscow to Tokyo.

Though the media had not yet picked up the scent, the ramifications of this event of unprecedented importance was a matter of grave concern to the frightened policymakers of the world.

The heads of state had good reason to be concerned even more than frightened. The sphere in the Gamma research center was a CTL—closed timelike line—generator, and this in turn was a time machine, although the techs never used that word, preferring the term "causality violation" for time travel.

Gamma Base housed a technical achievement that was the fruition of almost a half century of development of the most secret military undertaking since the Manhattan Project of World War Two, which had split the atom and developed the first atomic bomb.

Begun by German scientists operating at the Peenemünde Rocket Proving Grounds in northern Germany in the closing months of World War Two, the research into time travel was imported to the U.S. with those same ex-Nazi scientists, who, among other things, went on to work on the U.S. space program.

In the late 1950s the Toymaker project had succeeded in "translating" a rat through a CTL. In the process of translating, only a portion of the rat vanished, leaving a thrashing obscenity behind that lived for a few seconds before dying.

During the 1960s a refined version of the CTL generator, or time machine, had successfully transported animals of small biomass into the past. But the device had not been able to retrieve these test subjects from what the techs called "downtime," or the past.

The problem of sending live test subjects downtime and bringing them back to the present had eluded the scientists until well past the turn of the twenty-first century, when humans were translated a few days backward in time.

It was during this phase of experimentation that Lux Vadim, then at the helm of the Centurion Development Corporation, which had worked closely with DARPA in conducting secret projects, had gotten wind of what was happening at the secret desert base.

Intrigued by the advanced research he knew to be underway at Gamma and determined to exploit it for his own profit, Vadim, as president of Centurion, had pulled strings and called in long-uncollected political markers.

In the end Centurion had been awarded a lucrative contract for manufacturing critical components for the CTL generator and installing the systems. On fulfillment of the contract, Vadim himself had been able to witness the CTL generator in action, through the obtainment of a high-security clearance.

After his release, Vadim had satisfied himself that the time-travel device was fully operational.

He knew that if his Motherboarder operation fell apart, as indeed it ultimately did, and he found himself out of the religious-cult leader business, then he could use the CTL generator to escape back into the past, the one place where his pursuers would have little hope of finding him or bringing him back to stand trial.

Vadim had apparently succeeded in carrying out his plan, according to all evidence. Entering Gamma via his security clearance privileges, he had activated the CTL generator and disappeared downtime through a closed timelike line.

But spacetime, though it behaved like a fluid in some respects, acted more like a crystal lattice in others. The introduction of a destabilizing force might shatter the delicate latticework of causality with disastrous consequences.

Vadim was a loose cannon, careering his way through spacetime. Sooner or later, it was feared, he would throw the entire continuum out of balance. Causality could go haywire. Like a machine out of control, it might even blow itself apart.

QUINN FACED the smartwall.

The millions of pixels glowing on the huge liquid-crystal display plates coalesced into a montage of life-size high-definition images. Omnidirectional audio filled the room.

"The world of the 1990s was considerably different than our own time," the voice of the tech narrator told Quinn. "It was an era which witnessed the breakup of the Soviet Union and the fighting in the Baltic states and Yugoslavia."

The smartwall's giant digital video display showed Russian President Boris Yeltsin facing off against Russian tanks during the August coup of 1991.

The images changed, showing Serbian troops fighting their Croatian opponents in the slaughterhouse that had once been Yugoslavia before the Soviet breakup. Both sides ported the ubiquitous

AK-47 assault rifles commonplace in the world at the time as they fired across no-man's-land in trench warfare reminiscent of World War One.

"But these events, although of great importance to the history of our own century, nevertheless follow in the wake of an event that took place some months before the Soviet Union's disintegration. This was an event which, although not recognized at the time, has proven to be one of the most significant turning points of the late twentieth century."

Now the scenes on the smartwall shifted to show a panoramic display of attack helicopters filling the skies of what appeared to be a Middle Eastern city. Tanks and APCs rolled through streets lined with date palms in the shadow of spires and minarets.

The images segued to show a sinister-looking figure in a khaki uniform and black beret whose fleshy face sported a thick black mustache. Holding a semiautomatic pistol pointed at the sky in one hand, he gestured with the other hand balled into a clenched fist.

His dark, glittering eyes swept across the crowd that thronged the large square below the balcony on which he stood as he harangued the assembled populace.

"Saddam Hussein," said the tech's voice-over. "It was this Mideast despot whose invasion of Kuwait on August 2, 1990 began a domino effect that led to the formation of what is now called the first coalition to launch the assault known as Desert Storm, the avowed purpose of which was to free Kuwait from Saddam's iron-fisted rule."

The smartwalls segued to depict yet another battleground. This one was in the flat sand desert of southeastern Iraq. Here a montage of violent images and cacophonous sounds showed a cascade of brilliant lights over Baghdad as coalition fighter-bombers commenced the first salvos of the operation that had come to be known in its entirety as Desert Storm.

These scenes gave way to images of Scud missile attacks on Riyadh and Tel Aviv, and later to the crossing of the Euphrates by mechanized troops, the tank battle and the surrender of scores of thousands of Iraqi soldiers who had been pounded for weeks in their bunkers, expecting a land attack that had never materialized.

"For almost nine years, the Iraqis and the Iranians hurled wave after wave of their citizens at one another on this same desert battlefield. Saddam believed that he was facing a similar threat from the United Nations coalition confronting him in 1990-1991.

"Saddam was proven wrong in the course of events. The military might assembled against him put on a martial display never before seen. Within a matter of weeks, Iraq was bombed practically back to the Stone Age.

"But after the victory parades, and after the relief that so few combatants had died in the fighting," the narrator went on, "the war quickly faded from the headlines. The final death throes of the old Soviet Union and issues on the domestic scene soon drove events in the gulf completely from memory. America was fighting other battles, battles on its home front."

Now the scenes shifted to the urban riots that had plagued the last few years of the twentieth century. The slaughter in Los Angeles in 1992 was followed by scenes of the carnage in Chicago two years later, ending in the tactical nuclear explosion that had struck the Republican National Convention in San Francisco in 1998.

"Desert Storm had been forgotten," the tech's voice went on. "It would be decades before its true significance was realized after the domestic troubles had been settled. Now, as you may know, we have come to view it far differently.

"We know now that what happened in Iraq was as dramatic a turning point in world events as was the Battle of Trafalgar in 1805, when British warships decisively defeated a Franco-Spanish coalition and fixed the map of Europe for the next two centuries.

"Had American and Western powers permitted Saddam to control the flow of Middle Eastern oil, then North America would have been hit by an oil shock of a magnitude that would have made the severe OPEC embargoes of the seventies look tame by comparison.

"The domestic strife that marred the late nineties would have escalated to full-blown civil war. America might have collapsed under the weight of these destabilizing burdens, had the coalition powers not defeated Saddam soundly in early 1991."

Quinn rose from his seat. He walked toward the smartwall where the life-size image of Saddam Hussein appeared and studied the cruel features of the Iraqi dictator.

Here was an enigma, thought Quinn.

Saddam was a man who had held his country in thrall and hung on for years following the coalition's victory as the unchallenged master of Iraq.

"You think that Lux Vadim has gone back to the Desert Storm era?" Quinn asked.

"We're virtually certain," replied the tech, now stepping away from the smartwall. "Apart from the fact that in the Motherboarders' bizarre pantheon of avatars Saddam was equated with the reincarnation of the high priest of Mu—this we know was just a pose on Vadim's part—we believe that Vadim entertained a genuine, slavish admiration for Saddam.

"Furthermore, we know that Vadim, who is an expert on military technology, could stand to make a fortune if, back in 1990-1991, he could sell his expertise to Saddam. Can you imagine how sophisticated high-energy laser systems might have changed the course of the war? It boggles the mind to contemplate."

"But the past hasn't changed," Quinn responded at once. "Had Vadim been able to alter the past, then we would have a different history even as we speak. Yet history hasn't changed at all. Desert Storm is still the victory for the Coalition that it always has been. Saddam was defeated, as history shows. Nothing whatever has changed."

"That, I'm afraid, is open to question," replied the tech. "Subtle changes in the framework of causality might have occurred due to Vadim's temporal translation. These changes might not fully manifest themselves for years to come. Also, there is another issue to be considered—the Muan power crystals that Vadim believed to have been buried eons before in the Iraqi desert."

"They're just a myth," Quinn ventured, shrugging off the prospect as farfetched. "Part of the line of pseudoreligious bullshit that kept the suckers flocking by the thousands to join Vadim's Motherboard Church."

The tech shook his head. "That's not entirely correct. In fact, there is compelling evidence that such crystals did actually exist, just as Vadim claimed. Did you ever hear of the Ancestral Heritage Society? Of Operation Wotan?"

"Yes to both," Quinn answered with a nod. "It was a Nazi organization founded by Himmler. Wotan was a bizarre expedition, staged by the Nazis, to find the lost continent of Atlantis in the 1930s, wasn't it?"

"That's right," the tech affirmed. "The full story is still classified. It reveals that Nazi archaeologists did find something during the Wotan digs, and that the cache included a crystal of strange power. Ancient scripts identified another cache of far more, and far larger crystals buried somewhere along the Iran-Iraq border centuries ago. Both of these caches were said to have come from Mu."

"And you're telling me that Vadim is after the Muan crystals," Quinn summed up. "Why?"

"Because of their potential for use in the construction of the ultimate particle-beam weapons, weapons that can generate tremendous laser energies with incredibly small power requirements and that can be built in extremely small sizes. It is that, more than anything else, that we are concerned with.

"You see, Saddam Hussein was a mystic. He spent millions excavating what he believed to be the site of ancient Babylon and constructing a replica of the city-state in Baghdad. He believed himself to be the reincarnation of Nebuchadrezzar, king of ancient Mesopotamia.

"As incredible as it may sound, there is the possibility that if Vadim finds a way of contacting Saddam, he could convince him of his ability to find the Muan crystals and use them to create weapons of devastating power. Because of certain time paradoxes, that new reality could come crashing down on us tomorrow, or the day after, even if our 'now' stays unchanged."

Quinn looked past the tech and again studied the giant face of Saddam frozen on the large digital video screen. Across the gulf of years, it seemed to taunt him. Could Vadim get to Saddam? he wondered.

The answer, Quinn realized suddenly, was yes. Saddam had considered himself a messiah. Vadim would be his perfect apostle—an apostle of death.

21

Swarming like human ants in a futuristic hive, jumpsuited personnel busied themselves at tasks throughout the high-security technical installation.

Six stories beneath the burning desert sands, a bank of superdynamos capable of generating enough electricity to power a small city began to charge storage batteries each the size of a grain silo. Millions of volts of raw power drained into the batteries, which would release their load to energize gold-vapor lasers.

The nucleus of activity in the Gamma Base command center was the thirty-foot transparent poly-carbonate sphere from which Lux Vadim had vanished into the past.

To Quinn, who watched from the sidelines, it seemed as if the CTL generator were more like a living thing than a machine. It almost seemed to control the men and women who swarmed around it rather than the other way around.

Quinn was aware of the focus behind all the activity in the research center. The techs were preparing the time machine to send him back into the past where the mission he had been tasked with was to bring Vadim back to stand trial.

Only as a last resort or in self-defense was Vadim to be killed. As an incentive against a misapplication of the termination directive, Quinn's contract called for only half his completion bonus to be paid in the event of the felon's death, whereas bringing Vadim back alive would net him an additional twenty percent commission.

Before Quinn himself would be sent downtime, an unmanned temporal drone unit would be translated via the CTL sphere. Containing video and audio recorders, as well as sensors for data on the atmosphere, weather and other environmental factors, the drone had already been placed inside the sphere.

This phase of the process was necessary to ensure that Quinn, catapulted back in time to that identical spot to which the drone would soon be sent, did not wind up embedded in solid rock or find himself stuck in a cavern filled with poisonous gases.

Sampling the environment downtime, the drone's sensor data could then be analyzed for factors that a human subject would encounter on CTL translation.

"Energize," ordered the mission-control manager from his command console.

For the second time since entering the base after Vadim, Quinn heard the rising crescendo of power generators charging to peak loads deep in the bowels of the installation.

Step-up transformers were expanding hundreds of volts of input into millions of volts of output as power was sucked from the gigantic storage batteries.

Beneath the roots of the high mesa, radioactive particles were being accelerated in a ring a mile in circumference as a phased array of gold-vapor lasers were computer fired at a plasma comprised of vaporized uranium. Powerful field-effect magnets had imparted a counterclockwise spin to the plasma at a rate of millions of revolutions per second.

The bombardment of the spinning plasma core by the lasers held the secret of causality violation. For the space of a few brief instants, the controlled nuclear detonations would duplicate one of the most awesome forces in the known universe: the spinning black hole.

Gravitational forces generated by this phenomenon resulted in the creation of what the techs called "light cones." Through these flowed the closed timelike lines that were pathways backward into the past or forward into the future.

The key to controlling where a time traveler ended up lay in tipping the light cones over along their axis of spin. Once tipped over, a CTL could in theory lead through a light cone to any point in the past or future.

"Ready for translation," reported a technician monitoring one of the banks of data screens and lighted digital readout panels.

The instruments now showed that the artificial black hole had begun to tip the light cone created by gravitational forces produced by its mass and spin.

Using computer algorithms developed by a CIA technical focus group on time travel in the year 2012, the light cone could be pointed with precision toward any known year in the past or projected into the future by manipulating the spin of the simulated black hole.

"Engage autosequencing," the mission-control manager reported, his eyes moving from the CTL translation sphere to his own banks of screens and back again as a data block calibrated in microseconds completed the countdown to December 1990, the drone's destination.

"Autosequencing engaged," another tech replied as the supercomputer completed the tilting of the light cone. "Countdown in progress. Mark at zero-zero-niner-zero-five."

The large digital display panel registered the countdown toward zero. As the numbers cycled toward the point of temporal translation, the milky light that Quinn had observed just before Vadim translated back in time filled the clear-walled sphere.

Then suddenly the interior of the time-travel device went completely black. This phenomenon was due, Quinn knew, to the fact that gravitational forces within the artificial black hole had created an "event horizon." Beyond this barrier no visible light could escape through the clear walls of the CTL sphere, and in the absence of light, the human eye perceived blackness.

"Prepare for probe retranslation," the mission-control manager said after the CTL probe had disappeared downtime to the target date.

"Probe retranslation sequencing initialized," a tech replied, affirming the command. "Countdown in progress. Mark."

Events reversed themselves after this second countdown. A second bank of fully charged gold-vapor lasers powered up, and millions of volts were generated to culminate in the creation of a second tipped light cone. At the conclusion of the process, the probe reappeared inside the CTL sphere, once more back in the year 2035.

Technicians swarmed around the retranslated CTL probe. After removing the probe from the interior of the sphere, they connected interface cables to the probe's many input-output ports. The interface connectors linked the probe to the supercomputer systems at Gamma, downloading the sensor input into the high-level number crunchers that would translate the raw data into meaningful form.

"WE'LL COMPLETE your preparation while the data's being processed," the mission-control manager said to Quinn.

The mission-support team at Gamma Base had already attached medical sensors to Quinn's body and were checking his vital signs prior to temporal translation. The team had been responsible for managing the manifold aspects of Quinn's trip into the past, including detailed research into the era he would visit and furnishing the temponaut with all appropriate mission support materials.

Quinn already was dressed in fashions that were current during the latter half of the year 1990, to which he would soon, if the systems checked out properly, be translated. The leisure attire included sneakers with an old-fashioned vulcanized rubber sole that did not have the "memory" features common to twenty-first-century sneaker soles.

But the six-pocket trousers and black leather jacket were of an almost contemporary cut, though high-wear-rated plastic-paper hybrids were the materials of choice in the twenty-first century.

The mission-support engineer laid a wallet and money belt on the table. In addition to these two items, he placed a wristwatch and other forms of "pocket litter," as the spooks called it, on the table.

"The wallet contains a thousand dollars in worn currency," the tech told Quinn. "The bills have been artificially aged, and the serial numbers are authentic. There are also major credit cards, as you can see.

"The cards are a lot trickier than the paper money. We can't be a hundred percent sure the plastic will work downtime. We've manufactured duplicates of cards held by CIA imprest funds during the late twentieth century, but we've had no way to test them out."

Quinn opened the wallet, counted the bills and inspected the credit cards that Gamma had furnished him. There were a dozen of them, the old-fashioned type backed by a brown Mylar strip, without any three-dimensional laser photo of the holder on the reverse as current cards had.

These cards, Quinn recalled, would have been issued before more modern cards containing flash ROM chips came into use around the turn of the century, cards that were essentially miniature data banks and performed many more functions than their predecessors.

Thumbing through some of the other contents of the wallet, Quinn found some old-style two-dimensional photographs. He pulled them out and inspected them, noting the family portrait with Quinn posing in the center of the group.

"That's your 'family,'" replied the chief mission-support engineer. "Adam Jackson, your alter ego in 1990, is a family man. That's his family. Computer simulated, of course."

"Jackson looks like a happy man," Quinn told the tech. "Almost a pity that he never actually existed."

Quinn replaced the photos in the wallet and placed the wallet into one of the pockets of his trousers. He picked up the money belt and unfastened one of its Velcro-backed pockets. Inside the belt were several sheafs of bills in mixed denominations.

"You have thirty thousand dollars in that money belt," the engineer informed Quinn. "Because of our uncertainty about the performance of the simulated credit cards, it was decided to give you plenty of cash."

"Hope I don't get mugged," Quinn said, strapping on the money belt as he caught sight of the technicians inspecting the data downloaded from the newly recovered time probe.

"Just don't flash it around," the technician advised with a smile. He picked up another item on the table. This was a black leather carryall of medium size equipped with a shoulder strap. "Your 'special gear' is inside the luggage."

Quinn nodded. The support personnel had done a reasonably good job of packing a great deal of specialized matériel into a very small space. The case contained Quinn's stealth suit and VRG ensemble. In addition, it also contained a variety of weapons.

Niched in foam padding were a P-90 5.70 mm close assault weapon and a Glock 20 laser-equipped semiautomatic pistol. The Glock fired the 10 mm ammunition that was obtainable during the year 1990.

In addition to extra ammo clips for the weaponry, silencers had been issued, as well. The laser-targeting enhancements, though of a recent design, could be powered by batteries available down the time stream.

Quinn zipped up the black leather suitcase and replaced it on the table. "There's one possible glitch," the chief tech warned Quinn. "At this stage we are not at all certain about how electronic components will behave once translated. We've encountered problems with sensor probes sent back in time before. They malfunction unpredictably.

"As yet, we're at a loss to explain the malfunctions. It's possible that your gear won't work, or function only part of the time or at limited capacity. Then again, everything might function perfectly. Just make sure you factor this into your plans."

"Your warning is well taken," answered Quinn. "And I suppose the same would apply to any electronics taken down the time line by Vadim, too?"

"It would, yes," replied the tech with a nod.

"So you're saying there's also the possibility that I won't be able to track Vadim by reading telemetry from his skull transponder?"

"That's also correct," the tech replied. "You might wind up going by nothing but instinct."

The briefing was interrupted by one of the Gamma personnel whose voice over the speaker grille informed the mission-control manager that the inspection of the time probe had been completed.

"Put the data on my screen," the mission control manager told the caller.

He inspected visual and hypertext data, showing him that back in the year 1990, the area now occupied by a wing of the underground installation was an empty cavern with a side tunnel leading directly to the desert exterior.

"Looks like it's a go," the tech told Quinn, noting that no sign of toxic gases or other environmental hazards was revealed by the probe. "You'll find a map in your pocket that will lead you to the highway. Though we can't pinpoint the exact time that Vadim entered the time line of 1990, we think we can guarantee that you'll arrive *after* he did."

"Which means that it hopefully will be long enough following his arrival to avoid the risk that Vadim will be ambushing me and not too long afterward so his trail will have gone completely cold," Quinn put in.

"That's right," the chief mission-support engineer said, adding, "there are two main points you should know about. One concerns the phenomenon known as 'Velikovsky's Paradox' I mentioned before—electronic equipment can malfunction when causality is violated.

"Temporal translation shock syndrome, or TTSS, is the second, and it may be of even more critical importance. In a nutshell, a subject translated through a CTL can begin to deteriorate mentally and physically. There is no way to predict who will suffer from TTSS."

"You mean that Vadim might be cracking up back there in 1990," Quinn conjectured.

"That's right," replied the tech. "It also means that you might do the same. If that's the case, I'm afraid there's nothing anybody can do to prevent it."

QUINN CROUCHED within the time-travel device. The hunched posture was necessary because of the data brought back by the time probe.

The cavern's roof was low, and clearance with its walls was minimal. Should Quinn arrive at his destination in an upright position, then his upper torso would materialize inside solid rock, killing him instantly.

He looked out through the walls of the transparent globe at the activity in the command center. All external sounds were muffled by the thick spherical walls that seemed to separate Quinn from another reality.

"Systems initialized," reported the engineer via an intercom link. "Temporal translation in five seconds. Good luck."

At the zero mark, Quinn's perspective underwent a radical phase shift. The transparent walls of the sphere turned a seamless black, shutting out all external sights and sounds as a maelstrom of color began to surround the time traveler.

In the space of a heartbeat the Gamma Base mission-control center had disappeared, and Quinn felt the hard rock floor of the cavern beneath his bent knee. There was the coolness of the rock beneath his palms. The silence was so total it made his ears ring.

The Gamma Base techs had been right about the clearance, Quinn saw right away. He barely had enough room to walk on a crouch toward the cave entrance a few dozen yards up ahead. Apparently Vadim, through luck or foreknowledge, had avoided the hazards posed by the clearance factor on his own translation.

Drawing the P-90 bullpup from the quick-release rig on his thigh, Quinn proceeded cautiously toward the cavern's mouth. There was no way to be certain that he had actually traveled back to the time the techs had tried to put him in.

There was no guarantee either that Vadim was not waiting around a blind bend in the tunnel formed by the cavern walls, armed and ready to blow Quinn away.

As it turned out, though, the cave was deserted. Quinn saw no signs indicating Vadim's presence anywhere in the vicinity. Taking his BioTrak scanner from his carryall, he activated the unit but wasn't able to pick up a position icon on Vadim's skull implant. Replacing the tracer in his carrying bag, Quinn walked out into pitch darkness.

Beyond the cave, darkness primeval had fallen across the desert landscape. Quinn had just traveled back four and a half decades in time, but had he not known that there was a highway less than a mile from the cave, he might as easily have thought he had traveled back forty million years.

Shouldering his carryall, Quinn checked his wrist chronometer. By its glowing dial he saw that it was a little past two o'clock in the morning as he began walking toward the highway across the cool desert sands.

22

The occupant of room 502 checked out of the Endicott Inn outside of Tucson, Arizona, and climbed into the driver's seat of the rented Prisma sedan.

The powerful V-8 engine under the muscle car's hood roared immediately to life. The driver steered the vehicle out onto the highway, reaching forward to switch on the FM stereo radio.

Less than three days had passed since he had walked out of the cave in the Nevada desert after translating into a CTL terminating in 1990, and Lux Vadim had already immersed himself in his new time.

The basics came first—that was a rule Vadim lived by. In order to establish a new identity, he had attended to the basics and had done so thoroughly.

In his wallet was a set of credit cards. These identified Vadim as one Abbott Motherwell, a traveling salesman from Encino, California.

He also carried a recently issued passport for his new persona that was every bit as legitimate as the other assorted pieces of identification, including his valid Los Angeles driver's license and social security card.

The small, high-capacity Glock 20 with autotargeting laser he'd taken downtime with him in a shoulder holster was also concealed by his windbreaker. Hidden in his attaché case was the H&K 4.73 mm fléchette-firing autoweapon, plus several hundred rounds of ammo for both futuristic weapons.

The weapons stood ready just in case any unforeseen contingencies popped up, contingencies that might call for drastic action. Among these contingencies was the possibility that his sabotage of the CTL generator system had not been as crippling to a pursuit mission as Vadim had intended it to be. Therefore it was conceivable that WorldPol might send an agent back after him from Gamma Base, or even from some other secret time-travel research-and-development installation that he didn't even know about, for that matter. The spooks were a devious bunch, and anything was possible when dealing with them.

Vadim steered with one hand and continued to play around with the dials and buttons of the dashboard FM radio. He found a popular rock song, and began thumping his foot in tempo to the driving beat.

QUINN HAD REACHED the highway after slogging through the sand in the early-morning gloaming. The four lane highway was precisely where it was marked on the road atlas of the southwest United States provided by the CIA.

A distant dot on the flat horizon grew into a shimmering white splotch created by headlight beams and thermal distortion and finally resolved itself into the cab of an eighteen-wheel truck.

Sticking out his thumb in the timeless gesture of a hitchhiker looking for a lift, Quinn caught a ride with the trucker, a produce hauler from Oregon bound for Phoenix, Arizona.

Thanking the driver, who had regaled him with tales of Vietnam—what his era knew as "the forgotten war"—Quinn got off at the nearest town, Four Corners.

It was still early morning, and though the sun would soon rise and vehicles had already taken to the highways, a sense of quiet reigned over the land. Beyond the town the sawtooth ridge line of distant mountains was etched against an indigo sky.

A warm, bone-dry wind blew strongly along the main street of the small Nevada town, but Quinn knew that within a few hours it would become as hot as the air from an industrial oven.

Ducking into an alley, Quinn unshipped the BioTrak scanner from the queer-looking pouch that hung from his belt. Quinn hadn't seen a fanny pack since attending family gatherings at his grandmother's house when he was a kid. He had to admit that they could come in handy, though.

The tracer still didn't show any indication of Vadim's presence, though its range encompassed several miles in all directions. But then again, Quinn hadn't expected an easy go of it.

Two possibilities existed to explain the absence of any location readings on Vadim. The first was that the transponder implant had ceased to function due to Velikovsky's Paradox that the chief mission-support engineer at Gamma had mentioned to Quinn. A less exotic explanation was simply that Vadim was out of range, which was to be expected if he was moving away fast from his point of temporal translation.

Vadim was smart enough to suspect that he might be followed down the time stream. He would have had to have been a fool to have remained in Four Corners—if he'd come here at all—any longer than necessary to establish a new identity and prepare himself for the next leg of his trip. In Quinn's experience, whatever else Vadim might be, he was certainly no fool.

Putting the tracker back in the fanny pack, Quinn slung the black leather carryall over his shoulder and left the alley for the main street.

There on the sidewalk he stopped, wondering where to go next, when his eye caught the flashing neon sign of a car-rental agency located diagonally across the main street.

Just then a pair of headlights suddenly came into view at the far end of the street. Quinn stepped quickly back into the shadows of the alley as the police cruiser glided past and disappeared down the road.

The street was deserted again as he stepped back out and walked down to the car-rental agency, seeing the first glow of dawn paint the sky in lavender streaks on the eastern horizon.

As he neared the parking lot of the rental business, a dog barked from behind a chain-link fence that wound around the parking lot.

Quinn carefully studied the area, convincing himself that there were no perimeter alarms present before consulting his watch. It was a little before four o'clock in the morning. He had plenty of time to do what was necessary.

Passing the car-rental agency, Quinn headed down the street toward a strip mall with two of its stores still open. One of them was an all-night newsstand. The other was a combination burger joint and taco stand.

Quinn went into the newsstand first and scanned one of the newspapers. The date above the headline was December 14th, 1990.

The techs at Gamma Base had translated him back down the timeline with surgical precision. As indicated by the headlines dealing with the buildup of U.S. Forces in Saudi Arabia, he had arrived a few weeks before the beginning of the Desert Storm campaign.

"I can't sleep," Quinn told the guy behind the counter. "Maybe you've got something I can take."

The guy scratched his head and reached behind him to a line of over-the-counter drugs on a row of shelves. From one of the shelves he brought down a small plastic bottle containing some Ee-Zee Do-Zee nonprescription sleeping pills.

"These here work pretty good," he said. "I use 'em myself, chief."

Quinn paid for the sleeping pills, pocketed the small cardboard box and walked down the narrow pavement of the strip mall toward the burger joint. There he ordered one of their deluxe quarter-pound-patty hamburgers from a sleepy looking counterman.

As he paid for the burger, he noticed that the police cruiser he had been surprised by earlier had just passed by the strip mall. He made a mental note to keep an eye out for the local constabulary as the car passed out of sight once again.

In an alley behind a pile of empty cartons left out for trash pickup, Quinn dumped all the contents of the capsules of the over-the-counter sleeping medication and sprinkled them over the hamburger patty.

Reclosing the container, he walked back toward the car rental agency.

The dog inside the fenced-off lot started barking again as the intruder came near. Quinn looked around, established that he wasn't being watched and waved the hamburger under the dog's nose. The barking turned into a few halfhearted whelps before it ceased completely. The tantalizing aroma of food had overcome the animal's natural wariness.

Quinn tossed the hamburger over the fence and watched the dog forget all about him and go for the tempting meat. As he climbed the fence, the dog momentarily looked up from its meal, as though it were trying to decide whether the intruder was more important than the free breakfast.

The decision went to the hamburger and Quinn was not troubled by the dog who seconds later, began to wobble on its legs as the Ee-Zee Do-Zee powder that Quinn had spiked the patties with began to take effect.

Once he was inside the yard, he negotiated the parking lot quickly, past an assortment of sedans, station wagons and four-by-four vehicles, heading for the office premises. The office, housed in a converted trailer raised off the dirt lot on cinder blocks, was wired to an alarm system. Quinn quickly saw that he could circumvent the alarm with a phreaker, of which he had brought several varieties with him downtime from Gamma.

He unshipped the advanced, special-purpose electronic device and flipped it on. The phreaker's LCD readout indicated that the alarm system was neutralized a few moments later. He left the phreaker in place and continued on his run.

Once inside the office, Quinn succeeded in booting up the agency's computer system and slaving it to a palmtop master unit he removed from his black leather bag. He accomplished this by mating the Kosmos palmtop to the server unit via an interface attached to the serial port at the rear of the computer housing.

With the computer system phreaked, Quinn had no problem logging on to the company's data base. The data base of the agency branch in Four Corners was linked to the national data base via a submenu option, and although it required another password and access privileges, Quinn easily entered it via the palmtop master unit.

Calling up the records of automobile rentals that had been made during the past couple of days, Quinn was on the alert for any patrons who had paid cash exclusively.

As it turned out, there was only one such patron matching these parameters—a Mr. Abbott Motherwell of Encino, California. According to the computer, he had rented a Prisma luxury sedan the previous day and had paid for the rental with cash.

Quinn used the office phone to dial the number that Motherwell had given as his home phone number and received a message stating that it was no longer in service.

Another call placed to a telephone company information operator showed no listing for Motherwell, either. It was a good bet that "Motherwell" was in fact Lux Vadim. The destination listed for the car was given as one of the Arrow rental offices in New York City. The address of the office put its position on the west side of Midtown Manhattan.

Using the palmtop unit to power down the host computer while covering his electronic tracks so that no record of his unauthorized break-in remained, Quinn shut off the computer and put the palmtop master unit back in his carryall.

Just as he was about to leave, he spotted the weaving flicker of a flashlight beam and heard the crunch of footsteps outside on the gravel-topped surface of the parking lot.

Looking out the window, Quinn saw a uniformed police officer shining his flashlight down on the drugged guard dog. Another cop was already radioing in a report via a hand-held communications device. Quinn realized that he was caught in a zero-sum response loop unless he took the initiative and took it quickly.

Keys to the various rental vehicles were hanging on a board on the wall with rows of numbered pegs. He found the set whose tag identified it as belonging to one of the four-bys he'd seen parked in the lot on his way in.

There was a rear door leading from the office that would enable him to exit unseen by the police. Pocketing the keys, Quinn quietly opened the door and then closed it behind him. Exiting the office building, he crept through the shadows and retrieved the phreaker that had neutralized the office alarm system.

The sound of the four-by's engine being gunned alerted the cops near the fence. But by that time Quinn was burning rubber toward the padlocked gate, which buckled and tore loose as the heavy vehicle collided with it at high speed. The four-by's powerful engine sent the truck bumping over the pavement and out onto the street on oversize steel-belted radials.

Quinn already had the P-90 CAW propped against the window frame of the speeding four-wheel-drive vehicle. With the CAW set on full-auto burstfire mode, Quinn stopped the vehicle and hosed down the blue-and-white police car.

The police cruiser's tires popped with four loud, near-simultaneous bangs as the car sank down to sit on its naked wheel rims. Quinn screamed the four-by away from the police car as the deputies got off some shots from the Glock 9 mm semiautos they packed, but none of the rounds came close to striking the highballing truck.

As he roared down the main street toward the highway, Quinn heard the sounds of sirens on his tail as more patrol vehicles joined in the chase.

23

Halogen high beams knifed through the night as two police cars careered around a corner. They were coming straight at Quinn, and they were loaded for bear.

Instead of slackening his pace, Quinn floorboarded the gas pedal, pushing the four hundred and ninety horses under the vehicle's hood to their tolerance limit.

The four-by shot up the highway at speeds better than one hundred miles per hour until the velocity needle was red-zoned.

The two police cruisers separated slightly, not wanting to risk a head-on collision with the speedballing truck. But they were too slow to get out of the heavy vehicle's way.

The oncoming four-by made its own room as it bore down on the cruisers now breaking left and right. Metal shrieked, sparks flew and headlights blew out with loud pops as the truck's front end plowed right through the two vehicles.

The two police cars were bulldozed aside, the impact of the collision ripping off the front fenders of both vehicles and sending them skidding across the blacktop.

With a screech of tire rubber spun without mercy against asphalt until it burned and smoked, Quinn felt the four-by pull free of the embrace of twisted, ruptured metal and shoot up the highway. Mobile once again, the truck raced up the main street of the desert town, straddling the broken white line with two wheels in each lane.

The two deputies were unable to get their badly damaged cruisers started again. Grating and wheezing noises from under the crumpled hoods told them not to even bother trying to play amateur mechanic.

"That sumbitch got past us," the wheelman of one car told the base station as he repeatedly tried to get the engine to turn over.

"Ten-four," the base station replied. "We're setting up a roadblock up ahead. Got a chopper warming up for takeoff in case it's needed. Don't worry, the guy's toast."

Not far ahead, and directly in his path, Quinn could see a bus painted in police colors rolling into position at the head of the street. Two patrol cars pulled up to flank the large, heavy vehicle.

The SWAT guys took up positions on either side of the bus, their hats on backward, their flak vests strapped down and their weapons armed and ready. They were ready for business.

The M-16 automatic carbine rifles they ported might be outdated in Quinn's time, but the SS109 tumbling rounds the short-barreled weapons could fire in full-auto burst mode would kill you just as dead as a laser-guided caseless 4.73 mm fléchette round.

Not wanting to risk taking on the roadblock head-on and get a face full of hot lead, Quinn viciously wrenched the four-by's steering wheel. His knuckles whitened and sweat poured across his strained features as Quinn hung a tight, screaming, skidding left turn around the corner of the intersection at the next traffic light.

There were more police cruisers already in position there, he saw through slitted eyes as he came out of the wrenching turn. Deputies packing pump-action shotguns were already crouched behind the doors of the parked vehicles, their gun muzzles pointed his way.

Using the brake pedal and handbrake to pull a fast bootlegger turn, Quinn did a one-hundred-eighty-degree turn in just under two seconds flat. Acrid black smoke billowed from the four-by's burning tire treads, encircling the hard-spinning vehicle as the truck swung all the way around to point in the opposite direction it had been going.

As the four wheels of the rugged vehicle found purchase on the tarmac and the four-by shot back up the avenue toward the town center, Quinn heard the rear window implode and disintegrate as it was struck by part of a fan of 30.06-gauge shotgun pellets.

He heard the staccato, cracking reports of more small arms shooting as M-16 fire opened up, but took no other hits as far as he could tell as he poured on more steam and highballed the rig down the avenue.

This, at least, looked like one escape corridor that the sheriff's men had neglected to cover. A few hundred feet up ahead, Quinn could discern that the street passed directly under an old black trestle bridge and continued on a straightaway that ran at right angles to a railroad crossing a short distance beyond the bridge. Beyond the crossing, the street fishhooked into a turnoff onto the highway.

Reflexively Quinn reached out toward the dashboard to punch up a GPS map display so he could get some idea of where the highway network would take him once he was on it. In that instant he realized that it would be at least thirty years before such options were standard in American automobiles.

Even the rearview mirror was still actually a glass ''mirror'' instead of a zoom-capable digital display. And in that primitive analog rearview mirror, Quinn now saw headlight beams lancing and juddering toward him as more of the sheriff's deputies gave chase in the police cruisers that had been taken off the roadblocks and tasked with pursuit and interception.

For the next mile or so, until it passed the railroad crossing, the road ran ruler straight, with no intersections in sight. At the sides of the road were brick warehouse structures, the narrow lanes between them potential dead ends.

Suddenly the stop signals flanking the railroad crossing began to flash red and orange, and the warning sounds of an alarm bell filled the air. The yellow-and-black-striped wooden barrier was already being lowered to bar access to the railroad crossing as a freight train came barreling down the tracks.

The glaring headlight beams of the pursuing police cruisers were growing brighter in the four-by's rearview. The chase cars were closing in, eating up the road as the cops poured on the speed.

The constant clanging of the warning bell at the railroad crossing up ahead grew louder as Quinn came nearer. Added to the din was the mournful, eerie whistle of the diesel locomotive piercing the night from less than a mile away.

Risking everything on a single throw of the dice, Quinn double clutched the gear shift and floored the gas pedal for a final burst of speed. Tension twisted his features into a snarl of defiance, and rivers of sweat pasted his hair flat against his forehead.

The four-by growled as he goosed the accelerator, arrowing the big truck forward toward the railroad crossing at a speed in excess of the one hundred twenty miles per hour that its speedomoter stopped at.

An instant seemed to compress itself into the space of a lifetime for Quinn as the front end of the truck crashed through the striped barricade only a few feet from the bullet-shaped nose of the oncoming train. He saw the striped wooden barrier splinter in half and go flying to either side of the four-by and was aware of the black nose of the speeding diesel locomotive hurtling toward him, a huge black shape screaming out of the night like an onrushing specter of doom, its brakes screeching, its whistle howling, the cyclops beam of its headlight blinding his sweat-stung eyes.

The ominous shape grew larger and nearer until it filled the world, and the banshee scream of the air brakes merged with the scream of the truck's over-driven V-8 engine. Gritting his teeth, Quinn clutched the truck's steering wheel until his knuckles whit-ened, his booted foot stomping down on the accel-erator pedal.

The four-by passed broadside of the oncoming train, mere inches from the point of a shattering collision. The black death shape hurtling out of the night was now behind the four-by, and the truck's rear tires were bumping across the outer rails of the tracks to find purchase again on the blacktop surface of the road.

On the other side of the railroad crossing, the column of patrol cars came screeching to a sudden halt. Due to the velocity of the high-speed chase, the cars could not stop in time. As tightening brake shoes bit into spinning axles, the cruisers went crashing into one another, creating a multiple-car pileup on the road.

Car doors slammed as deputies climbed out of the immobilized vehicles, cursing their bad luck.

The train was thundering across the tracks now, but it would be a long time before the many boxcars cleared the crossing completely. Until that time, the surviving chase cars were stopped dead.

MISSION LOG THREE:

Terminal Velocity

24

Ah, global warming, Lux Vadim thought to himself as he strolled along the street identified on maps as Avenue of the Americas but which all New Yorkers simply called Sixth Avenue.

The ozone layer had not yet deteriorated to the point where the inhabitants of the five boroughs could grow cactus in mid-December.

The last time he had visited New York—in the year 2030—he recalled that window boxes with cactus were all the rage, their gaudy flowers rioting in the blazing winter sun.

But the weather was still unseasonably warm for December, and the visitor from the future walked the crowded streets of Midtown Manhattan comfortable in the windbreaker and turtleneck shirt that he had bought at a Fifth Avenue haberdashery located in the lobby of the Park Central Hotel, where he was staying.

Vadim felt a strange tingling as he turned the corner at Radio City Music Hall and followed Forty-seventh Street eastward toward Rockefeller Center.

Decades from now, his internationally famous face—familiar to any viewer of the electronic media of the day—would have turned heads had he appeared in public. But he was now downtime a few years before his birth in Iowa City, Iowa, and he was a completely anonymous face in the lunch-hour crowd of Midtown.

With this anonymity came a strange sense of hidden power. He knew things about the world and what surprises lay in store for it that those people he passed on his way had no inkling of.

Many of them would die for lack of an over-the-counter cancer medication that was available uptime for only a few dollars.

Other passersby would complacently go about their business, never dreaming as they planned for a better future that the worst recession since the end of World War Two was looming just around the corner, one that would snatch their livelihoods away from them almost overnight.

As the euphoria brought on by the Gulf War's easy victories faded from memory, economic miseries would put many of the trendy shops that Vadim was now strolling past out of business forever.

One of the other things he knew about was what lay just a few weeks away from his "now." As the headlines of newspapers proclaimed from the streetside stands he passed, the buildup of troops and war matériel in Riyadh, Saudi Arabia, code-named Operation Desert Shield, would soon turn into the twin blitzkriegs called Desert Wind and Desert Storm.

Before long these busy people swarming around him would be riveted to television screens. The obsession with the day-to-day progress of the war in the gulf would be unlike anything seen since the population had huddled around radios during the dark days of World War Two.

At first they would be terrified by the images of warplanes taking off from secret air bases to conduct precision bombing sorties over Iraq in the largest-scale American military invasion in over four decades.

Knowing all this in advance gave him a strange adrenaline high.

It was almost like having the gift of prophesy.

No, it was more that.

Prophets could only see their visions and utter their truths. Whether or not any attention was paid them had nothing whatever to do with the prophets themselves or the truths they uttered.

Unlike the Jeremiahs of the world, the Reverend Vadim had something better going for him than mere prophesy. He possessed the ability to change reality, to mold the stuff of causality to fit the visions of futurity that he saw cast on the present, to make the future into his own self-fulfilling prophesy.

The events in the Iraqi desert had not yet come about, despite the fact that his memory told him that they had already happened. No prophet could change the future, but he could do precisely that if he wished.

Lux Vadim could make Desert Storm turn out differently. Very differently. He could cause those coalition fighters to drop from the skies, render F117A Stealth planes visible to Iraqi radar.

He could retrofit the Iraqi Scud missile warheads with deadly biological payloads that would—just as Sadam had hoped would happen—draw Israel into the fight, which the conventional warheads had failed to accomplish.

And he could make certain that, instead of surrendering in droves, those Iraqi troops stood pat in their desert bunkers to make the allies pay with blood for every inch of desert they captured.

And he knew that if he could convince Saddam Hussein that he was who he claimed to be, then he could name his own price. He already knew what that price was: the Muan crystals of power, sitting in the desert, waiting to be brought once more into the light of day after their millennial sleep.

With the crystals of Mu in his possession, he could develop a time-travel capability in the twentieth century. He could mold reality like a sculptor molded a lump of soft, wet clay, twisting and shaping it to suit his whims and designs.

"My designs," Vadim heard his own voice say. Suddenly he realized that he had been speaking aloud. People nearby were staring at him as though he were a lunatic. What was happening to him? he wondered.

How much had he said? He caught sight of a beat cop standing nearby, who also was watching him, though not making any motion toward him. In another minute that might change. Vadim pushed past the pedestrians near him, his face burning, eager to get away from where he was.

He did not know that he was suffering from TTSS disorder and that temporal translation shock syndrome was making him deteriorate faster and faster each day he spent downtime. Lux Vadim did not realize that he was cracking up.

THE CAR WAS a Japanese import, so spanking new that the interior still smelled of vinyl upholstery. Quinn had paid cash for the vehicle in Dallas, Texas.

Purchasing the car in that manner might have raised an eyebrow or two at the car dealership. Unlike Vadim's rental strategy, though, curiosity went no further than that. And there was no documentation logged on a computer network, no identification that needed to be presented, and no clue as to Quinn's final destination.

Three days of hard driving after leaving Texas behind, Quinn had merged with the interstate highway to complete the final leg of his journey to New York, where he hoped to have a shot at apprehending Lux Vadim and taking him back to 2035 in order to pay for his crimes.

According to the schedule he'd been given at Gamma Base, the next CTL translation window, the first of several doorways to the future, would be opening up in Lower Manhattan near the Brooklyn Bridge in approximately ten hours.

Three CTL windows had been scheduled for opening in 1990; the first was the one from which Quinn emerged into the past. The second would be the New York window. The third window would open in Iraq, near the proposed burial site of the Muan crystals, in case Quinn had to go the distance with Vadim.

The possibility existed that Quinn had traveled half a continent in pursuit of a red herring. His only lead in chasing down Vadim to New York had been the destination on the rental car that he had copied from his hack of the Arrow Car Agency computer system back in Four Corners, Nevada.

Despite the possibility that he was chasing shadows, Quinn strongly believed that Lux Vadim was in fact heading for New York City.

In these culminating days of the Desert Shield buildup and the imminent launch of the Desert Wind coalition air strikes against Baghdad, the United Nations building on the East Side of Manhattan had become the focus of world attention as last-minute talks were held there. If Vadim wanted to contact Saddam Hussein, then Manhattan would be the perfect jumping-off point.

Here, as at no other time in history, high-echelon Iraqi government agents were collected in one compact area within the continental United States. The situation seemed made-to-order for Vadim to carry out his intended contact with Saddam.

But the proof of the pudding would be in the tasting. If Quinn could establish that the car rented by "Abbott Motherwell" had been returned to the Arrow agency parking lot in New York City, then he had strong reason to believe that Vadim was nearby. And he was willing to bet that he would have his confirmation.

IT WAS more than an hour later when Quinn pulled the Toyota sports car into the underground parking garage of the Remington House Hotel in Midtown Manhattan.

He gave the attendant his car keys and received a claim check ticket in exchange, then followed the directional signs toward the elevator. The elevator car took him up to the lobby level of the hotel, where Quinn next walked directly over to the front desk.

Due to the early-morning hour, the lobby was virtually deserted. An attractive black girl was seated behind the desk, wearing a pert-looking uniform. Quinn asked for a room and requested that some hot coffee and a sandwich be sent up.

The room was spacious and afforded a panoramic view of northern Manhattan. The skyscrapers marching toward Central Park were lit up in a spectacular grid of a million windows against the black rectangles thrust high into the night, and the headlight beams of cars passing over the bridges that spanned the Hudson and East rivers created a psychedelic light show.

A waiter soon appeared with the food and coffee he'd ordered from the hotel's kitchen. Quinn tipped the man and filled the hole in his stomach before doing anything else. As he finished his sandwich, he linked the Kosmos palmtop computer to the phone line and began to hack into the Arrow Car Rental Agency's computer system.

More powerful than a supercomputer of the 1990s, the Kosmos palmtop soon defeated the safeguards of the UNIX-based operating system that the Arrow agency's data base records were stored on. Once inside the system, Quinn began giving himself top-priority data-access privileges—it was almost child's play hacking these antique computer systems.

The data base at the New York end of the Arrow operation was far more extensive than at Four Corners. There were numerous entries. The Kosmos was able to filter these in only a few seconds, after which the small screen showed Quinn that a vehicle rented in Four Corners had been returned to the Manhattan branch on the previous evening.

Quinn logged the entry to the ten gigabyte memory of the Kosmos palmtop, shut down the system and disconnected the computer from the modular phone jack.

It looked as if the trail was warming up. Vadim might be somewhere in New York City. Quinn had a few more hours to find him before the time translation window opened up and only seconds to get him inside before it closed again and popped out of existence forever.

25

"My name is Abbott Motherwell," said the man on the phone. "I would like to speak with Ambassador Rafiq Mafkouz."

"The ambassador cannot take any calls," the woman with the exotically accented voice replied. "I will connect you with someone else who can help you."

The next voice that came on the line was a deep baritone. Its clipped diction and controlled modulation announced to Vadim that he was dealing with Iraqi Intelligence.

"This is Nazir Yamani speaking, special assistant to the ambassador," the male voice announced. "How may I help you, sir?"

"By permitting me to help you," replied the caller.

"Oh?" asked Yamani, a short, muscular man whose sharp, cold eyes betrayed a professional distrust of everything and everyone, suspecting another of the many cranks the embassy had received in recent weeks was on the line. "And what would be the nature of this help to which you refer?"

"That is something I am afraid I can only discuss with the ambassador, and in private, I might add," Vadim replied.

There was a brief pause during which no response was made to his last statement. Vadim figured that the Iraqi intelligence officer was gesturing for somebody else in the room to listen in, had himself switched on recording instruments, or was doing both.

"Mr. Motherwell, you will appreciate that the ambassador cannot see anybody at this time. The people of Iraq stand on the brink of war with the United States and several other countries. What you ask is impossible."

"Write this down," Vadim said, although he knew that there would be no need since the entire conversation was being taped by the Iraqis as a matter of routine. "Umar-19 is a weapons-development facility and test bed located in the mountainous region a few miles northeast of Qaiyara. As we speak, a project to develop a nuclear explosive device is stalled due to a lack of Kryton switches. These were delivered from a German manufacturer several weeks ago, but most of the switches turned out to be defective."

Now there was dead silence over the line. Vadim knew that he had finally begun to hook his fish.

"Make a note of this, too..." Vadim continued to describe, in graphic detail, situations and events that were at present among the most closely guarded military secrets of the Iraqi government. These were secrets that would not be fully revealed to the world at large until after the conclusion of the war in the gulf.

"Stop!" Yamani shouted, wiping cold sweat from his brow. Much of what he was hearing he had no direct means of verifying or disproving at the moment. However, the Intelligence colonel had personally heard certain rumors that far too closely matched what he was being told now to be attributable to mere coincidence.

At first Colonel Yamani had been inclined to dismiss this American caller as a crank. In recent days and weeks the embassy had been besieged by many lunatics, some hostile, others claiming to be helpful, even some callers bearing messianic messages or purporting to be inspired by the prophets.

But Yamani could tell right away that this man was of a different stripe then those mad ones.

An unmanning fear seized hold of the Intelligence colonel's heart, making him furrow his brow and nervously stroke his moustache as he realized that such words spoken on an open line, even by a person other than himself, could seal his own death warrant.

"What's the problem," asked Vadim, an edge of playfulness in his voice, "am I going too fast for you?" He was beginning to enjoy the feeling of control over his adversary. He knew fully well what the Iraqi was thinking. Indeed, his words had been calculated as a dominance strategy, intended to produce the maximum shock effect and quickly gain him the upper hand.

"Please say no more," Yamani replied, the tension evident in his strained voice. "This is an open phone line. I can make no promises except that someone will call you back shortly, Mr. Motherwell."

"That's what I thought," Vadim told the Iraqi before hanging up the phone. "I'll be waiting."

THE IRAQI AMBASSADOR sat across from the American caller who had contacted him some hours before.

Vadim had been called back promptly by the stunned Iraqis, just as he had surmised would be the case.

The information he had given Yamani was not only accurate, but it also encompassed a collection of compartmented data that was known, in its entirety, by a mere handful of men at the apex of the Iraqi Intelligence pyramid.

The "dangle" was too good to pass up. The very audacity and improvisational feel to the Intelligence initiative seemed to be an indication that the contact was genuine. Under analysis, it simply did not appear to be the kind of dangle operation that the CIA or any other Intelligence service would mount.

Mindful of surveillance, the Iraqis had implemented an elaborate plan to move the defector—for that is the only term that they could use to define the American caller—to a safehouse in the outer borough of Queens.

An effective variation on a time-tested deception ploy was carried out. An Iraqi agent, dressed as Motherwell, was sent to exit the hotel and get into Motherwell's car. All the while the real caller was moved to a waiting van parked in the underground garage of the hotel and spirited away down a darkened street.

Blindfolded, Motherwell was then driven around in circles. "Driving a square," as the maneuver was known to Intelligence operatives, would both disorient their guest so that he could not recall details about the route taken to the safehouse. It would also permit the Moukhabarat personnel to detect and evade any pursuers that might be on their tails.

Since there did not seem to be any pursuers, the van broke away from its circular route through the streets of Forest Hills and proceeded directly to the safehouse in the wooded section only minutes from Midtown Manhattan yet resembling the suburbs in most respects.

The entire operation, carried out flawlessly by the Iraqis, took only two hours. The ambassador was already waiting for him when the contact arrived at the safehouse.

"You have made some highly provocative statements, Mr. Motherwell," the ambassador was saying to the American. "I would like you to tell me why you have made them."

"To get your attention, of course. And I see that I've gotten it."

The ambassador's face turned beet red. He was not a man used to being spoken to flippantly and was given to frequent rages when incensed.

He had picked up a pitcher of water from the negotiation table and thrown it into the face of the Kuwaiti ambassador sitting across from him just the previous day, when the man had the temerity to ask for his stinking little country back.

"Sir, I warn you that I am not here to play games," he told Motherwell. "You are now in no position to joke with me."

"Okay," Vadim told the ambassador. "You want to know all about me, I'll tell you about me. I came here from fifty years in the future in a time machine. There are technological matters and historical matters known to me that could result in Iraq winning the coming war instead of losing it. In return for my services, I want something from Iraq.''

"This is getting us nowhere," the ambassador shouted, rising to his feet and throwing open his arms in a dismissive gesture.

Picking up on the cue, the Iraqi hardmen looking on reached for their weapons, sensing that Mafkouz had reached critical mass. They anticipated the order to send a few silenced rounds into the head of a man who was obviously insane.

"You are in very deep trouble, my game-playing friend," Mafkouz growled, seconds away from giving the order to have the man killed where he sat. "You, as well as your CIA handlers, will learn that we have little sense of humor in these difficult times."

"Uh-uh," Vadim said with a smile, shaking his head. "*You're* going to learn something—that I'm here to cut a deal not screw around. Now you listen to me. You've taken my keys when you searched me. One of those keys unlocks a safe-deposit box back at the hotel. In that box you will find some items. Analyze them."

The ambassador's rage began to drain away a little. There was something in the confidence with which this man spoke that made the Iraqi feel that he was not as insane as he appeared on the surface.

Could it really be that there was a germ of truth in the wild story he was telling?

"Why?" Mafkouz asked simply. "What's to be gained from that?"

"Just do it, my friend," Motherwell told him. "Do it if you want to grasp the life raft I'm offering the pile of sand you call a country. Do you know what kind of massive assault you're about to get hit with? Of course you do. You have to know.

"Let me tell you, Mafkouz, it's going to be worse than anything your Intel people imagined. It's going to be pure hell. Hundreds of thousands of your troops will die in the desert like rats burned up in their holes. In the end you will see Kuwaiti war wagons chasing them across the desert. And for Saddam, it will be the beginning of the end. Unless, of course, you do what I tell you."

The Iraqi stared hard at this man and glanced at Colonel Yamani with equal intensity. A few moments ago Mafkouz had been prepared to have Yamani arrested as a spy and executed for treason along with the CIA dangle. But now he had begun to feel a strange fear that gnawed at his entrails. For this man was not a madman and he did not appear to be a fool, either. He was something else entirely, and that thing, Mafkouz was starting to realize, might just be a prophet of God.

"We will do as you ask," the ambassador said after another moment's deliberation. "But if you have wasted our time, I promise you that your death will be painfully slow."

Vadim smiled toothily. Despite the threat Mafkouz had just made, he knew that he had the Iraqis scared.

Vadim could feel their fear hanging in the close air of the room; he could smell it like a dog can smell it on the skin of a man. He began to feel high again, high on his ability to control the Iraqis with his knowledge.

The thought momentarily struck Vadim that this euphoria was out of place, that he was not acting like himself, that his speech and mannerisms had changed from his normally cautious deportment and demeanor.

Vadim realized he had undergone a personality change, but he was enjoying the high too much to care about it, and the realization that he was cracking up under TTSS disorder was the furthest thing from his mind.

"There's one more thing," he told Mafkouz. "Somebody else, also from the future, may be in this time, too. Be careful. Because he is one very dangerous man, and he will kick your asses before you even know what hit you."

26

Among the flash ID that the mission-support team had provided Quinn before his time translation from Gamma Base were CIA and FBI badges and cards, as well as police shields of major American cities, including New York.

For the past few hours Quinn had been canvassing the leading hotels in Midtown Manhattan with a photograph of Lux Vadim, a.k.a. Abbott Motherwell. It was deep December and the days were short. Darkness had fallen quickly.

Some time after nightfall, Quinn was still pounding the New York pavement, but had yet to get a break in his bid to track down his elusive quarry.

Beginning with the most expensive hotels on Park Avenue, Quinn worked his way down his list, while he headed downtown at the same time. He was acting on the assumption that Vadim would frequent only the best establishments.

Quinn had two or three more of the premier hotels on his list as he arrived at a hotel in the vicinity of the high forties. It was already past the dinner hour, and the rush-hour crowds had abated. Something resembling calm had drifted over the city as a light rain had begun to fall, although with Cristmas decorations everywhere, snow might have been more in character.

Just off Fifth Avenue, the hotel Quinn approached sported a liveried doorman and a red carpet outside, the added touches of elegance probably intended to make up for the seediness of the neighborhood, which included a drug rehabilitation center and rows of drab-looking office buildings.

Farther down the street was a cabstand where a group of cabbies stood around discussing the day's news and smoking cigarettes.

Like everywhere else in the borough of Manhattan, the block also had its fair share of homeless persons who lurked on the fringes. He saw a group of them scrounging through a Dumpster piled high with trash at the corner of the block in the shadows cast by a streetlight that had either died or been smashed into malfunctioning.

Other derelicts hovered at the edges of the red-carpeted entrance to the elegant midtown hotel, where Quinn could see a group of well-dressed Japanese businessmen being helped to a waiting taxicab by the liveried hotel doorman.

It was strange how life's throwaways could live in the midst of society and yet be treated as though they didn't exist. They were like ghosts inhabiting another plane of reality, the living dead drifting through their own universe, half in and half out of the world of the living.

As Quinn walked up the street toward the brightly lit hotel entrance, he eyed a car pulling up in front of the hotel. The vehicle braked to a stop just beyond the entranceway where a yellow strip and signs declaring No Standing were conspicuously posted.

What attracted Quinn's attention to the vehicle were the diplomatic plates it carried, identified by the letters *DPL* for the diplomatic corps.

He stopped and watched, unseen and apparently unnoticed by the occupants of the vehicle, two of whom climbed out of the car's back seat and walked briskly past the doorman, through the doors and straight into the hotel's lobby.

On the night wind, Quinn caught a snatch of conversation in a language that sounded Middle Eastern before the hardmen ascended the stairs and were out of earshot entirely.

Remaining behind the wheel of the stationary vehicle, the driver switched off the ignition. Quinn saw the taillights wink off, then a flicker of flame limn a cruel slash mouth and aquiline nose as the wheelman lit up a cigarette and sat smoking in the darkened vehicle's interior.

A gut check told Quinn that it was no mere coincidence that he and the stocky enforcer types who had gotten out of the car with the diplomatic tags had arrived at the Park Central hotel at approximately the same time.

But if in fact those men were Iraqi Moukhabarat operatives, what was the purpose of their visit? Were they coming to talk to Vadim? To snatch him? To terminate him? Or was there some other aim in their visit to the Park Central, one that had nothing to do with Nomad's mission downtime?

Regardless of the reasons, Quinn knew that he had to act quickly or lose what might be his only solid lead. For Vadim was surely close by, probably in the New York City environs if not in the hotel directly across the street—a smart move, as it would not be the first place that a pursuer familiar with his modus operandi would look for him. But he would not remain long; his final destination was Iraq itself.

There were two homeless men foraging in a pile of trash left in the Dumpster he'd spotted earlier. He noticed them stealing glances at him as they went about their scavenging activities. Now he saw that one of them was eyeing him directly, making no attempt to conceal the mixture of hostility and avarice that crossed his face.

The derelict spit on the ground. "What you lookin' at?" the guy growled at Quinn, meeting his glance and holding it menacingly.

Keeping the car parked outside the hotel in view, Quinn crossed over and got in the homeless man's face, noting the ugly purple lump that had deformed the lower lid of one of his eyes.

His partner had stopped what he was doing and was staring at Quinn, too. He also launched a gob of spit at the sidewalk.

Their combined rage was like a force field that he could feel radiating at him like heat from a furnace. Their anger was as palpable as the odors of their soiled clothing and unwashed bodies.

"I'm looking at two guys who stand to make ten thousand bucks apiece for about five minutes' work," Quinn replied calmly.

The look of rage immediately softened as the hooded eyes widened, and in its place there was the glimmer of astonishment which in a heartbeat changed to doubt. They had been screwed by everyone. Here was another guy trying to screw them. It had to be that way. No other explanation was possible.

"Yeah, sure," the first homeless man said. "Show us your money, man."

Quinn did. "Now that I've got your attention, I'm gonna tell you what I need," Quinn declared. "You tell me if you can do it. Then you get the money—it's as simple as that.''

"What do you need?" the other homeless man asked.

"There's a car across the street," Quinn told them. "Don't look at it. I want you to get the attention of the dude behind the wheel. I want you to hold his attention until you see me nod. That should take three to five minutes. Can you do it?''

The answer was yes. Quinn paid each of the homeless men ten one-thousand dollar bills, and shortly thereafter they crossed the street obliquely toward the car.

Keeping the hotel entrance in constant focus, and reasonably sure that the wheelman had not noticed him, Quinn also crossed the street on the diagonal, but away from the two men he'd recruited.

Moments later the derelicts had crossed directly in front of the vehicle with the diplomatic plates. They right away began to launch into a convincing shoving match that ended with one of them going sprawling directly across the hood of the target vehicle.

The homeless man who had taken the tumble jumped to his feet and took a wild overhand swing at his partner, continuing the fight directly in front of the car.

Quinn had taken a miniaturized tracking device from his pocket as they had crossed the street. He was ready to deploy the tracker the moment the altercation broke out.

Quinn saw that the driver had stuck his head out the window to shout at the two men flailing at each other on his hood, his attention completely focused on them. In a matter of seconds, Quinn had attached the magnetized tracker to the interior of the rear wheel housing.

Catching the eyes of one of the combatants, Quinn nodded slightly. His two recruits immediately stopped their diversion and in a matter of seconds had melted away into the shadows.

Out the corner of his eye, Quinn saw the driver get out of the parked car and look around suspiciously. The Iraqi was not only staring at the backs of the two homeless men as they ran down the rain-slicked street but looked all around him, as well.

These actions told Quinn that he was more than just a civilian; he had suspected a diversion after the initial shock had worn off and was checking the surrounding area for signs of surveillance.

Taking care not to make eye contact with the glowering driver, Quinn headed up the red-carpeted stairs toward the lobby entranceway of the Park Central.

As he reached the double glass doors, he could see the two men who'd left the car nod to the desk clerk and turn back toward the hotel entrance. Again avoiding direct eye contact, Quinn kept moving toward the front desk.

Examining some travel brochures on a Lucite stand, Quinn kept his eye on the lobby entrance, checking to make certain that the two hardguys had actually left the premises and also sweeping the lobby for indications that he was being surveilled by a third party.

Reasonably confident that the area was sterile, Quinn went up to the deskman. The ID he flashed was an NYPD detective badge with a perfectly forged photo-identification card in the lower half of the leather holder.

"What can I do for you, Lieutenant?" asked the desk clerk. He sensed trouble, and his face wore a forced smile. In his experience trouble and cops usually went together.

"Those two men who just left," Quinn said. "What was their business?"

"Well," the clerk replied, "they were removing something from the hotel's safe. We have safe-deposit strongboxes for use by guests."

"But they weren't guests," Quinn prodded the nervous deskman.

"No, they weren't. But they had a letter of authorization from one of our guests and the keys to the strongbox. So I had no reason to prevent them."

"No, of course not," Quinn said, taking something else from the pocket of his black leather jacket. It was a photograph of Lux Vadim. "Was this the guest whose property they had authorization to retrieve?"

"Yes," said the deskman, nodding. "That's him, all right. Mr. Abbott Motherwell, suite 745."

"Is Mr. Motherwell in right now?" Quinn asked. The desk clerk turned around and scanned the racks containing room keys behind him.

"No, he's not. His key is gone."

"Ring his room, please," Quinn asked.

After a few minutes with no response, Quinn debated having a look at the room. He weighed the possibility of what this strategy might yield against the potential of those Moukhabarat types leading him to where Vadim might be at a remote location.

The more he considered it, the more it was likely that Vadim was somewhere else, and that the men were now going to that very place.

"Don't discuss this visit with anybody," Quinn warned. "If Mr. Motherwell returns, say nothing. This is official business and it could involve criminal charges if it came out you didn't cooperate."

"My lips are sealed," the desk clerk told Quinn, who slipped him a fifty-dollar bill to ensure that they stayed that way. The desk clerk's experience with cops also told him to make sure he kept his promise.

"YOU WITH the FBI or the CIA?" asked the cabbie. Quinn had gotten into his hack a few minutes ago and said that he would pay extra to be taken exactly where he wanted.

The passenger grunted something unintelligible, and in the rearview, the cabbie saw him take up a device resembling a hand-held computer. Flipping up an antenna, the fare started punching up a storm on the keypad as the device emitted a series of beeps and trilling sounds.

With a mixture of satisfaction and relief, Quinn saw that the tracker was giving him a strong reading on the location of the car he was tracking. The icon representing the vehicle moved slowly along a grid of streets and avenues as it rolled across the Fifty-ninth Street Bridge into the borough of Queens.

The techs at Gamma Base had promised Quinn that the tracker would interface flawlessly with the array of Navstar satellites that had been installed in the latter years of the twentieth century to create the first operational global positioning system.

The GPS system would enable the tracker to interpret signals bounced off the satellites from the satcom-capable subminiature bug, giving the device in Quinn's hand tremendous range.

Keeping his eyes on the tracker's screen, Quinn asked the cabbie why he had asked him if he was either with the FBI or the CIA.

"Look, buddy," the cabbie went on conspiratorially. "I ain't stupid. I been hackin' a cab for like twenty years. Before that, I was into some heavy doings in Nam and I know a spook when I see one. This a bust or somethin'? You can level with me."

Quinn searched his memory for the criminal enterprises taking place in the early 1990s. He recalled that the Colombian cocaine cartel had been prominent in the headlines of the era. The Cali-based narcobarons had been engaging in a guerrilla-style war against their own government for some years.

Indeed, the cartel was still active uptime, even after merging with the Japanese Yakuza by 1999, although in Quinn's time biopharmaceutical and hardware drugs had replaced coke as the mind-altering substances of choice. The names, faces and places changed, but the human need to alter consciousness would never stop, Quinn reflected.

"Okay, I'm gonna level with you, chief," Quinn told the cabbie. "You're right on the money. I'm with the FBI. All I can tell you is that a major Colombian drug lord is about to go down for a hard fall."

"Christ, I fuckin' knew it!" the driver shouted, slamming his palm against the steering wheel as he turned onto the Fifty-ninth Street Bridge. "We're heading into Queens. Lot of Colombians down there."

"There you go, partner," Quinn said, hoping that his patter would keep the cab driver satisfied, but doubting it if New York cabbies of 1990 were anything like their loquacious counterparts of his own era.

Quinn again fixed his eyes on the tracker unit and continued to direct the cabbie according to the movements of the icon on the screen. Thanks to a gridlock condition at a traffic intersection in Forest Hills, they were able to make visual contact with the vehicle Quinn was pursuing.

Quinn put the tracker on standby mode and kept his eyes on the car. It was just a few hundred feet along, its taillights glowing red as it sped up the gleaming wet street.

27

The Iraqi ambassador examined the electronics items brought back by the search team he had dispatched to the Park Central. The team had just returned after conducting evasive maneuvers intended to dodge surveillance, reporting no apparent sign of pursuit or attempts at interdiction.

Mafkouz was astonished as he studied what he held in his hand. The items all appeared to be of radical design. Having been trained at a French technical university and knowing something of electronics himself, the ambassador was impressed, although he took care not to allow any hint of excitement on his face to betray his inmost thoughts.

He handed the devices over to the technician seated at the table. The man adjusted the lighted magnifier he wore clipped to his eyeglasses and began to disassemble the unit's case with a small, battery-powered screwdriver.

With the case open, he inspected the circuitry with logic probes, using a chip extractor to pull integrated-circuit chips so he could examine them close-up, immediately noting that the dates of manufacture stamped on the chips were decades from the present.

"Well, what is your impression?" asked Mafkouz after impatiently watching the tech conduct his inspection.

"This is extraordinary," he replied. "These components are at least twenty years ahead of anything available today. I've never seen anything like it!"

He held one of the chips up and pointed to the label adhering to its surface. The label bore a strange pattern of interlocking light and dark squares.

"Do you see this label?"

"Yes," the ambassador answered with annoyance. "Get to the point."

"This is a special two-dimensional bar code. I have only recently read an article in a technical journal concerning it. Ordinary bar codes are of a type called 'Code-39.' This is a new type containing many pages of data on the chip, which to my knowledge has not been used commercially. If I can decipher it, then we may know still more."

"What about the possibility of a secret governmental project?" asked Mafkouz.

"Impossible," the tech replied, shaking his head from side to side. "It will need verification, of course. Both in reading the bar code and in reverse engineering, which can only be carried out by a fully equipped laboratory. But my initial impression remains that this technology is like nothing currently produced anywhere on earth, either in secret or the open market.''

"Very well," Mafkouz assented, nodding to the technician by way of dismissal.

After the Moukhabarat agents saw the electronics specialist to the door, he turned to Vadim.

"It appears that these technical artifacts lend credence to your story," he admitted. "I will ask for further instructions and recommend that your proposition be aired at the highest levels.''

"In the meantime," Vadim pressed the Iraqi UN ambassador, "I'd like to get back to my hotel. I'm getting a little tired of sitting around cooling my heels.''

"In the meantime, sir," Mafkouz replied with an edge in his voice, "you will be the guest of the People's Republic of Iraq. For your own safety, you will remain here where we can protect you until further notice.''

Mafkouz made no response to the man's protests but spoke to his staff before leaving the room. The Iraqis had no intention of allowing their new ally to go elsewhere. If it turned out that he was what and who he claimed to be, then he was now an essential part of the Iraqi war effort, far too valuable to even be left alive after his usefulness had ended.

THE SAFEHOUSE was situated on a dead-end street in a wooded section of Queens, not very far from the Long Island border.

The location had been chosen with considerable care for the clandestine purposes to which the Iraqis had put the house. The access lane to the property could be kept under constant surveillance. Though the wood-lined street was dark, men wearing night-vision goggles could be stationed throughout the perimeter, hidden among the trees.

In the virtual screen of his VRGs, Quinn received power-on confirmation that all systems diagnostic checks had been carried out. His stealth suit and battle mask were now interfaced with the bullpup autoweapon he clutched in his gloved hands.

Quinn stole through the darkness, invisible Q-switched lasers scanning the operational perimeter. Within a matter of moments he came upon a covert watcher armed with an assault weapon. The man was patrolling the wooded stretch surrounding the safehouse.

Garbed in paramilitary camos in a forest green pattern that were made of chamois to cut down on rustle as he moved against tree branches and leaves, the watcher was wearing conventional NVGs and carried a sound-suppressed short-bareled M-16A2 weapon.

He moved with the caution of a professional soldier, but after a few minutes of real-time video surveillance, Quinn did not detect a high level of field craft. He had not expected to, since perimeter walkers were generally selected from a pool of throwaways and were valued one step above watchdogs.

Since Quinn enjoyed an overwhelming technological superiority over his opponent, whatever wood craft he possessed would not make a difference to the final outcome, but a guy who was on the ball might still cause some problems despite this uneven match situation. Above all, it was necessary that the sentry be taken down quickly and silently.

With the VRGs directing Quinn toward his quarry with a glowing red line superimposed over the real-time video display, he was able to duck-walk close to the watcher in the woods.

The sentry heard sounds of movement and was alerted to the presence of something coming in the darkness. Grasping his weapon at hip-fire position, he pivoted fast, jerking the gun around. He swept the area from where the sounds had come but saw nothing but shadow in the green view field of his NVGs. Quinn's stealth suit had broken up the thermal signature to blend perfectly into the background.

Putting the death dot on the target icon representing his quarry, Quinn squeezed the trigger of the P-90. The silenced weapon hardly moved in his black-gloved fist as a 3-round burst of sound-suppressed 5.70 mm steel chewed up the watcher's head at nearly point-blank range with hardly any recoil.

Quinn stalked on past the terminated sentry whose dark blood was seeping into the leaf-matted earth. He was tracking the house, his virtual screen crunching numbers to compute the optimum access points for penetration of the Iraqi stronghold.

In a pulse beat, two options were highlighted on the virtual screen. One route in was via the drainpipe, hand over hand and up to the topmost story of the house, at which a lone window was lighted against the night.

The other route to Nomad's target objective was through its rear entrance, a strike vector that would take Quinn across the ground-floor level of the house.

Several feet along, a message appeared on his virtual screen: "Warning—perimeter defense system encountered."

The VRG screen highlighted in red the area around the house that was ringed by an invisible cordon of perimeter sensors. These had been emplaced to detect the presence of intruders and trigger an alarm inside the structure.

"Intrusion-detector system is field-effect resistance type" the data block at the top of the virtual screen added.

Unshipping a phreaker from a gear pouch, Quinn activated the small black cylinder with a series of keypresses.

Instantly three black wire prongs popped out of one end while a small antenna rose from the other. Quinn pushed the phreaker down into the earth on the near side of the highlighted line signifying the field area.

"Perimeter defense neutralized," flashed the message on his virtual screen a few moments later, and the red highlighting changed to a blue to indicate its neutral status as the phreaker overrode the sensors and transmitted signals indicating that the invisible electromagnetic field remained unbroken.

Quinn stepped across the invisible sensor line without tripping any intruder alarms in the perimeter detection grid. He was positioned a few feet from the side of the house. Quinn stopped and panned up to the lighted window on the top floor. Punching a series of commands on his wrist-top keypad, he sent invisible laser beams lancing across the glass windowpane.

The laser beams were able to pick up the faint vibrations of sounds within the room against the glass.

The VRGs' audio processors could then magnify these vibrations many times, adjusting for clarity.

". . . You will be guest of the People's Republic of Iraq. For your own safety, you will remain here where we can protect you until further notice."

Next Quinn heard a string of strident protests. A new command set entered at the wrist-top keypad threw a voice-analysis graph on the screen.

"Match probability ninety-seven percent that speaker is target Reverend Lux Vadim," the screen reported.

The original speaker next began talking in a foreign language as he addressed others in the room, who answered him with a series of monosyllabic replies. Another coded command set put the VRGs' microprocessor into simultaneous translation mode.

"Language spoken identified as Iraqi dialect of Arabic."

Text is:
Speaker One: "Watch this man and make certain that he does not leave, Jameel."
Speaker Two: "Do not worry, Excellency. If this venomous serpent attempts to leave, we will snap him like a dry twig."
Speaker One: "Make certain that this is so. Your lives depend on it."
Speaker Two: "We will not fail you, Excellency."

With that, there was the sound of a door opening and closing. Quinn continued to monitor the room as the lights above the entrance came on and Mafkouz, accompanied by another man, got into a parked vehicle outside.

The headlight beams snapped on, and the car rolled down the gravel-topped dirt road toward the main route that ribboned past the woods in which the safehouse was located.

Quinn waited until the vehicle had left the premises, then proceeded to enter the house. Grasping the drainpipe, he hoisted himself up, using special grippers on his gloved hands and boot soles for support. A few minutes later the taxing climb brought him to a smaller side roof that ran below the lighted window.

To one side at shoulder level was a small porch or portico that was encircled by a wooden railing. Quinn swung one leg across the railing and was soon crouched on the porch facing a darkened window.

As his VRG screen redrew, it flashed him the glowing red 3-D wire diagram of a darkened corridor running the length of the upper story of the house.

The window was taped with conductive circuit traces and was wired to an alarm system that would be activated if the glass was broken and the traces cut. There would be a magnetically operated switch on the window, too, which would operate similarly if the window were forced open.

Unshipping a second flavor of phreaker, Quinn placed the black oblong against the windowsill, where it was held securely by spiked anchors ejected at high speed.

As he punched the phreaker's activation code in at the small keypad on the oblong, a text box popped onto his VRG screen informing him that the alarm system had been deactivated. Jimmying the window, he raised the sash and entered the corridor.

With the P-90 CAW gripped in his right fist, he crept along the darkened hallway on a stealthy half crouch toward the door set midway along its length and which was indicated by the flashing display on his VRG screen.

The door was located at the top of a flight of stairs that led down toward the ground level.

Quinn paused for a moment, scanning the downstairs level for passive sonar data on the threat environment. The scan revealed that there were three other men downstairs, all of them armed. He could deal with those odds.

Quinn stood outside the locked door and took a deep breath. He lifted his booted right foot and kicked hard, hearing the sound of splintering wood as the door flew open.

28

The three men inside the room were frozen in shock.

Two of them were the Iraqis that Nomad had seen getting out of the vehicle he'd bugged outside the Park Central. The third man was Vadim himself, and the petrified look on his face was that of a man who knew his time was up.

Although the Iraqis were stunned at the sight of the black-clad figure whose head was encased in the weird battle mask of advanced design, the Moukhabarat agents had been trained to react quickly under conditions of high stress.

The first gunman was in the act of dipping for the SIG-Sauer P-220 .45 ACP pistol holstered at his chest in a speed rig as Quinn put the flashing pipper on the glowing blue target-acquisition reticle that formed a box around the Iraqi's head.

The instant the pipper touched the edge of the target, the P-90 CAW wheezed as a brace of silenced 5.70 mm needle-nosed rounds augered through space. The burst struck the target within a micro-inch of the death dot's position.

The shot pattern was tight and lethal. Three bullets ripped away the target's left eye, taking most of the temple and upper jaw with it in a splatter of crimson gore.

As the Iraqi's face disintegrated into a bloody mist, momentum thrust him sideways. The body crashed through a window and disappeared amid a shower of breaking glass. It hit the sloping rooftop with a dull thud, rolled down and crashed to the ground twenty feet below.

Quinn saw Vadim dive behind the sofa as he acquired the second target that the VRG had ranked next to die. The other Iraqi gunman had been a half second slower in dipping for his hand cannon, so the VRGs' battle-management computer had assigned him the second kill priority.

But by now the Iraqi already pulled his 9 mm Colt semiautomatic pistol from the pit holster worn halter fashion across his chest. Holding it in a match grip, he whipped up the deadly little Colt, yelling for backup as he squeezed the trigger to the point of let back.

He was already history as Quinn cooked off another burst of 5.70 mm needlepoints from the P-90 bullpup. Computer targeted, the rounds blew off most of his hand and part of his wrist and sent the pistol cartwheeling through space.

As blood spurted out of the stump of the Iraqi's wrist where the hand had been torn clean off, Quinn put the pipper on the guy's heart and automatically triggered another burst of P-90 fire into his upper left chest zone.

The put-away burst struck its mark with high ballistic-energy transfer. With his punctured heart draining its life out inside his chest cavity, the triggerman became dead weight and crumpled against the couch behind him, ending up with his face in the cushions and his hindquarters jacked clownishly up in the air.

Vadim was wide-eyed with fear as Quinn grabbed him by the collar and hauled him to his feet. Vadim could not recognize the man behind the tactical mask of the VRGs, but he had no doubts as to where he had come from.

"You're from my time!" he stammered in panic. "They sent you to kill me!"

"They sent me, Vadim," Quinn snarled. "But if you die—which I sincerely hope you do—my job is to make sure a jury of twelve orders the sentence carried out. Now get going."

"I recognize your voice," Vadim cried out. "You're—"

"Shut up." Steel whipcord fingers closed around Vadim's hand as Quinn shoved him toward the open doorway, cutting him off. There was no time to waste. More shooters were now on their way.

The audio signatures of voices came from the ground level at the foot of the stairs, and threat icons representing three running figures moved through the graphical schematic of the house on the VRG screen.

With the P-90 bullpup in tracking mode, Quinn moved toward the stairway when suddenly a door at the end of the hall flew open. A dark-haired woman toting a SPAS 12 combat shotgun jumped out, the black stinger at belt level.

Quinn had acquired the new target but hesitated a split instant because the shooter was a woman.

She, on the other hand, had no such qualms.

The SPAS 12 clutched in her fists roared, belching scorching fire and lethal steel.

Quinn's armored stealth suit stopped most of the fan of deadly pellets as he shoved Vadim behind him. Targeting fast on the wild-card shooter before she could jack another shell into the pumpgun's chamber, Quinn put the death dot on the killbox and launched a put-away burst from the plastic doughnut in his fist.

She flung out her arms with a muffled groan as the quick burst plowed up her chest and exited her back, splattering the wall behind her. Her eyes clouded over, and she slid down the wall to wind up in a sitting position, blood pooling around her.

Then she went terminal.

With Vadim still in tow, Quinn turned his attention to the stairway where the heads of the first two Iraqi backups were coming into view.

The pipper changed color and flashed, indicating acquisition as it touched a portion of a human cheek framed in the cross hair sights on Quinn's virtual screen. But the target moved out of range a second later, jerking back his head.

"Acquisition lost," reported the VRG screen, "Retarget."

Quinn ducked back around the banister as a salvo of 9 mm SMG fire came angling up the stairwell, the rounds ricocheting off the corners of the wall and fragmenting as they rebounded back into space again.

Quinn momentarily reholstered the P-90 and whipped two neural disrupter grenades from munitions pouches. Arming the electronic flash-bangs and setting time-delay parameters by clicking "chords" on the buttons studded along their sides, he flung the black cylinders down the stairs. The bouncing, rolling grenades initialized moments later.

Disorientating high-frequency sound and flashing light pounded through the lower level. The potent combination hit the Iraqis on the floor below like a flurry of hammer blows. The SMG fire ceased abruptly as Quinn hustled down the stairs, pulling Vadim after him by the arm.

Immune to the effects of the submunition burst due to the protection offered by his VRGs, Quinn found the Iraqis staggering about in a dazed condition.

They saw him coming through a haze of cordite smoke and each tried to draw a bead, their limbs shaking and their vision blurring due to the neural assault. But the Iraqis were already lunch.

With the VRGs having prioritized the kills, Quinn swung the targeting pipper up to the first, second and third target, taking them all down with mechanical precision under hammering 5.70 mm automatic fire.

Retrieving the neural disrupter grenades, Quinn deactivated them and stowed the reusable rounds in his gear pouch. An added bonus of the disrupter effect was that Vadim himself was somewhat incapacitated.

This made him easier to manage as Quinn hustled him out the door of the safehouse and into a truck parked outside. But Quinn knew that with Vadim's minimal exposure the disorientating effect would soon pass.

Quinn sliced through the metal collar protecting the steering column with a laser cutting torch and hot-wired the ignition cables. He jump-started the engine and pulled away from the house, peeling rubber.

Quinn had removed his VRG helmet, and as the truck began steamrollering down the gravel-topped access road toward the highway, Vadim reacted with shock as he finally recognized who his captor was.

"Quinn!" he shouted. "I should have known it would be you."

"Shut up," Quinn warned as he pushed on the brakes to slow the truck as he approached the highway.

"Listen," Vadim urged his abductor, "why bother with me? Back here in this now, we can both get rich."

"I'm already rich," Quinn retorted, checking both sides of the highway.

"I mean *really* rich, Quinn," Vadim insisted. "The kind of wealth that only monarchs know about. The kind of wealth that goes hand in hand with absolute power. With what we know, we can rule this entire planet."

"I told you to shut up, Vadim," Quinn finally gritted through his teeth. "You're a psychopath. We're going back to where you came from."

He wrenched the steering wheel and bounced the four-by from the dirt road onto the highway, high-balling the vehicle in the direction of Manhattan.

Deciding to make a desperate break for freedom, Vadim wrenched open the passenger door and tried to bail out. As he saw the road streaking past below the open door, he hesitated long enough for Quinn to grab him with one hand.

While he grappled with the prisoner, Quinn almost lost control of the truck. The heavy vehicle swerved to one side, careering toward the ditch beyond the shoulder before Quinn managed to yank the struggling Vadim back inside.

Slamming hard on the brakes, Quinn managed to stop the truck in the middle of the road, regretting that he had not taken the necessary steps to subdue his captive right away as the truck skidded to a lurching, diagonal halt across the median line.

"No!" Vadim protested as Quinn produced a pneumatic injector the size of a thimble from his pocket.

The injector was filled with a powerful drug that would paralyze Vadim for the duration of the trip. Holding the squirming passenger as tightly as he could, Quinn pressed the snout of the injector against the side of his throat and dispensed the fast-acting drug.

Vadim went limp a second later and sagged against the car seat. Quinn reached over the prone man, pulled shut the passenger-side door and thumbed down the locking tab.

Taking his foot off the brake, he resumed his route down the highway. A check of his wrist chronometer told Quinn that there was now less than an hour remaining until the CTL window materialized.

He would have to make tracks if he were to reach it before his destination popped out of existence again.

IT WAS EARLY in the morning when Quinn reached the end of his run at the foot of the Brooklyn Bridge on the Manhattan side of the span.

Out in the harbor, the fog-shrouded silhouette of a moored freighter rose from the gunmetal-colored water like a ghost ship. Across the river on the Brooklyn waterfront were old warehouse buildings dating back to the Civil War.

The area appeared to be completely deserted. Quinn knew that this initial impression could be deceptive. There could be homeless people, drug addicts, cops or any number of other city denizens in the vicinity. Nevertheless, a continued VRG check of the area gave Quinn no indication that anyone else beside himself and Vadim was lurking nearby.

Vadim had begun to stir by now.

Quinn knew that he would soon begin to come out of his drug-induced stupor. That was all right, too. The reverend could soon be as frisky as he liked in the custody of WorldPol uptime in the year 2035.

Unshipping the Kosmos unit, Quinn punched up the button marked Aut-Or, which put the powerful computer into automatic orientation mode.

A graphical screen popped up on the flat display panel. The flashing icon revealed the exact spot where the CTL window would materialize. The digital clock at the upper right was counting down from 4:02 minutes.

Quinn needed to hustle.

He pulled the semiconscious Vadim from the passenger side of the parked truck. Locking Vadim's arm beneath his, he forced his groggy captive toward a spot within the shadows of the bridge underneath one of its stone-and-concrete supports.

As the countdown on the Kosmos computer reached the zero mark, the air became charged as though an electrical storm were coming. Winds began to churn up as the local disruption in the electromagnetic field caused by the tilting light cone created a vortex effect. Candy wrappers and sheets of newspaper were blown off the dusty pavement and began spinning crazily through the air.

Soon jagged blue bolts of static electricity crackled and writhed like snakes as the fabric of space and time began to warp back on itself, opening a tunnel forward into the future. The CTL window had materialized.

With a secure lock on Vadim's arm, Quinn dragged his quarry toward the rainbow-edged circle that hung like a hole ripped in space.

Just before Quinn shoved Vadim inside that force field, headlights appeared from down a narrow street running perpendicular to the bridge trestle, illuminating them in their blinding beams.

In a split instant, the cops, who had seen the strange lights from down the street, had come to investigate. Twisting free of Quinn's grasp, Vadim booked toward the police cruiser.

Reacting quickly, Quinn pulled the P-90 from its breakaway rig and stepped from the mouth of the CTL window. The glaring headlights were extinguished with the shattering of glass and the double pops made by air rushing twice into a vacuum. More fire from the bullpup totaled the cruiser and sent the cops ducking for cover behind a stone buttress.

Tracking for his quarry, Quinn saw to his chagrin that Vadim was gone, probably making his escape along one of the many narrow, cobbled streets that snaked past warehouses hunkering in the shadows of the bridge. Suddenly there was a crack, and a bullet ricocheted off concrete as the patrolmen opened fire.

Knowing he had to move fast but not wanting to cause injury, Quinn pitched a neural disrupter at the shooters and went off after his quarry as they sank down to the ground, writhing in pain as their nervous systems went haywire.

He was away from the strike zone in seconds after retrieving the grenade, following Vadim into the shadows. But the shadows had swallowed him up, and Quinn heard the shriek of sirens in the distance, getting closer by the second.

29

Saddam Hussein, the supreme ruler of the sixteen million people who made up the Republic of Iraq, a man who claimed direct descent from the legendary warrior-potentates of ancient Babylon, dismissed the whisperer with a curt wave of his hand.

Major General Izmir Zambrani, chief of the state security agency, the feared Iraqi Moukhabarat, had just informed Saddam of the final analysis of the artifacts that had recently arrived in Baghdad via diplomatic pouch.

The technical specialists employed by the Iraqi state security service were the best in the country. Having been educated at Western universities through a government-financed program and enjoying privileges that the average Iraqi would never know, they were loyal to the ruling regime.

The unanimous opinion of the technical focus group was that the electronic components were of radically advanced design specifications. It would not be possible to produce such components at the present time, simply because the precision laser tools and integrated-chip production techniques necessary had not yet been devised.

The focus group's report cited one instance in which a single microchip no larger than the circle made by looping the thumb and forefinger was found to have the capabilities of a Japanese supercomputer just purchased by Iraq.

Nobody, not even the Americans, could duplicate such an engineering miracle. Such a device could only come from the future. There was no other explanation possible.

Although the artifacts had been received weeks before, the report from the hastily assembled technical focus group had been delayed. None of its members had forgotten that safety, in Saddam's Iraq, lay not only in numbers but in making certain that the report would not be perceived as threatening.

The memory of what Saddam had done to Iraq's minister of health and member of his cabinet, Dr. Riyadh Ibrahim, was still fresh in the minds of all who served the Iraqi president. According to reliable accounts, Saddam had asked his advisers to speak frankly regarding their options in the face of occupation by the Iranian army during the Iran-Iraq war.

All around the council table had repledged their support to Saddam, giving him a unanimous show of faith. All except Ibrahim, who, at Saddam's urging to speak his mind without fear, expressed to the leader the candid opinion that he should at once step down in favor of a democratically elected president.

Saddam politely thanked his adviser and smiled at Ibrahim. Then, quickly drawing his pistol, he shot him between the eyes. The doctor's wife, inquiring after her husband soon after the incident, was told by Saddam that he would return her husband the following day.

Though Saddam was true to his word, the results were not to Mrs. Ibrahim's liking. Security agents placed a large black plastic bag containing the bloody, hacked-up pieces of her husband on her doorstep.

The technical focus group had arrived at their collective decision about the authenticity of the components almost immediately. What had taken the assemblage weeks of deliberation was the precise nature of how to frame their report so as to make certain that their necks were not forfeited in the process of giving it to their leader.

Saddam would read the complete report, which, said Zambrani, would be on his desk on his return to his office in the presidential palace in the heart of Baghdad.

For the present, Saddam was otherwise occupied.

Early that morning the president of Iraq had risen, washed and prostrated himself on the polished terracotta floor to say his daily morning prayers. He had then embarked on a tour of the countryside, visiting a town peopled by the peasant class, from whose ranks he had risen to control the entire country.

Saddam had just gotten out of one of the cream-colored Mercedes sedans that made up his entourage after climbing the steep, dusty road to his hometown of Tikrit. An Iraqi film crew was waiting to record the leader as he walked among the people.

The sunbaked town was located some one hundred miles northwest of Baghdad in a region straddling the Tigris River. Sporting his trademark black beret and attired in the olive drab uniform of the leader of the Iraqi armed forces, Saddam strode through the dusty streets of his birthplace.

Here, amid narrow cobbled alleys and mud-brick peasant houses, he had imbibed the bloody spirit of revolution under his uncle Khairallah's tutelage and dreamed his first dreams of one day ruling the nation then ruled by Abdul-Karim Qassim, the dictator who had successfully overthrown the centuries-old Iraqi monarchy.

As the cameras watched him, Saddam sat on a mat woven of reeds and smoked a hand-rolled cigarette of strong local tobacco with one of the villagers.

The old man spoke to him of earlier days, days when he had known him as a young ruffian, for even then the child whose name meant "he who confronts'' was a cause of trouble. But Saddam's mind was occupied elsewhere, and his thoughts had turned in another direction entirely.

Storm clouds were brewing over the ancient lands. The Western powers were assembling a massive army on the territory of the spineless Saudi dogs who had turned their backs on the pan-Islamic republic that Saddam sought to meld together from the disunified peoples of the region.

But listening to the old man with the wizened face, Saddam began to relax. Some ancient spirit from the parched clay soil reached up and entered him, suffusing him with a sense of all-embracing tranquillity.

There was power in this land, hidden power that had whispered seductively to Saddam when he had been very young of great works he could accomplish. Now the desert was speaking to him again. The ghosts of Babylonian warrior-kings called out to him from their eternal slumber beneath the baking earth.

These ghostly voices were telling Saddam that he could win if he believed. Not in Allah, but in the baneful might of his own strong right hand, just as his predecessors had done thousands of years before.

THE MAN whose identification papers had him down as Abbott Motherwell blinked in the dazzling sunlight of the Iraqi afternoon.

The plane trip across the Mediterranean and the tip of North Africa from Malta had been longer than he had expected a shuttle flight to be. The trip had been a culmination of a zigzag across the globe with Iraq as its ultimate destination.

Lux Vadim had no intention of being followed or intercepted, and the twists and turns had been designed to thwart pursuit.

Quinn was both deadly and inhumanly efficient, almost like a machine. The Iraqis had been fools and had not paid attention to the warning he had issued them at the safehouse in Queens.

Between the two forces whose conflicting interests pulled him in two completely opposite directions, Vadim could find himself torn apart if he wasn't extraordinarily careful.

His escape from Quinn in the final seconds before the closed timelike line window opened had been nothing short of a miracle. A few heartbeats longer, and Vadim had no doubt that he would right now or very soon be facing a jury of his peers in the year 2035. Nor did he doubt that they would convict him of mass murder, and the judge would order the death penalty without blinking an eye.

Like a cornered rat back in Manhattan, Vadim had cowered in an abandoned building, fearing the manhunter out of time. Whether due to the dense material that had been used to construct the old building foundation at the turn of the twentieth century or to Velikovsky's Paradox—the effect of causality violation that made electronic components unreliable—the BioTrak transponder embedded in Vadim's skull had not functioned normally.

Days later, for the first time feeling out of danger, Vadim had reestablished contact with the Iraqis. The embassy in New York had given him instructions to wait at a certain phone booth at a certain time.

The call had come through right on the money.

"What the hell happened, Motherwell?"

The voice on the other end had belonged to Ambassador Rafiq Mafkouz. Vadim had enjoyed the recognition that the ambassador was a frightened man. He had the deaths of a half dozen or so Moukhabarat operatives to account for and had no explanations.

Vadim had appreciated the ambassador's predicament. Being at such a loss in Saddam's government could well cost Mafkouz his head. The knowledge that he was the sole man who held all the answers had given Vadim an added measure of satisfaction.

"I warned you about Quinn," Vadim had declared testily. "You weren't paying attention. I told you he was dangerous. Now you know just how dangerous I meant."

"I apologize for doubting your word," Mafkouz had replied, his anger again in check. "It appears that there is much we do not understand. But I am relieved to find you well."

"So am I," Vadim had answered with a sarcastic snort.

"I can now tell you that our experts have had the chance to go over the materials supplied by you," Mafkouz had continued. "They have now been deemed conclusively genuine. My, ah, superior is quite impressed."

"I want to meet with him," Vadim had pressed. "Personally."

"That can now be arranged," Mafkouz had replied with hardly a pause. He had already come to his decision, Vadim knew, and had been expecting the American's demand this time. "Tell me your location. We can have someone fetch you in no time."

"Uh-uh," Vadim had answered the Iraqi, getting the uncomfortable feeling that he had spent enough time at this location already. "That's not how we're playing it this time around."

"Oh? And how exactly are we 'playing it'?" Mafkouz had responded with more than a trace of annoyance.

"By *my* rules," Vadim had answered. "Tell your 'superior' that I will take steps to get myself out to his headquarters within a few days. I will make contact with him at that end, and a meeting can then be arranged."

"That may not be wise," Mafkouz had remarked right away. "Other, ah, parties may be injecting themselves into the situation. You may be watch-listed."

"There are no other parties," Vadim had challenged. "I told you that before. There is only one man, and he can't afford to go to any outside parties. He would be laughed at or put in a lunatic asylum. Two, three days," Vadim had said. "Put the word out," he'd added before hanging up the receiver.

He had cradled the handset's earpiece in its metal hook and left the area as quickly as possible to embark on the circuitous approach to his destinations. And he had made it, he thought as he exited the dusty landing strip. He should be much safer in this armed camp of a country whose leaders had it in their best interest to protect him.

Motor transportation proved easy to find. His credentials identified him as a reporter for a major

cable news network. Hordes of reporters from print
and electronic media, representing every shade and
nuance of the political spectrum, in addition to every
newspaper and magazine with a national circula-
tion, were descending on Baghdad in these final
weeks before Operation Desert Storm commenced.

Lost in the crowd of foreigners, Vadim had what
amounted to perfect cover.

The Iraqi locals were benefiting by the influx of
foreigners, too. On the outskirts of the deserted air-
strip were posted several men with vehicles who made
it clear that they would drive him wherever he wanted
for only a few American dollars, for Iraqi dinars
were accepted only as a last resort.

Vadim chose one of these entrepreneurs and got
into a beat-up Ford sedan that bore the battle scars
of many harsh years of negotiating narrow alleys and
driving on poorly paved desert roads under the heat
of the blazing desert sun.

It was a wonder that such old jalopies existed at
all, but there seemed to be hundreds of them everywhere in good operating condition despite the rough
environment and in the face of a probable shortage
of spare parts.

Communicating to the driver that he wanted to go
to the Baghdad International, Vadim settled back
into the hard cushions of the back seat. The side of
his head throbbed where the transponder implant lay

just beneath the skin, although he knew that this was probably only a psychological reaction and not an actual pain.

Vadim cursed that pea-size implant inside him, but knew that there was no way to safely remove it. He hated the thing because it linked him to Quinn and he knew that Quinn was out there tracking him, maybe even in Baghdad. Or soon to be, if not yet in the country.

But Vadim would soon be in the protection of Saddam. Even Quinn couldn't reach him in the heart of Saddam's police state. No, not even Quinn was good enough to pull off a stunt like that.

30

Though Vadim was not aware of it, the object of his fear and loathing had arrived in Baghdad not long after his own arrival.

After leaving New York, Quinn had made the rest of the trip free from detection.

Unlike Vadim, whose paranoia had caused him to see his pursuer lurking around every corner, Quinn knew that the events of the previous night would go down in the books as unsolved and end at that stage.

The cops back in Manhattan had reacted quickly in the aftermath of the confrontation at the Brooklyn Bridge.

From Battery Park to Chinatown, the screech of sirens had competed with the moaning of the chill wind New Yorkers called "the Hawk" as patrol cars had converged on the crime scene in response to a report of officers in trouble.

Reports were sketchy, and barring the insistence of the two harness bulls that a strangely dressed man in a "space helmet" was dragging another man into "some kind of space warp" that had opened up in thin air, the incident went down as a botched drug shooting. Proceeding along that official line, the dragnet launched by the NYPD was bound to fizzle as Quinn's path quickly grew cold.

Police choppers had been ordered airborne, their searchlight beacons crisscrossing the skies above Lower Manhattan while squad cars had patrolled the dark, narrow streets, sending lights of their own lancing into shadowed alleyways and basement entrances.

But by the time the sun had risen, the manhunt was called off. Had the officers at the scene of the bizarre incident been seriously injured or killed, it might have been a different story, but since they had suffered superficial injuries, the focus of the police had turned to new problems, chalking up the stories about "space warps" and "aliens" to the effects of stress.

Though it had been a far cry from aerospace plane travel, which could reach any spot on the globe within two hours, Quinn's plane trip from New York's JFK airport had been fast by the standards of the late twentieth century. The SST, practically a prehistoric relic of pre-ASP air travel in his own era, was the height of opulence and speed downtime in 1990.

He had booked the next available flight out of JFK, which had landed him at Orly Airport in Paris,

France, in about two hours. From there, he'd had to travel the rest of the distance to Baghdad, via a slower 747 turbojet, adding an additional six hours to his overall trip.

Quinn now sat in the back seat of a taxicab driven by an Iraqi who, after attempts at conversation, had graduated to suggestions of taking Quinn to meet some women he knew. These ladies could provide delights such as not even the fabled courtesans of the court of Nebuchadrezzar were equal to delivering. Quinn had politely yet firmly refused and turned his thoughts to other, less pleasant pursuits.

Once again Quinn had staked the success of his mission on journeying to Baghdad in pursuit of the rogue time traveler. Yet Quinn's choice of his Middle Eastern destination, like New York City before it, was based on much more than just playing a hunch.

Every aspect concerning Vadim's patterns of movement and behavior pointed to Baghdad as his final destination. The clandestine contact and subsequent meeting between Vadim and the Iraqis in New York City had confirmed this hypothesis.

Vadim was obsessed with the Muan power crystals and knew that he had only a matter of weeks to get his hands on them.

Operation Desert Shield, which was stockpiling men and matériel in forward staging areas around Riyadh, Saudi Arabia, in the greatest airlift in history, would soon give way to the Desert Wind and Desert Storm phases of the attack on Saddam's Iraq.

The commencement of the aerial strikes on Baghdad would begin in a matter of days.

After these violent events were set in motion, Saddam would not be conducive to listening to Vadim's stories, verifiable or not. He would have other problems on his hands.

The window of opportunity for Vadim to take possession of the Muan crystals was between now and the commencement of Desert Wind on January 16th, 1991.

This told Quinn that of all the possible places in the world to search out his quarry, Baghdad was the first on the list.

Quinn's reflections were interrupted by the jolt of the taxi as it came to a halt directly in front of the Baghdad International hotel.

Quinn realized that the driver had been telling him something, but he had been so wrapped up in his thoughts that he hadn't been paying the Iraqi any attention.

"Hotel is full up, mister," the driver was saying. "You have reservation? If not, Ahmed can show you nice, small pension. Very clean, very reasonable price."

Quinn didn't think he'd have any problem getting himself a room at the hotel, but he thought the cabbie's suggestion might be a good one to keep in mind.

Taking down the address of the place mentioned by the driver, Quinn tipped him substantially and hauled his carryall into the hotel lobby.

AS HE HAD EXPECTED, the International hotel was packed to the rafters.

Media personnel from around the globe had converged on the few world-class hotels in Baghdad like a swarm of desert locusts. Throughout the jammed lobby, media people were typing up reports on laptops, conducting interviews and, also predictably, packing the hotel bar with a record crowd of foreigners.

Quinn made his way to the front desk, where a harried-looking concierge said something into a phone as he made eye contact with Quinn. Hanging up, he came forward.

Quinn asked him for a room.

"Do you have a reservation?" he asked. Quinn already caught the look in the man's eyes that was a mixture of pity and scorn. A "yes" answer would have undoubtedly provoked the predictable response that without one, he might as well sleep in the street.

"No," Quinn answered the deskman. "But I have something better."

The concierge looked down at what the newcomer was sliding across the top of the front desk toward him. It was a traveler's check and the sum across its face was five thousand dollars. The deskman knew enough about such matters to realize immediately that it was genuine.

The expression in his hooded eyes underwent a quick transformation as he surreptitiously glanced from side to side to make certain the transaction was not being seen.

"Well," he said, reaching for what amounted to a small fortune in Iraq, "there *is* a small room available, sir. I am afraid I had overlooked it initially."

The traveler's check was safely tucked away in his coat pocket as he turned and handed Quinn a room key. "Enjoy your stay in Baghdad, sir," he concluded.

"I'll do that, partner," Quinn told the Iraqi. "And you do something for me. Keep your mouth shut about our little arrangement. If you can do that, there'll be a fat bonus for your discretion when I check out."

"My lips are sealed, sir," the Iraqi replied with a smile. His dark eyes followed Quinn as the new guest walked toward the elevator.

The concierge wondered who the newcomer really was, for he was certainly no reporter and could not possibly be a tourist, either. CIA perhaps, or even Mossad. Maybe KGB. Or perhaps he was just a freelancer, this final choice seeming the most likely one.

Not that any of it really mattered to him.

In Saddam Hussein's Iraq, the acceptance of the bribe from the newcomer was in itself sufficient grounds for treason, and once charged, summary execution was a virtual certainty.

The deskman's elation at his sudden good fortune was tempered by the dawning fear that he might have been seen accepting the gratuity in exchange for a room.

As the concierge daydreamed about what the money would buy him and how he would safely get it out of the country into the Egyptian bank where he kept an account, the new arrival was entering his room.

Quinn found the accommodations comfortable after a long time in transit.

The bar downstairs would serve both as a place to feel his way around and begin his search and a place to unwind. In the meantime, Quinn unpacked his bags, paying special attention to the padded carrying case for his laptop computer.

In one of its pockets, blending in well with the other electronic components used by writers on foreign assignments, was nestled the tracker. It was similar enough in appearance and functioning to a hand-held personal computer of the late twentieth century to be overlooked by baggage handlers.

Due to the Velikovsky Paradox, the BioTrak unit functioned only intermittently and unreliably. But because it was impossible to know when it would malfunction, there was no telling when Quinn might get a tracking icon from the implant in Vadim's skull.

Sitting on the edge of the bed, Quinn keyed on the tracker, and its screen instantly came to life. To Quinn's shock and amazement, the icon representing Vadim was positioned only a few hundred feet from the very spot where he sat.

Vadim was somewhere in the hotel!

31

The shocking realization that Vadim was right there at the International, almost literally under his nose, hit him with the force of a hammer blow.

Having originally resigned himself to a lengthy, dangerous and potentially fruitless search in a city that was the heart of one of the most brutally repressive police states on the face of the earth, he was unprepared for this surprisingly good turn of luck.

Still, it *did* make a kind of sense. Like himself, Vadim was probably posing as a journalist, too. It was the best kind of cover to have in such a situation, the classic cover of soldiers of fortune because of the ease of forging press credentials and the freedom to move around provided by such a cover.

Before making his way downstairs to the hotel lobby, Quinn stowed his baggage in the room's closet. His VRGs, stealth suit and other specialized gear were all stowed in his carryall, although broken down into compact, modularized form. The collapsible field equipment was hidden among his laptop, tape recorder and the other journalist's equipment.

If these exotic items were found and examined while Quinn was out of the room, they would undergo a delayed self-destruct, killing whoever happened to be unfortunate enough to be within the small radius of the explosions. Hopefully that would give Quinn some lead time to engineer an escape.

Quinn had also disguised his appearance since leaving New York for the Middle East. His hair was cropped close against his skull and shaven at the edges to create a widow's peak. He had dyed it blonde, too, while tinted aviators helped to mask the shape of his face.

Effective disguise depended as much on acting ability as on physical alterations. Besides making cosmetic changes to his features, Quinn had changed his walk and mannerisms, as well. Body language could be more of a giveaway than appearance, especially at a distance.

As he crossed the hotel lobby, his eyes scanned the area from behind the smoked gray lenses of his aviator shades. Although the lobby appeared even more crowded than when he had come in earlier that afternoon, Vadim seemed not to be anywhere in sight.

Quinn thought of methods he might try to discover Vadim's room number through the bribable deskman. But without knowing the alias used by his quarry, it would be difficult not to attract the wrong kind of attention. A second bribe might have a boomerang effect, spooking the man into calling in the Moukhabarat.

Bypassing the front desk entirely, Quinn crossed the lobby and went into the packed bar.

He spotted Vadim almost immediately.

In the sudden space created by the shifting of the crowd in the packed bar, Quinn spied his quarry seated by himself at a table, drinking alone.

Quinn was only able to watch Vadim for a minute or two before the press of bodies once more obscured his line of sight. Pushing through the jostling, shoulder-to-shoulder crowd, Quinn got another look at the table a few moments later.

But Vadim was not the only patron sitting at the table anymore. He had been joined by two newcomers.

Elbowing his way through the noisy crowd of multinational media people, Quinn made his way to the bar, which was just close enough to the table to give him a chance of eavesdropping on what was being said there.

Ordering a bourbon and soda, Quinn reached up and appeared to be adjusting the tinted aviators he wore. What he was really doing was activating the farfoon built into the lightweight tinted glasses.

Sounds picked up by the subminiature microphone array located on the glasses' sweat bar fed into amplification circuitry within the hollow wire frame. Output was via tiny directional speakers at either side of the earpieces.

"I'm afraid you have no choice," he heard one of the men at the table say to Vadim. "The matter has been decided at the very highest levels."

"You people screwed me once before," Vadim protested in undertones. "I don't want it to happen again. What the hell kind of guarantees do I have?"

"This is Iraq, Mr. Motherwell," the other man vouched, his voice deeper and calmer than the first speaker's. "Here it is somewhat different than in America. In this country we can provide absolute protection. Forget about your difficulties in New York."

He waved his hand as if to brush away a thought that was as unimportant as a bothersome mosquito.

"Anyway, my terms were a meeting with Saddam," Vadim specified. "You're telling me something different."

"What we are saying comes directly from the leader's own lips," the first speaker resumed, annoyance obvious in his voice. "You must understand that in this current crisis situation we must be extremely careful. The safehouse will be secure and comfortable, and your stay in Baghdad will be brief—I can promise you that.''

"No.'' Vadim rejected that statement with a shake of his head. ''I don't think so. That's not the way I'm playing it.''

The Iraqis at the table exchanged meaningful glances with one another.

The first one spoke up again. ''You do not understand, Mr. Motherwell. As I said, this is Iraq, and we act with the leader's full approval. I am afraid you have no choice but to accede to our request.

The Iraqi leaned back in his chair and Quinn saw Vadim's glance move down a few notches to come to rest just beneath his left armpit. Quinn knew that he was staring at the butt of a handgun.

Do not force us to take measures that will prove regrettable,'' he added. ''Cooperate with us, and I can assure you that all your goals will be met. We are as eager to do business with you as you are with us.''

"Okay,'' Vadim conceded, standing up and reaching into his pocket. ''Just let me pay the bar tab.''

Quinn had turned sideways and saw Vadim start to cross toward the cashier's table, but the second Iraqi had already risen to his feet and quickly stood beside Vadim, his hand clutching the foreigner's arm.

"The bill has already been taken care of, Mr. Motherwell. Our car is waiting outside. Come with us, if you please.''

Quinn watched the trio edge through the capacity crowd toward the entrance as he downed the last of his drink. He had seen enough to know that the Moukhabarat had beaten him to the punch.

Again Quinn was one step behind Vadim.

As before, he would have to play a game of catch-up ball.

THE DRIVE THROUGH Baghdad took them down a meandering labyrinth of narrow, snaking streets, sun-drenched plazas and whitewashed two-story buildings concealing cool interior gardens.

The official vehicle came to a stop at the end of a street that was blind at one end and dead-end at the other.

To one side, near the terminus of the cul-de-sac, stood a brick building, fronted by a high gate of wrought iron. Armored security cameras on motorized swivel mounts were posted atop the gate, providing security personnel inside with real-time video of the approach to the building.

One of the Iraqis jabbed his finger at a doorbell, and a few moments later a buzzer sounded as the lock on the gate snapped open with a loud metallic click.

Bracketed by the Moukhabarat agents, Vadim was swept through the gate by his two handlers. Inside the vestibule, Iraqi red berets porting AKM rifles snapped to attention as the trio entered the building.

Vadim's escorts conducted him along a short breezeway with locked steel doors and the Spartan look of a military headquarters.

"Stop here," Vadim was told, and the Iraqis rapped smartly on a door at the corridor's end. The door was promptly opened by another uniformed soldier, and Vadim was brought inside the room.

An official in a uniform was waiting there, sitting at a desk of polished mahogany. From the moment Vadim entered the room, the man watched him with languid eyes, black beneath the hooded lids, eyes that nevertheless missed nothing they saw.

Darkly complected, he sported a thick black mustache. Black hair was slicked back over a fleshy, pockmarked face. "Sit down," the uniformed individual said commandingly to Vadim. He introduced himself as Major General Izmir Zambrani of the Iraqi Intelligence and Security Service.

"Let us get right down to business," Zambrani said gruffly to the new arrival. He spoke with the upper-class accent of the English schools he had attended, the privilege of being born into the ranks of the Iraqi elite.

"It is in the interest of both of us to conclude this phase of your stay in Baghdad as quickly as possible, wouldn't you agree?"

"I agree," Vadim told Zambrani. "Therefore I can't understand this cloak-and-dagger bullshit you people seem to be addicted to. You've authenticated the sample materials I've provided. Why this charade?"

Major General Zambrani lit up a gnarled cheroot and leaned back in his chair, which creaked as he shifted his weight. He regarded his visitor for a long moment through his languid black eyes as he blew a pungent cloud of gray-blue smoke at the ceiling.

"Put yourself in our position," he said. "We receive a contact from a man claiming to be from the future. He offers to provide us with revolutionary weapons technology in order to help us defeat our foes and realize our great leader's ambition of a pan-Islamic republic.

"As proof of his claim, this man next provides us with various artifacts, again supposedly manufactured in the future. Incredibly a cursory investigation shows some promise that they are quite as advertised."

Blowing more smoke at the ceiling, Zambrani went on, "But then, as we await final word, our 'visitor from the future' is abducted under violent and mysterious circumstances from the safehouse where we have taken him for his own protection, and then disappears entirely from view."

"Look, I told you about Quinn," Vadim interjected with a jab of his finger toward Zambrani's barrel chest. "The world police force of my time sent their best operative after me. To bring me back."

"Yes, so you have claimed," Major General Zambrani replied with amusement, meditatively stroking his mustache as the trace of a smile played across his lips, "and a contemporary New York City police report citing certain strange events later that night lends added credence to this story.

"But despite all of that, and the fact that the materials you submitted for scrutiny are beyond the ability of our technicians to satisfactorily explain or reverse engineer, we must still consider the possibility of a CIA dangle operation being run.

"It would be a bold gambit, and one built on an unlikely chain of events, I grant you that, but we must be careful. President Hussein himself needs this assurance before granting you the privilege of the personal interview that you request."

"All right," Vadim reacted, "let's get it over with." There was no point in arguing with the general, he realized. He was in the hands of the Iraqi state security service in the heart of Baghdad, and they were suspicious as hell. He supposed he would be, too, if their places were reversed. He would just have to play ball by their rules. For the present, at least.

"Splendid," declared Zambrani, extinguishing his cheroot. "Then let us begin. I will ask you several questions and you will reply. Take your time answering," he concluded. "Take all the time you require. We have all night."

32

In the dazzling sunlight of the Baghdad afternoon, no passerby would take notice of the dark-tinted aviator glasses that the Westerner wore as he walked down a street in a residential section of the ancient city.

The glasses doubled as eyephones, linked via microwave telemetry to the tracker unit that Quinn carried in one of the big thigh pockets of his six-pocket jeans.

As Quinn walked along the Baghdad street, the icon showing the location of Lux Vadim was superimposed over the images of the surrounding streets and buildings. Invisible to anyone besides Quinn, the tracker icon had been leading him toward his quarry since he had left the Baghdad International almost an hour ago.

Having taken a taxi to the outskirts of the neighborhood, Quinn set the eyephones to a local scan mode and proceeded the rest of the way on foot. As he approached a street that doglegged left to a dead end, Quinn saw a box form around the tracker icon.

This indicated that the quarry was within two hundred feet of his position.

Reaching into his side pocket, Quinn used his thumb and four fingers to keystroke in a two-key "chord" command to redraw the screen of his eyephones. The overlay underwent a phase shift as the tracker computer offered Quinn a glowing wire grid map of the neighborhood.

The boxed tracker icon was now blinking from a point with grid coordinates that placed Vadim in the brick building fronted by a wrought-iron gate at the dead end at the top of the street.

Just then, Quinn noticed that a uniformed Baghdad policeman was watching him from across the street with what seemed to be an undue amount of curiosity.

The man's uniform consisted of brown pants and short-sleeved shirt open at the neck. A billed cap and a Sam Browne belt holstering a wheel gun and ammo completed the outfit. After a few seconds the policeman came walking over to him.

"American, yes?" he asked Quinn.

"Reporter. Trying to learn about Baghdad. The people's Baghdad."

"Your passport and press card, please," the policeman demanded, extending his hand. He eyed the American while the documents were produced, and he scanned the identification carefully before handing them back.

"The people of Iraq do not want war," the cop lectured him. "It is George Bush and the Zionists who force war on the innocent Iraqi people. You write that in your story. You tell Americans the truth about Iraq."

Quinn assured the policeman that he would honor his wishes to the letter, grateful that the man had apparently just happened by and was merely curious.

It could just as easily have happened that he might have met up with a Moukhabarat operative, and the situation would have been considerably different. An Iraqi spook would have looked beneath the surface at once, and even if Quinn had his disguise down to the hilt, his nose might have sniffed him out.

When the policeman had turned the corner, Quinn passed the street on which the safehouse was located. Suddenly remembering something that had been at the back of his mind, Quinn reached into one of his pockets and brought out a folded slip of paper.

The street name on the paper matched the one he was on. Confirming this with a quick glance at the signs painted on the walls per Middle Eastern fashion, Quinn walked past the mouth of the dead end and continued along the street in search of the address that Ahmed the cabbie had given him on his arrival.

The address, he soon discovered, belonged to a white stucco building a few houses down the street. He knocked on the door and in a few minutes was greeted by an old woman in a shapeless dress. Her snow white hair was pulled tightly back against her head, and the skin of her face had a waxy, almost translucent quality about it. She looked at him quizzically, her brown eyes wrinkling into crow's-feet at the corners.

"I'm looking to rent a room," Quinn told her. "Ahmed told me I might find one here."

The old woman nodded and gestured for Quinn to follow her. She led him into the cool, shadowed interior of the house and up a short flight of stairs by which Quinn saw a flash of green from a small walled garden hidden from the street.

"Here is the room," she said, her English heavily accented. "Sixty-five American dollars a day. Breakfast included."

Quinn smiled as he counted out the money into the old woman's hand. In her case, looks were probably deceiving. She had known enough to overcharge the American, and had known that he would pay, in light of the crunch of rentable rooms in Baghdad.

Going to the window, Quinn pulled up the sash and spread the wooden shutters that kept out the harsh afternoon sun.

A rush of street noise and baking heat assaulted him as he looked out. But the view was better than he had dared hope. Directly below the window was a clay-tiled roof that was spaced mere inches from the other rooftops of the neighboring houses.

From the window Quinn had a direct line of sight of the cul-de-sac where the Iraqis were keeping Vadim.

"I'll be back soon with my baggage," Quinn told the old woman, who nodded and walked back downstairs with him.

His arrangements made, Quinn returned to the International and retrieved the pieces of luggage containing his VRGs, stealth suit and other combat gear, ascertaining that these had not been tampered with in his absence.

This time he took a cab directly to the street that the Iraqi bed-and-breakfast was located on, but not directly to the house itself.

Getting out of the cab, Quinn negotiated the street and was soon inside the house. The sun was already riding low on the horizon, bathing the mud-brick, plaster-walled buildings with a bronze light.

Iraq would be dark soon.

With the coming of night the killing ground would be ready.

AFTER the big crescent moon had set over the rooftops of Baghdad and the dusty street was silent except for the occasional barking of stray dogs, a shadow moved low across the rooftops.

Having donned VRGs and stealth suit, Quinn exited the window of his room. From there had jumped to the roof of the adjoining house and scanned the area.

Painting the operational environment with invisible lasers and programmed to respond to the transponder in Vadim's skull, the VRGs showed the target icon as he subjected the night to a high-speed scan. The scan revealed the heat signature of a rifle-armed sentry posted on the flat rooftop of the safehouse.

Quinn used his wrist-top keypad to focus on the target, and the VRGs flashed him an image of an NVG-equipped shooter in black togs and black watch cap. He was equipped with a long-barreled automatic weapon, a sniper's gun.

Crouch-walking toward his quarry to keep his profile low against the horizon and prevent him from being skylighted, Quinn moved stealthily toward the sniper position.

The passive infrared night-vision goggles worn by the sentry were blind to the random heat-diffusion patterns produced by Quinn's stealth suit.

Popping up a heartbeat and pulse-rate graph on the virtual screen, Quinn was confident from reviewing the patterns that the sniper was completely unaware of the deadly shadow stalking him.

A digital display showing Quinn's distance from the target cycled down to zero at the top of the VRG screen as Quinn approached the sentry to within a few scant feet of his position.

Standing to one side of the prone shooter, Quinn popped up the reticles on his virtual screen. Lifting the lethal black doughnut in his right hand, he watched the death dot glide across the electronic view field.

The pipper tracked across the screen, and the sound-suppressed weapon went off the moment that Quinn put it into the center of the cross hairs that framed the blacksuited figure hunching on the roof.

The sniper grunted, tried to get up but never made it. He rolled over on his back with arms outflung, and the spiking lines on the vital-signs graph flattened out, indicating to Quinn that pulse rate and heartbeat had both dropped off to zero.

With the sniper taken down swiftly and silently, Quinn phreaked the perimeter sensors on the roof and unlocked the access door.

He was inside now, on the top level of the safe-house. His VRG screen reconfigurated, showing a glowing 3-D wire diagram of the building's interior based on laser probes, as well as the location of the transponder implant worn by Vadim.

A warning message popped up as Quinn was half-way down the flight of stairs leading to the floor below, indicating that a threat signature with armed personnel parameters had been identified by the VRGs' on-board microprocessor.

In real-time video mode, Quinn saw the Iraqi commando in fatigues come striding into view as he mounted the stairway. The red beret was toting a Krinov assault weapon, the short-barelled SMG version of the heavier Avtomat Kalashnikov autorifle.

Quinn got set to put him down with a silenced burst when the stairs creaked under his booted foot. The Iraqi whirled in place, already bringing the Krinov into firing position, reacting instead of thinking, as he had been drilled countless times to do.

Quinn's reactions were quicker and, set on Auto-target mode, the VRGs automatically triggered a 3-round burst of 5.70 mm fléchette fire as soon as the target was acquired.

Legs buckling under him, the commando sagged to the floor with a thud that was loud enough to alert a sentry on the level below.

Quinn heard the sound of footsteps and moved quickly away from the body that sprawled in its own pooling blood. There was no time to drag the corpse of the takedown out of sight. Already sweeping the stairway as the other trooper came into view, Quinn raised the P-90 and took down the third kill of the penetration with a precision-targeted head shot.

At close range, the high-velocity needlepoint rounds sheared off the upper left quadrant of the Iraqi's skull, sending plugs of bone and brain matter spattering on the wall behind him with a dozen wet slaps. The sentry sagged to his knees, producing little in the way of noise besides the telltale death rattle.

Quinn waited, scanning the strike perimeter with multiple-mode VRG scans in real time.

The operational area remained secure.

He proceeded on toward the boxed tracker icon, which the data block at the top of the screen indicated was situated beyond the door coming up on Quinn's right.

Beyond that door Quinn would come to the end of the line. But he was well aware that the mission parameters had changed considerably since the New York phase of operations. Under the circumstances, there could be no guarantee that he would be able to bring Vadim back to stand trial for his crimes.

In that case, Quinn would carry out his fallback directive and terminate Vadim before he was able to assist Saddam in winning the Gulf War by gaining possession of the Muan power crystals.

Quinn booted in the door and surveyed the strike zone. The target icon of his VRG display was positioned squarely on Vadim.

Inside the room with the time traveler were an Iraqi in a military uniform and several paramilitary types. Receiving target prioritization, Quinn shot the officer first as he went for the .38-caliber wheel gun holstered at his hip, killing him with a fléchette burst in the heart.

Another computer-targeted burst settled accounts with the men in paramilitary uniforms. In the confines of the room, the bursts of high-velocity autofire from the silenced weapon caused the bodies to open up, spewing blood as they jerked convulsively.

Vadim saw Quinn and cowered with fear.

"No!" he shrieked. "Don't kill me! Please don't kill me!"

Lux Vadim realized that he was about to die.

Quinn dragged the pipper across the virtual screen and put the death dot on the cross hairs framing the cowering man's left chest and pulled the trigger. A silenced burst of 5.70 mm fléchettes augered through space and struck Vadim in the heart zone, flinging him against the wall with arms out-thrust.

Suddenly Quinn's VRG screen lit up with multiple threat warnings. Almost simultaneously a heavily armed squad of Iraqis was busting through connecting doors at either side of the room to Quinn's left and right.

More threat readings indicated that another squad of armed Iraqis was mounting the stairs.

In the same instant, Quinn saw that Vadim was stirring on the floor, and Quinn realized that he had been set up.

Vadim had been wearing body armor, which, if made properly, could even withstand hits by the high-penetration-capable 5.70 mm rounds fired by the P-90.

Now Vadim laughed with maniacal glee, but Quinn reacted to the sudden shift in the tactical situation by pulling a high-blast-yield incendiary grenade from a pouch at his side and tossing the ballpoint-pen-size black cylinder into the center of the room.

Quinn dived out into the corridor, and a tremendous explosion followed. He flattened himself against the wall and spun his body around to face the squad of armed men double-timing up the stairs. He whipped up the P-90 as a firestorm swept the room behind him.

With the op zone having reached the point of meltdown, Quinn tossed an APERS minigrenade into the group of Iraqis storming the stairs as he raced back toward the rooftop level, his VRGs indicating that more men were already on the roof.

Black smoke was now rising toward the sky in a thick plume as fire licked up from the window of the blast-damaged, hell-visited room.

With the VRGs set on Autotarget mode, Quinn took down more Iraqi opposition on the rooftop with lightning quick bursts of precision targeted fléchette fire.

Reinforcements were already on their way as the Iraqis mustered up more troops from a nearby army barracks. Quinn raced across the rooftops of Baghdad, alone in hostile territory as the dragnet was deployed.

future you envision,'' spoke the angel before vanishing in a haze of incandescent brilliance.

When Saddam awoke, he saw a star glittering brightly in the dark heavens above Baghdad as brightly as the Star of Bethlehem. Surely this was another omen, he knew, and resolved to follow the path shown him in his dream.

And so, despite his fiercer instincts, which called for a more brutal reception for the American, Saddam had taken Abbott Motherwell into his presence and had welcomed the newcomer as a guest in his house. Saddam was prepared to listen to what Motherwell had to say.

The American spoke of the shattering events that were to follow his arrival within a brief matter of time. He spoke of how Iraq would be attacked shortly after an historic ultimatum dictated by President George Bush had expired, and how the coalition forces would launch an air assault that would rain death and destruction down on Baghdad on a scale never before seen.

He spoke of things even more incredible still. Tens of thousands of Iraq's soldiers would perish in the unrelenting air strikes. Unlike during Iraq's war against Iran, during which they had fought bravely and died willingly for Allah and glory, his troops would be reduced to whimpering dogs by the might of coalition firepower.

B-52 Stratofortresses, F-16 and Tornado fighter-bombers and F117A Stealth planes would be among those aircraft that dropped thousands of tons of bombs on the bunkers in which they hid.

Hell itself would seem to touch the earth as fuel-air explosives with blast yields exceeded only by nuclear weapons were dropped, making the desert shudder to its roots as fiery mushroom clouds billowed up into the sky.

His Russian tanks, which lay buried beneath the sand, would be reduced to flaming hulks in the Desert Wind air strikes, and the elaborate network of sand berms, revetments and firetraps that had worked so effectively against the Iranian human-wave attacks would be bypassed entirely in a lightning armored push that would see coalition forces in striking distance of Baghdad within days after the ground assault commenced.

The billions of dollars' worth of advanced weaponry he had purchased from American, Japanese and European suppliers would prove worthless. Those same contractors who had assured Saddam of bombproof bunkers were even now supplying coalition military commanders with the blueprints and suggestions on where to best strike them.

Saddam would turn to the desperate gambit of launching Scud attacks on Israel in an effort to turn

Israel against the Arab states and snatch victory from the jaws of defeat as those nations banded together.

But this bleak strategy would end in failure, too, as precision bombing by night and by day would destroy the Scud launchers on the ground. And batteries of improved Patriot missiles would knock them from the skies as they arced in on their trajectories toward Tel Aviv and Riyadh.

Then would come the ground assault, where coalition forces would find Iraqis surrendering by the thousands.

Occupied Kuwait would fall quickly and troops fleeing Iraq's formerly subjugated neighbor would be killed like cattle running through a slaughterhouse pen on the highway to Basra, leaving a morass of smoldering vehicles and charred, putrefying corpses.

With the fall of the elite Republican Guard units in a swift tank battle outside the southern city of Basra, the allies would be poised to enter Baghdad itself.

At that time, his army decimated, his people having gone for weeks without food, water, electricity or medicine, Saddam would have no choice except to accept the coalition's terms of unconditional surrender.

Never since the days of the ancients mentioned in the Bible and the Koran had a ruler heard such doomsaying by a prophet from God. But Saddam, who had earlier read Motherwell's debriefing under the late Major General Zambrani, knew all of what the American was telling him. But he continued to listen.

Among Saddam's other time-honed abilities was one that even his enemies would come to understand and grudgingly admire. This was patience.

One of the many blessings that Allah had bestowed upon Saddam was the gift of seeing the truth in men's eyes as sculptors are said to see the finished statue in blocks of uncut stone. He had used this ability on several occasions, penetrating the artifice of his enemies and revealing the evil or the goodness that lay in their hearts.

The gift had served Saddam well during the time of the great purge on his coming to power. He recalled with joy how he had convened a meeting of the Baath Party Regional Congress. "We have treason among us!" he had shouted from the podium to the assemblage, then began to call out the names of twenty accused plotters. Led away by armed police, their treachery was soon punished by death.

The gift was the most important test of all, the litmus of truth to Saddam. As Saddam listened, he used the gift to peer deep into the soul of the American. To his own amazement, Saddam saw that this man Motherwell was speaking truthfully and without guile. The gift never lied, and it did not do so at present. Now he was certain that this was no CIA dangle operation.

This was a miracle of Allah!

But there were new revelations yet to come, Saddam quickly learned. For soon the American had begun to tell him things that he had concealed even from Major General Zambrani's probing mind.

"Zambrani wouldn't have believed me," Vadim told Saddam as he faced the mustached figure who sat across the polished desktop smoking a cigar while watching him with a penetrating gaze. "Only you will understand what I am about to tell you," Vadim said.

He knew that Saddam would understand him. For the first time in his life, Vadim felt himself in the presence of a mind that thought like his own.

"Out in the desert between Basra and the Iran border, there lies buried a treasure trove of the ancient Babylonian kings," Vadim continued. "It is called 'The Abraxas Hoard.'"

"Show me where, exactly," Saddam said through his interpreter, pointing to a map on the wall behind him with a stubby finger, his eyes widening in their sockets as the gift filled them with heaven's own unearthly light.

Vadim rose and made a circle with his fingertip over the area that he was referring to. Saddam nodded. This, too, was a sign from Allah that the American was destined to work a miracle.

"I am familiar with the area you point out," Saddam replied through his interpreter. "You may be aware that I have been involved in certain archaeological excavations to bring the past glory of the Iraqi people to the recognition of the world. It is an area rich in hidden caves and ancient ruins."

"It is also the repository of unique crystals of extremely ancient origin," Vadim explained, picking up the thread of narrative. "They can be used as a means of generating tremendous energies.

"Bombard them with laser radiation of the proper frequencies, for example, and no light will be reflected back. All of the photonic energy in the light will be retained by the crystals, as though they were storage batteries. But the capacity of the crystals is tremendous, maybe even limitless.

"I know how to turn them into weapons of incalculable power," Vadim added. "With them you could turn the tide of the coming defeat. I have already sketched out how the American Stealth aircraft can be detected on radar. Once targeted, they could be vaporized in the skies."

"And what do you want in return?" asked Saddam, his eyes again boring deep into the soul of the American who had been brought to him by the angels of the All-Wise.

"To share in the glory," answered Vadim truthfully, "and to share in the spoils of victory."

Saddam nodded at the visitor and blew smoke at the ceiling. For the first time since their meeting had begun, Vadim saw a smile play across the face of Saddam Hussein as the Iraqi president leaned forward and extended his hand in the eternal gesture of a man who was about to strike a deal with another.

THE SUPREME COMMANDER of coalition forces stationed in the gulf theater of operations, General H. Norman Schwarzkopf, picked up the handset of the telephone on his desk.

The air-conditioned office was comfortable although the desert heat outside was a broiling one hundred four degrees Fahrenheit. It would cool soon enough, he knew, well in time for the land invasion, but for now it was the nearest thing to hell the general ever wanted to know about.

Informing the major on the other end of the line that he would receive the visitor, the general turned in his swivel chair and set his eyes on the door. First impressions could tell a great deal, and he would need all his wits to respond properly to what was about to walk into his office.

"Please pull yourself up a chair," he said to the visitor who entered, instantly sizing him up as a man who was not, in a phrase he was fond of using, "bovine excrement."

"I don't know why I consented to see you, but here you are. Now, you got exactly ten minutes of my time before I kick your butt out of my office, so you better make it good," Schwarzkopf said without smiling.

Quinn had done some sizing up himself as he'd entered the military commander's office. Schwarzkopf in the flesh was even more of the bear than his nickname described. There was a keenly penetrating perception evident in those blue eyes, and Quinn knew that the general could spot deception the way an Arkansas sheepdog could sniff gopher on the wind.

"General," Quinn began, "right now there could be one of the sickest minds in criminal history sitting with Saddam just as I'm doing with you.

"This is a man who has preached the twisted gospel that Adolph Hitler and Saddam Hussein are messiahs and that humanity is a disposable means to their ends.

"I was able to track him down and locate him twice, but each time he slipped through my fingers. I need your help for a third try. And, General, if the man I'm after isn't caught or killed, Saddam will win in the gulf."

All the while Schwarzkopf had not taken his eyes off his visitor. He had already been briefed—verbally briefed with no written or electronic documentation—on how this man, identified by his papers as Adam Jackson, had appeared out of nowhere and asked to see him.

He was carrying a CIA identification card that was authenticated as a valid Agency document yet bearing a coded agent's number that computer extrapolation had concluded could be issued fifty years in the future.

His weapons and tactical gear were also highly advanced, decades ahead of anything the military had now, yet clearly based on classified designs currently on the DARPA drawing boards and prototypes in the Agency's secret labs.

The man was an enigma, and Schwarzkopf didn't like enigmas. He liked, in fact he needed, solutions.

The most disturbing aspect of all to the Bear was the fact that if this man was really from the future, then he knew all about the "Hail Mary play" that the general was planning, a masterfully conceived military flanking operation that was already in progress and required the utmost secrecy in order to work as intended.

Those military plans were the linchpin around which the prosecution of the entire Gulf War turned. Military victory or crushing defeat for the coalition depended on Saddam's thinking the allies would hit him in one place while in fact they were hitting him where he least expected the strike to come.

This meant that somebody who knew these plans in advance could blow the entire operation. Still, the general thought, Jackson had been thoroughly vetted by the Intelligence people. And besides that, his gut feeling told him to go with this guy, as screwy as the story he told seemed.

"I don't believe it myself," Schwarzkopf said evenly, "but I believe *you*. I'll have a crack Delta squad go out with you to get this wacko."

"No good, General," Quinn replied, shaking his head dismissively. "I took a big chance in coming here to see you personally. Not because I distrust you, but because of the dynamics of causality violation."

"Whoa there, guy! You just lost me," Schwarzkopf protested. "What was that again?"

"Time travel, General," replied Quinn. "It's tricky, very tricky. In my time, about fifty years from now, we've only begun to scratch the surface of the phenomenon. But what's been discovered is that the fabric of time is very fragile, a lot like a crystal lattice in which every part is linked to the rest of the continuum. Even small actions can create large rifts farther down the time line.

"That's one reason why my target has to be brought back alive, if at all possible," Quinn went on. "Killing him in this 'now' might have worse consequences for my time than allowing him free rein. But this dynamic principle also means that the involvement of three or four additional personnel could also have negative consequences. I'll need your help in getting near the area I think Vadim will go for, but the rest of the way I have to go alone."

"Okay, partner, I'll back you the whole nine yards," Schwarzkopf said finally after silently sorting out what Quinn had just told him. "I don't know how you did it, but you just made a believer out of me. In fact, I've got a new piece of big-ticket military hardware that I think will be just the thing to get you where you're going."

34

The SWATH craft cruised through the darkness that hung like a shroud over the seamless black waters of the Persian Gulf.

Riding the surface of the inland sea a few miles off the rugged coastline that encompassed Kuwait, Saudi Arabia and Iraq, the black craft seemed to stride the waves like a slumbering leviathan roused from the ocean's depths.

The twin pylons of the small waterplane twin-hull SWATH craft were part of an advanced-design military prototype. Among the most highly classified weapons in the military arsenal being assembled to assault Iraq, the SWATH craft was the maritime equivalent of the F117A stealth fighter.

Its matte black hull constructed out of radar-absorbing materials, the SWATH vessel also incorporated radical geometries into its design configuration. Above the waterplanes of its twin hull was a deck area that was disk shaped.

All sonar, radar and laser-targeting fairings were of a conformal hull design, scab- and blister-podded to match hull contours so that radar echoes were kept to a minimum.

Its propulsion system borrowed quieting technology from Trident submarines, while rocket launchers, deck guns and other weaponry were all kept hidden behind retractable panels prior to combat deployment.

The SWATH craft was what the techs called "low observable." Its radar cross section was only about the size of a raft of seaweed floating on the ocean.

To the Iraqi coastal defense radars scanning the Persian Gulf for signs of enemy incursion, the SWATH vessel was as good as invisible.

Quinn had boarded the stealth ship from a clandestine dock facility on the Saudi Arabian coast. The crew had been told nothing about the passenger who had come aboard under strictest secrecy. Quinn was ushered to the captain's quarters and kept sequestered as soon as the ship was on its way to its secret objective.

He now awaited the captain's signal that it was time to move to the staging area. From there, Quinn would embark on the final leg of his journey into the southeastern desert of Iraq. It was there that he hoped to intercept Vadim before he could finalize his plans.

For the third time since leaving Gamma Base in pursuit of his quarry, uptime in the year 2035, Quinn was betting the farm on being right about where Vadim would next be found. But Quinn had been correct in the two previous judgment calls. Like those earlier actions, he was now proceeding on the basis of sound analysis.

The time traveler's burning obsession to find the Muan power crystals of the Abraxas Hoard, said to be buried in the sand desert west of the Iraqi city of Basra, had been overwhelming. It had been a driving force behind his every move so far. Quinn had every reason to believe that this motivation would continue to drive Vadim toward a predictable climax.

Furthermore, secret intelligence reports originating from highly placed ground assets channeled to him by General Schwarzkopf had indicated that Saddam had not only met Vadim but had installed him in his palatial residence as a guest. Psychologically, the two psychopaths were a perfect match. Both were megalomaniacs with delusions of grandeur. Both claimed to have been inspired by no less than God Himself. Add to that Vadim's hero worship of Saddam, and it was not difficult to envision the Iraqi dictator's placing every means to retrieve the crystals at his honored guest's disposal.

Vadim would be there, Quinn knew.

It was a certainty.

And Nomad would be there, too, waiting and watching for the right moment to move on his quarry. This time he would not leave the strike zone without either bringing Vadim back to the future or taking him down in this 'now,' for the desert jackals to pick clean his bones.

THE FLIGHT DECK of the SWATH ship was located beneath the hull area. Circular in shape, it ringed the central core of the advanced-design vessel, which contained living quarters, command-and-control stations and the craft's propulsion system.

Sections of the deck could be raised to facilitate the launch of helicopters, tilt-rotorcraft or VSTOL aircraft such as the Hawker Harrier.

The flight deck crew paid only minimum attention to the black-garbed figure whose head was completely enveloped by a tactical helmet of strange design. Selected from the most highly qualified navy personnel available, the crew of the SWATH vessel had signed secrecy oaths preventing them from divulging anything having to do with the ship on which they served on penalty of a federal prison term.

Since the ship itself was ultraclassified, the crew was prepared for any contingency and also prepared to promptly forget about everything they had seen while working their duty cycles.

The personnel who readied the Seahawk helicopter for immediate takeoff on the flight deck assumed that the man who was about to get into it was testing out some new gear and that the rest was none of their business.

The chopper parked within the elevator section of the flight deck marked off with yellow-and-black hazard tape was a multipurpose workhorse that Quinn knew would soon be a Gulf War veteran.

The Sikorsky SH-60B helicopter was a vertical takeoff and landing aircraft with all-weather operational capability. Its terrain-following forward-looking infrared, or FLIR, targeting and navigational system would permit it to engage in low-trajectory flight at high speed across the Iraqi desert.

The Seahawk had been readied for a black-coded mission that would take it deep into Iraqi airspace flying under the radar curtain.

The pilot had been instructed to descend to a hover, drop combat matériel, allow his passenger to debark and then swiftly return to the SWATH vessel where the crew would be debriefed. What the pilot did not know was that the crew would then be rotated Stateside to keep as tight a lid as possible on the clandestine mission.

The engines began to whine as they were charged to full power, the chopper's rotors began to turn, and

Quinn climbed through the open hatchway into the crew compartment. The drop master strapped him to an elastic safety tether and indicated a seat against one of the bulkheads.

As the props revolved up to speed and alarms sounded to warn personnel on the flight deck that the movable section would soon begin to rise, Quinn stood. Still tethered to the bulkhead, he looked out through the open hatchway and saw the flight deck fall away as the Seahawk was lifted above the level of the outer deck.

Once the takeoff platform was stationary, the pilot received final clearance for takeoff and applied pressure to the collective pitch stick while simultaneously manipulating the cyclical controls.

The four-bladed rotor mounted atop the helicopter supplied lift and the chopper began to rise straight up with the speed of a freight elevator.

Thirty feet above the deck the Seahawk's pilot applied lateral thrust by means of the powerful rotor at the end of the tail boom.

The combat helicopter then nosed forward through the night. It was soon knifing over the sand desert of southern Iraq on its way to the most secret drop zone of the entire Gulf War, perhaps in the history of all war.

THE MECHANIZED COLUMN ground through the desert wastes. Hours before, the vehicles had set out under cover of darkness from the Republican Guard barracks located in the city of Basra.

Making up the column were two MICVs of the German Fox class. These armored vehicles were painted in a desert camouflage format.

Each of the military infantry command vehicles carried a contingent of elite commandos. All were fully indoctrinated members of the Republican Guard, the most highly trained and combat-capable echelon in the Iraqi armed forces.

Outfitted in desert camo combat fatigues like the other men who sat with him in the lead MICV, Lux Vadim consulted the backlit dial of his digital wrist chronometer.

Since they had set out from Basra, he had been eagerly looking ahead to accomplishing the crowning achievement of his life.

By the digital readout he could see that it would only be a short time before the column reached the dig site. It wasn't really appropriate to call it a "dig site," Vadim mused, because there would not be a tremendous amount of digging involved in the recovery of the Muan artifacts.

Once the sensor instrument that the Iraqis had built to his specifications indicated that they had reached the site of the cache of Muan treasures, including the lost power crystals, drilling tools would bore an entry hole into the cave that lay just beneath the ground.

According to legend, the burial cave was formed entirely of natural crystals. It was an enormous geode, whose walls were encrusted with mineral deposits of quartz, selenite and other semiprecious gemstones that had built up, layer upon layer, over the course of millions of years.

The desert was vast and the region in which the cave was located was uncharted. But Vadim knew precisely where to look, and with the advanced sonar probe the Iraqis had built for Vadim, it would be child's play to find what he sought. In only a little while, Vadim knew he would be face-to-face with the greatest treasure trove of all time, and the source of almost limitless power.

35

The chopper reached its drop zone without incident.

The Seahawk's stealthy, hedgehopping flight path had brought it in under the enemy's radar curtain. Its FLIR terrain-mapping and navigational system confirmed that the dry wadi that was its destination now lay directly below.

The night skies over Iraq had been made deliberately busy that night with incursions into its airspace by U.S. "ferret" aircraft to draw the attention of enemy sentinels.

Once trip-wire radars were turned on, EW-12A Raven aircraft equipped for electronic countermeasures missions used active jamming techniques to render them useless.

Once over the drop zone, the pilot manipulated cyclical and pitch controls to bring the nimble chopper to a low hover only a few feet above the flat surface of the desert floor.

The all-terrain-capable fast-attack vehicle, or FAV, went out the open hatchway first.

The rugged military dune buggy bounced twice on its oversize tires before coming to a complete stop. It finally settled down amid a cloud of powdery desert grit that its impact with the ground had sent swirling into the cold night air.

The FAV was followed by the modularized drop packaging containing the specialized gear Quinn had drawn from coalition stocks back in Saudi. He had programmed the VRGs to integrate this new equipment into their targeting system.

Flashing the thumbs-up to the drop master, Quinn followed the gear drop down to the desert floor, cushioning the impact of landing with boot soles and corded calve muscles.

Rising quickly to his feet, Quinn watched through real-time video on his virtual screen as the Seahawk ascended to its low-trajectory cruising elevation. It then turned and headed back to the safety of the SWATH awaiting its return in the dark waters of the Persian Gulf.

Quinn had plenty to keep him occupied now that he had touched down on the almost lunar landscape of the Iraqi desert. His first order of business was to trundle the FAV down into the shallow bowl of the wadi.

When this feat had been accomplished, he dragged the modularized gear storage containers down the sloping side of the dry hole and placed them in close proximity to the dune buggy.

Spring-loaded latches were thumbed up and the gear containers were quickly broken down. From the shockproof storage cases Quinn unloaded the weapons systems that he had requisitioned for the clandestine night mission.

Hefting the multiple AT4 manpads unit to his shoulder, he checked out the computer interface between the armor-piercing rocket launcher and his VRG system.

After he had punched in commands on his wrist-top keypad, the VRGs' on-board computer was ready to go through a simulated-fire exercise routine.

It took less than five minutes for the computer simulation of multiple AT4 rocket launches to cycle through the diagnostics routine. Autotargeting and kill-confirmation tests were also conducted until the combat readiness of the equipment was validated.

Powering down his VRGs and placing them in standby mode, Quinn got down to what would certainly be the hardest part of the entire mission to handle: *waiting.*

Hunkered below the lip of the wadi, Quinn scanned the flat, nearly pitch-dark terrain and bided his time until his dangerous quarry made his appearance.

QUINN HEARD a beeptone sound in his ear.

"Attention," read the data block that had popped up over a glowing multicolored wire diagram of the desert landscape. The three-dimensional diagram duplicated every dip and rise of the wasteland surrounding him.

"Multiton vehicles of MICV configurations sighted. Range is one-point-five-five miles. Heading is south by southwest."

Quinn experienced a sudden rush of exhilaration as he watched the blue icon representing the two MICVs trundle slowly across the red schematic of crosshatching lines that was superimposed over the real-time video of the undulating desert landscape.

Numerical data showing speed, distance and estimated time to contact were also displayed on the borders of the virtual screen as a glowing digital readout.

There could be no doubt about what he was looking at. On board this convoy was Lux Vadim.

Somewhere close by, probably within a radius of only a few miles, lay the objective that the convoy was headed toward. The destination of the column had to be the site of the Muan power crystals, the legendary Abraxas Hoard.

Minutes later the mechanized column had advanced from the farthest edge of the VRGs' sensor range into the middle distance.

Keystroking in new commands at his wrist-top keypad, Quinn dissolved the graphical display on his virtual screen. The wire diagram overlay vanished in the space of an eye blink.

Quinn's video viewing mode was now real-time with image-intensification enhancement to penetrate the blackness of night. Zooming the image of the halted column, he watched the convoy of trucks grind to a sudden halt. Camo-fatigued Iraqi troops were soon jumping from the rear hatch of both MICVs and taking up flanking positions nearby the halted column.

Within moments the VRGs flashed Quinn the message "Sighting of target confirmed," and augmented this display by highlighting with a glowing double blue contour line one of the figures that had emerged from the armored personnel carriers.

Having confirmed his target with the new data, Quinn prepared to move away from his secure position. Keeping his profile low, though he was certain he had not been spotted by the opposition, he crawled down into the shallow bowl of the wadi and started up the silent-running FAV.

Minutes later the black-clad striker rolled the dune buggy stealthily across the desert floor, steering along the computer track that glowed on his VRG screen.

With headlights damped, the FAV was invisible against the black horizon. Quinn's targets would not see or hear him approach until he was right on top of them.

VADIM, along with the Iraqi special forces personnel, had donned passive IR night-vision goggles before debarking the MICV.

The use of the NVGs was deemed an operational necessity to defeat detection by surveillance platforms of various types. Light sources of any kind would prove an invitation to disaster, and passive IR goggles did not require an external light source in order to function.

In the weeks following the United Nations resolution to sanction force unless Saddam pulled his entrenched troops out of Kuwait, the skies above Iraq were cluttered with layer upon layer of aerial and suborbital reconnaissance platforms of various configurations.

At the lowest altitude level of the recon network were F117A Stealth fighters armed with infrared imaging systems.

Higher up, at a cruising altitude of approximately seventy thousand feet, were TR1 recon birds piloted by combination U.S. Air Force-CIA crews and equipped with both IR and electro-optical imaging technologies.

Orbiting silently and invisibly at the highest end of the surveillance ring were the recon satellites, which were sensitive enough to read the numbers on a license plate from eighty thousand feet. Rhyolite-class radar satellites featured pulsed Dopplar imaging systems that were highly accurate through cloud cover.

Without the benefit of passive night-imaging technology systems, the special detail mobilized in the Iraqi desert would almost certainly be spotted by Coalition watchers.

Saddam understood the value of operational secrecy and was as fanatical about strict adherence to this principle as he was about everything else.

Through the luminous green stereoscopic view field of his NVGs, Vadim scanned the desert terrain surrounding him.

The map he carried was based on ancient Vedic texts, which were in turn based on far more ancient writings of Babylonian priest-scribes dating back to 1000 B.C. He had used the map as the basis for his navigational calculations. According to it, the natural cavern containing the Muan power crystals was located nearby, possibly within a radius of only fifty-odd feet.

The sonar probe built to his specifications by the Iraqis resembled a conventional metal detector. Its operating principle involved bouncing high-frequency sound waves off the desert floor and comparing the echoes that returned by means of a

small but extremely powerful computer microprocessor.

In a matter of minutes, Vadim's sweep of the flat
desert floor ended as a high-pitched tone sounded in
his ear.

It alerted him to the fact that he was standing directly above a hollow in the earth's crust some thirty
feet in diameter, according to the probe's LCD readout.

He knew he had found what he had been search-
ing for.

"Here," he called to the Iraqis, barely able to re-
strain the excitement in his voice, though he knew
that on the desert even the slightest sounds carried
great distances and immense care had to be taken to
evade surveillance.

"Dig right here."

Soon, using jackhammers powered by a portable
compressed-air pump that the crew had brought
along, and silenced with special foam casings, the
Iraqi combat engineer team had broken through the
thin layer of surface rock.

Peering down into the hollow using an infrared
flashlight to illuminate the cavern, Vadim immediately noticed the sparkle of the encrusted mineral
deposits that the ancient texts spoke of as lining the
cavern walls.

With a feeling of mounting excitement, Vadim called for a rope to be provided for him. It was lowered down to the floor of the cavern. Then he climbed down into the darkened depths.

There on the ancient rock floor, he found what resembled a large stone sarcophagus. The object was roughly fifteen feet in length, three feet wide and five feet in height. It was sealed with a stone slab that had been precisely cut to merge seamlessly with the dimensions of the repository.

Vadim tried to push aside the heavy stone cover but was unable to do so unassisted. He would not have been surprised to find that the slab weighed in excess of half a ton.

Only when he called for two of the Iraqis to help him was he able to make any progress in moving the heavy slab. It finally slid to one side, grating noisily against the sides of the repository.

Shining infrared torches down into the space below the slab, all three men gasped as they peered down into the interior of the container placed there millennia before.

The sight that greeted their startled eyes was like nothing any of them had ever seen, or even imagined possible. They had found the Abraxas Hoard.

36

Real-time video scanned the strike perimeter.

Through the computer-enhanced night-imaging system of the VRGs, Quinn saw the activity at the dig site with a sharpness and clarity comparable to viewing conditions in broad daylight.

Nomad had reached a forward observation position just as a stone sarcophagus, its sides carved in high relief, was hoisted up out of the cavern using a portable electric winch.

The sides of the receptacle were decorated with hieroglyphic writing of a kind with which Quinn was totally unfamiliar. It seemed to be a cross between Chinese pictographs and Egyptian hieroglyphs.

Once completely removed from the cavern, the large, heavy object was then loaded on the Iraqi deuce-and-a-half, and the hole in the earth covered up with plywood, then mounds of sand to camouflage the scar in the desert.

Preparing to go ballistic on the Iraqis, Quinn took notice of every aspect of the operations zone that might impinge on his attack strategy. Of primary importance to him at the moment was the fact that there were no lights of any kind positioned around the dig to illuminate the excavation site.

All personnel were wearing night-vision goggles of an image-intensification type. Quinn guessed that this was deemed necessary because the Iraqis did not want to risk the threat of being easily spotted by the array of surveillance systems in the air in these tense weeks before the gulf conflict began.

That was tactically sound thinking from one standpoint. From another perspective, though, it revealed shoddy planning. Use of passive night-vision equipment might successfully hide the excavation detachment from planes and satellites, but it would also give Quinn a sizable tactical advantage. With his VRGs and stealth suit combination, he could see the Iraqis clearly, but they would have a very hard time spotting him.

The FAV had taken him in close to the strike objective. He would have to negotiate the rest of the distance on foot.

The optimum opportunity window to hit the opposition was opening right up.

Some of the Iraqi detail had already returned to the sanctuary of the armored MICVs, and Quinn wanted to take his targets down while they were without the protection of the hardened vehicles.

Raising the shoulder-fire AT4 system, Quinn set his VRGs to autotarget mode. Their on-board computer crunched numbers and prioritized the targets according to range, position and threat-management force levels.

Putting the pipper on the first of the MICVs, Quinn felt the launcher buck atop his shoulder. Scorching blue flame belched from both ends of the launch tube, lighting up the desert for an instant as his battle-management system propelled the first of the four HEMP rocket rounds toward the target.

The boom was followed by a seething fireball that mushroomed up into the night as the first MICV was hit broadside. The rocket's penetrator head pierced the light outer armor covering the war wagon's turret.

The hollow-shaped charge detonated in a rapidly expanding ring that produced a superheated thermal pulse. Exerting pressures approaching two hundred tons per square inch, a high-speed spike of semimolten steel augered its way into the interior of the armored carrier with lethal consequences for the crew.

Iraqi Republican Guardsmen inside the armored vehicle were killed where they sat as blast effect tore their limbs from their bodies and ripped the flesh and sinew from their bones.

Atop the other MICV, a .50-caliber machine gun belched flame and spit hot lead as its frenzied bolt clatter echoed through the night.

Questing for vengeance, glowing tracers whipped toward the spot where a sudden flash of fire had marked the launch of the HEMP warhead seconds before. Darkness had swallowed up the shooter, and Quinn's stealth suit was invisible to the night-vision goggles worn by the Iraqis.

Rapid tracer fire pulses mercilessly raked the desert sands. But the fire was blind, its inaccuracy heightened by the fact that the surviving Iraqi MICV was already in motion, and stragglers scrambled to board the heavy transport truck on which the Muan artifacts had been loaded just before the rocket attack had commenced.

Swinging the AT4 launcher again into position, Quinn put the VRG death dot broadside of the MICV, which was kicking up sand and leaving deep tracks on the desert floor as it moved away at the highest speeds that it could muster.

Quinn felt the shoulder-fire launcher buck again as back-blast sent a plume of luminescent gases spraying into the night. His virtual screen tracked the round as it left the pipe on its lethal trajectory toward its fleeing target.

One more thunderous explosion marked the destruction of the second MICV, whose crew died in a manner just as brutal as the Iraqis in the first destroyed armored vehicle, now burning vigorously on the desert floor.

A few troops who had escaped the death rain were peppering the desert with heavy-caliber AK-47 fire.

Because Quinn's thermal-image-defeating stealth suit denied them target acquisition through their night-vision goggles, the troops could only use the muzzle-flash of the rocket launcher to sight their 7.62 mm autobursts on.

Quinn defeated this tactic by sprinting away from his last position as soon as he had launched his second computer-aimed AT4 round, and the small-arms fire fell wide of the intended mark.

Using the VRG targeting screen to acquire the third and final vehicle of the convoy, Quinn got a target confirm on the heavy transport truck and launched another round. The truck blew apart in a pyrotechnic shower as a third explosion lit up the night with a thousand shooting stars. Quinn put his fourth and final HEMP round into the deuce-and-a-half, intending to ensure that the Muan artifacts were completely destroyed and put well beyond the reach of Saddam Hussein or anyone else who intended to benefit from their lethal power.

Tossing aside the spent multiple launcher tube, Quinn sprinted across the fire-scorched sands toward the strike zone, the P-90 in his fist cybernetically linked to the VRGs' tracking screen.

Iraqi stragglers were still alive in the burning hell of the wreckage-strewn killground. In the flickering light of multiple fires they could see the dark figure silhouetted against the flames licking up from the strike perimeter. Wide-eyed with panic, the troops hurled massed 7.62 mm autofire at the figure darting between the funeral pyres of the burning wreckage like a specter thrust up from hell. The battle-crazed Iraqis believed the deadly shadow that was visiting destruction on them must surely be a spirit of the ancient dead who had been angered by their transgression of the desert burial site.

With his VRGs set on autotargeting mode, Quinn had already prioritized the handful of the enemy left alive on the ground. With the targeting pipper resting on one Iraqi commando, the P-90 directed silenced 5.70 mm burstfire on its lethal trajectory through poison clouds of toxic smoke billowing up from the burning wreckage.

As one Iraqi went down in a spray of blood, Quinn already had the next target within his sights and automatically launched a brace of needlepoint 5.70 mm fléchettes.

A third Iraqi rose to his feet, jacking off flaming hip-level bursts of his Kalashnikov Avtomat as he ran into the night, screaming like a man gone insane.

The VRG pipper flicked across the runner's rib cage, and a quick burst penetrated his back, twisting up his legs beneath his body in midstride and sending him flying onto the bloody desert sands.

Through his VRGs Quinn scanned the killground for survivors. Only one man showed vital signs still intact. His features turned into a bizarre mask by the flickering light of the burning vehicles, Vadim pulled a pistol from a belt holster and held it outstretched in a two-handed combat grasp.

Shakily he rose to his feet, brandishing the 9 mm semiauto at the mocking shadows.

"I see you, Quinn!" he shouted at the battle-helmeted specter who strode through the flames on the desert toward him, rising up out of the inky darkness of the desert night. "And if I see you I can kill you!"

But Quinn didn't stop.

He kept striding closer as Vadim squeezed the trigger of the semiautomatic pistol. A parabellum bullet cracked as it rushed past Quinn's face, followed by another and then a third round in quick succession.

Still Quinn came forward and stopped a few paces away from Vadim. The targeting pipper flashed on the center of Vadim's face as Quinn stared into the muzzle of the raised handgun.

For a heartbeat Quinn debated whether to take justice into his hands then and there. But termination was a directive to be carried out only as a last resort, and Quinn still had a chance to bring his quarry back alive.

Vadim squeezed the combat pistol's trigger again, cursing his shaking hands as a bullet made the desert dust spout near Quinn's booted feet.

Quinn moved the death dot from Vadim's head to the frame of the black Beretta pistol that he clutched in his hands. The P-90 whispered once, and a computer-targeted 5.70 mm round lanced out with surgical precision, knocking the handgun from Vadim's quavering grip.

With an inhuman snarl of rage and fury, the injured man hurled himself at Quinn. As Vadim came at him, fists balled, Quinn raised the P-90 and brought the buttstock smashing down against the side of his head with savage force.

Grunting in pain and gushing blood from the ugly gash in his scalp, Vadim dropped to the sand in a senseless, moaning heap.

A few minutes later Quinn had secured his hands behind his back with cable ties, propped him in the seat of the FAV and strapped him down securely.

His VRG screen was already counting down toward the crunch point as he gunned the dune buggy's powerful engine and raced away from the strike zone across the undulating desert terrain at maximum speed.

Superimposed over the real-time image-enhanced video display of the desert landscape was a glowing red 3-D wire diagram that snaked away to a triangle at its end. It was at the coordinates represented by that triangle icon that the CTL window would appear in just a little while.

Suddenly a data block popped up on Quinn's VRG screen. "Warning," the data block read. "High level of electromagnetic radiation detected...explosion imminent!"

37

Extracting every last possible bit of speed from the dune buggy, Quinn roared across the desert.

Less than a mile from the strike zone, an explosion of tremendous magnitude lit up the night with a blinding incandescence. Thunder boomed and echoed across the desert. Shock pulses sent shuddering force waves coursing through the bedrock of the desert floor.

The Muan crystals had caused the titanic blast.

Absorbing energy from the explosive strikes of Quinn's rocket attack on the Iraqi convoy, the crystals had remained undamaged within the protection of their stone sarcophagus. But the unstable materials of which they were composed had reacted to the energy bombardment by reaching a sort of critical mass.

Deflected upward by the desert floor, the vertical column of blast energy geysered up into the night in a hellfire stream. Its almost nuclear heat fused the sands below into a solid sheet of glass.

The intense light given off by the powerful blast had not gone unnoticed by either coalition surveillance assets or the Iraqis themselves.

From an Iraqi military installation based at Jalibah, warplanes were scrambled to investigate the explosion in the desert that was believed to have been caused by an American nuclear weapon. As the overdriven FAV screamed across the desert, the warbirds were already airborne.

Before long, Quinn's destination drew near.

In the darkness of the desert a mile or so ahead, Quinn's VRGs detected the presence of an electromagnetic energy vortex. Its configuration matched that of a CTL window that opened onto a light cone tilting back toward Quinn's future.

A three-dimensional grid diagram in glowing red cross hatching flashed on the striker's virtual screen. The double-ended, hourglass-shaped funnel on the computer display was a warp in the fabric of space and time, a rift in causality opened temporarily by the black-hole generator at Gamma Base.

The CTL window was the doorway back uptime to the year 2035.

When Quinn was less than five hundred yards away, the energy levels had warped the space-time continuum to the point where the CTL window was visible to the naked eye.

Real-time video showed Quinn a glowing portal in space, funneling down into infinity through a throat tinged with scintillating lights of spinning rainbow colors. Around its edges flashed an ever-changing light display, gleaming and glistening like an aurora borealis.

THE PILOT of the Iraqi MiG 29 and his wingman in the cockpit of a Sukhoi Flanker overflew the scene of the strange, high-magnitude explosion that had taken place in the southern desert. They could witness the intense rainbow-colored lights below. The sortie leader radioed his base that he also saw an unidentified vehicle heading toward the anomaly and asked for instructions.

"Attack the vehicle!" he was promptly informed. "Mark the position by jettisoning a radio beacon and then immediately return to base."

"Roger," replied the pilot of the MiG 29. He instructed his wingman to execute a turn and descend to strafe the target with Vulcan cannon fire.

"I copy that," the wingman reported, and readied his firing systems.

QUINN'S VIRTUAL SCREEN lit up with threat warnings as the two Soviet-built fighter planes approached on a low-trajectory attack vector that skimmed their underbellies only a few dozen feet above the surface of the desert.

Thirty millimeter fire from the Vulcan cannons mounted on the plane's wingtips hammered down toward the vehicle with an eerie moaning roar, narrowly missing the FAV as the MiG roared overhead.

Quinn stomped hard on the brakes and then used a spring-loaded knife to quickly cut the restraints securing Lux Vadim to his seat. There was no way to outrun the supersonic fighters in the FAV and no nearby cover in which to hide from their deadly armament.

A hard shove sent Vadim sprawling to the desert floor before Quinn also jumped out of his seat. Within a matter of moments, the Sukhoi's cannon fire walked along the desert floor and punched into the dune buggy with devastating results.

The 30 mm rounds chewed up the chassis of the open-topped vehicle before an incandescent tracer bullet penetrated its gas tank, igniting the high-octane fuel inside the tank. The FAV blew apart in a pyrotechnic shower of twisted, flaming metal as the gasoline vaporized, turning into a spreading cloud that ballooned skyward with an earsplitting boom.

The countdown window at the top of Quinn's VRG screen gave him less than three minutes before the CTL window would disappear. At that point his pipeline back to his departure year would be blocked, probably forever.

This CTL window had popped into being at the final preplanned location. Gamma Base would not open another one. Quinn and Vadim would be stuck in the past with no way out.

The lead Iraqi strike aircraft, the MiG 29, had taken a few minutes to complete its turn, due to the high speeds it was traveling, which carried it long distances in a short time. But the MiG was now heading back toward Quinn's position.

In the hellish, flickering light cast by the nearby fire of the burning FAV, Quinn's stealthiness was compromised. He could be seen and so he could also be effectively targeted.

Setting the P-90 on full-auto mode, Quinn tracked the bullpup weapon upward toward the attack planes with the VRG on automatic target-acquisition mode.

A heartbeat before the pilot could launch his deadly rounds, the P-90 cycled out a full clip of fifty 5.70 mm needlepoints at the nose assembly of the low-flying attack plane. Computer aimed at the cockpit, the needlepoint rounds penetrated the Plexiglas canopy, smashed through the pilot's helmet visor, and struck the pilot in the face, caving it in and splattering the instrumentation panel with an obscene crimson shower.

Still more sustained autofire from the rotoring P-90 ricocheted off the plane's controls and bounced around the cockpit at high velocity like a swarm of ravenous metal bees.

As the dead pilot's finger relaxed on the joystick fire button, the MiG veered suddenly out of control. Yawing sharply to one side, the stricken fighter turned belly-up, then pitched steeply down toward the desert floor.

The jet exploded a few moments later as its spin-out terminated in a violent crash, scattering pieces of burning wreckage and fiery aviation gasoline all over the desert floor to a radius of sixty feet from the impact zone.

In the blinding flash of the explosion, Quinn grabbed up the groggy Vadim as the second attack plane completed its turn and screamed back toward the kill basket.

The CTL window was now at the peak of its warp energies and would soon disappear. When that happened, the gash in the space-time continuum would close like a fast-healing wound. Quinn had only a few pulse beats left in which to reach the time window and translate out of Iraq and up the time line to 2035.

Half pushing, half dragging the bleeding, semiconscious Vadim toward the CTL window, Quinn struggled to reach the crackling, sparkling tunnel in time as the Sukhoi fighter raced toward them at subsonic speeds.

FLYING DOWN through licking fire and blinding smoke, the pilot could not see the two figures scrambling across the sands through the cockpit windscreen.

Then, with unexpected suddenness, bulleting out of the black smoke plume, the pilot saw the figures who had almost reached the mouth of the incredible vortexing light that had opened up in the night.

Without wasting another second or stopping to think, the Iraqi wingman put the flashing pipper on the targets and punched the joystick fire-control button, raining down heavy-caliber Vulcan fire on the two fleeing figures below.

QUINN HEARD the sound of keening, moaning death from the fast-rotoring electric cannon and the rapid thudding of the heavy Vulcan rounds as they slammed into the desert sands inches from his body.

He dared not look back, although he knew that in a second or two the lethal strafing fire would reach him. Mustering a final burst of speed, he shoved Vadim ahead of him into the mouth of the CTL window as it began to shrink in size and then leaped inside himself, feeling a line of fiery pain rasp across his side.

SOME TWENTY FEET overhead, the Sukhoi pilot thought he had seen at least one of the brilliantly glowing tracer bullets strike one of the running men as both disappeared into the fairy ring of radiantly sparkling lights that hovered over the desert floor.

A heartbeat later he saw the apparition shrink down to a tiny, glowing dot in the night and then vanish completely. At that point the Sukhoi streaked over the black emptiness of the desert below, and the pilot could see nothing more until he was able to complete his turn.

When he flew back over the area once again, he saw only the sand and the wreckage of the blasted vehicle and the crashed MiG. The two running targets he had been chasing at low altitude had disappeared completely. It was as if the desert itself had swallowed them up into its bottomless depths.

Perplexed, he turned and headed back toward Jalibah on full afterburner after deploying a marker beacon as instructed.

But their fate was no longer his problem. The Sukhoi fighter pilot had carried out his duty and would now turn in his after-action report. It would be up to others to deal with the ramifications of these puzzling events.

MORE THAN FOUR DECADES from that moment, yet only a few seconds after Quinn and his quarry had entered the CTL, the techs at Gamma Base saw the blackness inside the CTL sphere vanish and the rounded hull of the thirty-foot orb suddenly clear.

Within the transparent bubble, they saw two human figures materialize, the taller of whom held a tight restraining grip on the other.

The technical support staff rushed to the sphere, now seeing blood streak the curved, transparent walls.

Flanked by the contingent of bullpup-equipped commandos who had been standing at the ready, a medical crew helped both arrivals from the sphere. One of the occupants of the sphere immediately slumped to the floor of the operations center.

Quinn was bleeding heavily from his side as the medical support team administered emergency treatment to the serious bullet wound. Blackness had begun to close in. Quinn's final sight before darkness swallowed him up was of the Reverend Vadim laughing maniacally, like a man who had completely lost his mind.

"A stitch in time saves nine," he shouted over and over again as he was handcuffed and read his legal rights, then taken away for processing. "A stitch in time saves nine. But they won't save you, Quinn!"

The Peacekeepers are dispatched
to shut down the fighting
with brute force in . . .

2030

by MICHAEL KASNER

In Book 3: **FINGER OF GOD**, the Peacekeepers are up
against a ruthless and bloodthirsty enemy, with the specter
of nuclear holocaust looming on the horizon.

Armed with all the tactical advantages of modern technology, battle hard and ready when the free world is threatened—the Peacekeepers are the baddest grunts on the
planet.

Take
4 explosive books
plus a
mystery bonus
FREE

Mail to: Gold Eagle Reader Service
3010 Walden Ave.,
P.O. Box 1394
Buffalo, NY 14240-1394

YEAH! Rush me 4 FREE Gold Eagle novels and my FREE mystery gift. Then send me 4 brand-new novels every other month as they come off the presses. Bill me at the low price of just $13.80* for each shipment—a saving of over 10% off the cover prices for all four books! There is NO extra charge for postage and handling! There is no minimum number of books I must buy. I can always cancel at any time simply by returning a shipment at your cost or by returning any shipping statement marked "cancel." Even if I never buy another book from Gold Eagle, the 4 free books and surprise gift are mine to keep forever. 164 BPM AEQ6

Name	(PLEASE PRINT)	
Address		Apt. No.
City	State	Zip

Signature (if under 18, parent or guardian must sign)

*Terms and prices subject to change without notice. Sales tax applicable in NY. This offer is limited to one order per household and not valid to present subscribers. Offer not available in Canada.

1991 GOLD EAGLE   AC-92R

**In the aftermath of a
brutal apocalypse,
a perilous quest for survival.**

by **JAMES AXLER**

The popular author of DEATHLANDS® brings you an action-packed new post-apocalyptic survival series. Earth is laid to waste by a devastating blight that destroys the world's food supply. Returning from a deep-space mission, the crew of the Aquila crash-land in the Nevada desert to find that the world they knew no longer exists. Now they must set out on an odyssey to find surviving family members and the key to future survival.

In this ravaged new world, no one knows who is friend or foe . . . and their quest will test the limits of endurance and the will to live.